Feast of The Pale Leviathan

by
John Chrostek

Feast of the Pale Leviathan

ISBN

First Edition

Front cover art: Digital Collage by John Chrostek.

Back cover art: Last day of Pompeii (1890), Henry J. Pain (American, 19th Century).

Published by Deep Overstock, Portland, OR.

deepoverstock.com

For Amanda, my love, and all my friends
trying to keep their heads above the water

"Every part of the universe is 'body' and that which is not 'body' is no part of the universe."

-Thomas Hobbes, *Leviathan: Leviathan or The Matter, Forme and Power of a Commonwealth Ecclesiastical and Civil*

"Things don't have purposes, as if the universe were a machine, where every part has a useful function. What's the function of a galaxy?"

-Ursula K. LeGuin, *Lathe of Heaven*

"As the Crow Flies/
It's There the Truth Lies/
At the bottom of the well."

-Tom Waits, *Starving In the Belly of a Whale*

"This Old World is dying/
Don't It seem Like A Good Time/
For Swimming?"

- Adrienne Lenker, *Donut Seam*

I. Adrift

September is a knife, cutting the stagnant summer heat open and letting the chill seep in and float like sweet death above the river. Owen felt the change coming, felt the ceiling of the sky about to snap and knew he was running out of time to cash in his one free ride coupon to Wally's Waterworld, a local river tube establishment he'd been to several times in his childhood. His mother sent him the coupon a month and a half before as a present, tucked into a grocery store greeting card with a blushing rat in a blond wig and a formal dress on the front. It said "Say Cheese, Son! It's Your Big Day." There was no writing on the interior of the card to indicate what the big day mentioned within was meant to be. It was a weird gift, something of a disappointment from a woman with a current net worth above seven figures, but he understood well enough what it meant. Compared to his elder brother Alan, successful, handsome award-winning surgeon Alan, he was still a child in her eyes.

The coupon was for two free admissions, but today Owen had come alone. He parked in the far corner of the dirt and gravel car lot and walked barefoot over hot stones to the shuttle boarding zone that led to the main grounds of Wally's. He had arrived right on time, finding a parked shuttle bus (a squat yellow decommissioned public school bus) with an open door and a driver nowhere to be found. Pleased to have avoided a lengthy wait, he climbed on board and scoped himself out an empty seat.

The bus was packed with hectic families oozing excess children, happy couples taking selfies and murmuring into each other's ears, bundles of teens scrolling their phones or laughing amongst themselves. A pod of office workers on a team-building exercise, all adorned in the same mandatory lime green t-shirts and squinting in the brutal sunlight, dawdled like farmyard cattle as they waited for their group to fully assemble. A trio of elderly women in warmly colored one piece swimsuits pointed mockingly at the bus driver as she hustled her way back across the lot. Owen wasn't the only person at Wally's that day without a smile on his face, but as far as he could tell he was the only one entirely alone.

Fine by him. Being on his own wasn't going to keep him from having a good time. He'd come prepared. Tucked into his drybag were enough goodies to guarantee a perfect summer's day: sunscreen, trail mix, his old Zune in a waterproof case with wireless headphones, a Cherry Berry Bomb growler from his favorite micropub and a one pound bag of magic mushrooms he'd bought off a friend of a friend. It didn't matter that he was alone. A solitary trip could be richly rewarding with sufficient adventurous energy.

"Hey mister," cracked a little voice from the seat in front of him. It was a girl, maybe seven or eight, with bouncy little pigtails and a missing front tooth in her big earnest grin.

Owen looked up through his knock off Ray Bans and smiled back. "What's up, kid?"

"Nice hat!"

Owen chuckled. He was wearing a bucket hat he had purchased ten years ago, the last time he had come to Wally's. It said "*WALLY'S*" in an upward arc beneath a cartoon representation of Wally himself, bright blonde mullet and handlebar mustache framed around vibrant polarized sports sunglasses. He was uniquely proud of the hat. "Thanks!"

"What's your favorite food? Mine is hot dogs!"

Beside the child, her father, a joyless middle aged man with the pursed, wrinkled lips of a turtle turned and looked disinterestedly at the conversationalists.

"Honey, leave the man alone, he doesn't want to talk about hot dogs with you."

"Okay!" The girl flipped 180 degrees in her seat and immediately on landing began to talk to the children in the row in front of her. Owen leaned up against the scuffed window and watched the dense treeline break open, revealing Wally's Water World in all its sun-washed glory.

Past the painted arch entranceway and nestled between unthreatening woodlands and the glistening river, the docks looked like oaken fingers jutting out from the ochre soil of the main square. Damp stacks of one and two-person tubes were piled up against a row of little maintenance shacks sitting just beside the water, with more stacks being offloaded by two bored teenagers from a rusty white pick-up truck the park must have purchased three decades ago. In uneven lines along the small square the food and amenity booths were decorated with copyright-protected cartoon characters. Far more of these stands were shuttered up and decrepit than Owen remembered. He wondered how much longer this park had until it shuttered for good. Would tubes still float downstream a hundred years from now? Twenty years?

The busiest of the remaining stands was a food stall called The Bull Winkle, manned by three sweaty, overworked men all wearing flag bandanas.

Owen waited until it was his turn to order. "One hot dog, please."

After slathering the bastard in ketchup and mustard to hide the burnt exterior of the sausage, he grabbed a seat at an empty picnic table and chowed down. It's not a good idea to trip on an empty stomach, after all. Nowhere to go when you're already gone.

By the time he'd finished eating the hot dog and cleaning himself of the aftermath, the majority of shuttle passengers he'd ridden over with had taken to the water. The square was mostly empty now, an employee here and there standing about aimlessly in the thick of the end-summer sun. No one was paying much attention to anything at this point.

Owen reached into his drybag and fetched the crinkled sandwich Ziploc bag that held the mushrooms. He poured the dry husks out into his hands and scanned them for mold. All clear.

His mind wandered to Ciara and Bobo. They were out there, underneath the same bright sun without him, Bobo's tiny white ear hairs like princess curls blowing in the pale breath of a park valley. Ciara, watching Bobo run, smiling, radiant and present in each second of the day like it was effortless. He wondered what jokes she might have made, what book she would have brought with her to read, but the thought was painful. He would never know for certain, and what use was wondering? She had sent him back her ticket without a letter goodbye. Their last words together had already passed him by.

Another life, another way, slipped through his fingers.

Same as it ever was.

Owen ate every bitter, withered mushroom in the bag and sat at the table for fifteen minutes before walking over towards the river and grabbing a tube to ride in. The water was chilly on his bare feet and he struggled for a moment to push himself past the discomfort. He stepped back from the water and put his earbuds in. He had left his phone tucked safely away in his car to avoid getting wet, but he held little such worry about the Zune he got for his birthday in 2007. It was brimming with illegally downloaded music, and somehow still retained its battery life for ages. A Library of Alexandria that played with matches.

He put on Fleetwood Mac. Tango in the Night. *Come here to the seaside…*

The river felt a little less painful and a little more bright, and soon he was floating downstream. His stomach quaked and groaned, and he felt the urge to burp build up within him. He was alone on the water's edge for as far as the eye could see and he was falling head first into everything one breath at a time.

Then I remember…

ò

Light on water. Light splinters off the moving surface, becoming color and shine, becoming a bird call elongated like a hook across the long blue sky. The green lungs of the sweetgum and willow oak exhaled in praise of autumn's oncoming grace, remembering the lightness of ambering leaves, self-immolation as a transcendental act of faith.

The body feels the water on its skin. The chilly signals of the fingers, twitching and bobbing below the water, remember the world and now too does the brain. The body is floating on the water on an inner tube under the summer sun. In the scattered distance, other bodies, other tubes all float downstream. Children paddle kick with manic glee to accelerate their floats. Laughter dances on the water like dragonflies. The bodies round the coming bend, whirl along with the tide in clusters and pairs, organic and alien, many and one.

Owen remembers himself. He remembers his sunglasses. His arms raise up unbidden from the water to take them off. The sunlight above is blinding. It is a beautiful, radiant pain he cannot face. He puts them back on, no tension in his body, numb like a sleeping leg but painlessly so. Time settles down again atop the pollen and moss. Owen's throat is dry and tastes of stale mustard. The sun is past its center-point in the sky and the Zune is playing Boys II Men. He has been gone for a while.

A patch of shallow rapids and a graveyard of foot-stones draws closer. A pubescent boy in a short-sleeve wet-suit limply fights to dislodge it from the stones. He reaches out to the other side of the shallows where an older man stands fully upright, his own raft held up around his waist, talking to a disinterested young mother lolling by on the other side.

"Wanna connect, Dad?" The boy calls out to no avail. "Dad?"

The father finally notices his son as Owen pauses the music, turns the next bend and passes them by. In the water's glow, Owen sees visions of his own father taking the family to Wally's for the first time in the late nineties, dunking Owen below the water before throwing him skyward like a rock. The big shark smile on his father's face that always felt like a blessing until it sharpened to a knife. He always made everything colossal, explosive. His passion, his anger. Even the muscles of his heart.

Owen hadn't come here to hurt. He was too loose, too liberated to soak in old pain for long. He reached into his bag and grabbed the growler. He barely felt himself crack it open and take a swig, but he felt the bitter cool, the cherry pucker. It was enough to stop his thinking and get him back to drowsily eating the sunlight as it rained down on him.

II. The Watcher

At the end of Wally's Water World's main river course, three tributaries meet before the tidal flow picks up and feeds the freshwater to the bay. At that spot lies the exit dock where the rafters shallow up and dry off. For close to five miles prior, signs on either side of the tributaries warn floaters to keep sharp and drift slowly and steadily to the right. If someone isn't careful, they can get caught in the current, unable to swim to shore.

Patrick, the twenty-year-old lifeguard working the exit dock, looked up over his phone at the visitors drifting into view like clockwork. He was texting with a guy he met at a college varsity swim match named Evan. Evan had these charcoal eyes that burned up all the light in the gym and revealed nothing about what was going on beneath the surface. To catch those eyes was to be transfixed by the possibilities, the implications, the pleasant worry of Evan's intentions for him.

The weight of them made Patrick feel sick to his stomach in the best way. He couldn't help chasing that feeling with everything he had.

How's work? Evan texted. He was so curious, so attentive.

Shit sucks, lol, Pat replied. *Nothing ever happens here. I don't even know how this place is still open. I think it's a money laundering thing.*

That's boring. Anybody drown today at least?

Pat giggled. *No, no bodies yet.*

:(

Evan was typing for some time. In the distance, a

middle-aged woman fell backwards walking out the river, her coworkers laughing at her expense.

Pat's phone buzzed. Evan had finally replied.

Would you fuck a hot guy's corpse?

"What the fuck?!" Evan muttered to himself. His thumbs quivered over his keyboard like they were caught in the middle of a crime.

~~*What the fuck is wrong with you?*~~ Too confrontational. It was clearly a joke. A weird joke, yeah, but he was teasing. Was Evan a provoker? A bit sus? Did he think this wouldn't make Pat squirm at all?

~~*I'm not that desperate.*~~ What sounded more desperate than that?

He looked out at the horizon, unsure of how to proceed. Did he really like this kind of talk? Grim jokes were one thing, but this was beyond button pushing. This was internet weirdo stuff. Was this really what he was looking for right now? Some dumb, hot edgy swimmer boy to fuck with his head and make him feel small? Couldn't anything be simple anymore?

Then it hit him. The perfect reply.

I like my bodies warm.

Pat felt good about that one. He set his phone down, watching the last stragglers of the afternoon bus drift to shore. A father and son hit land, the son out way ahead of his father, not looking back. Family drama, he guessed.

He didn't notice the strange man standing just beside the watchtower, dressed in a full body maroon cloak, fingers extended in stiff contortions towards Pat. He didn't feel the curtain of life shimmer all around him, projecting a new reality just a half-step more charmed and vital over his senses.

His phone blinked coolly to life in his hands. He saw a picture of Evan, shirtless, shining like onyx on his screen.

"Oh, my god," Pat whispered, entranced by the illusion of the moment, totally oblivious to the man in sunglasses drifting past the shore, beyond the reach of the Jet Ski, beyond the decommissioned railway bridge and out, slowly, towards the yawning sea.

III. The Maw

Owen was unsure when exactly he had fallen asleep, but as his eyes adjusted to the sight of the distant shore he knew he had awoken far too late. Panic ran roughshod through him. A heavy fog hung around him, obscuring but a thin window of horizon, the flickering relics of the coastline barely cutting through. He shouted for help as loud and as long as he could muster. Nothing visible stirred in response save the ocean waves and the strange shadows that danced below the duskwater. The ocean churned.

His heart was pounding viciously, desperate to escape him and fly to safety. Had no one seen him floating out this far? How long, if ever, would it take until his absence mattered to the world?

He began to cry, mourning his own pathetic life, but his vocal chords were brutalized and could barely sustain the sound.

The bay was long gone now, the heavy fog following Owen away from shore. A solitary sea bird hovered soundlessly, for a moment or an hour, overhead.

The sun was setting. The sea-fog bloomed a rare and luminous orange Owen had never seen before, like the warm thin shadow of hell. He realized, in his dazed mania, that he had seen almost nothing of this world. He wanted to travel, to look upon the wide world, or so he thought, but really, most of his days had been spent pacing back and forth between old haunts and shoddy apartments. Themed work parties. Falling asleep on the couch with his jeans still on.

When he did see new places, new things, the wanderlust faded, a hunger sated, and that was that. There was always a tomorrow. Always a way out, a way forward. Until now.

Owen began to pray. He had forgotten his childhood hymns from Catholic school, strung bead-words gone unheard since before his father died. Even when he was young and he believed in the teachings as taught to him, when he mourned and raged and collapsed into himself and found nothing but silence where light had been promised, those words had been little comfort.

"Dear Lord, if you can hear me, please, send someone my way. A cruise ship, a fisherman. I'm not ready to die. I'll be good, I swear. I'll do right by others. I'll do something. I don't want to die. I can't die. Not like this. I need to see Ciara again. I want to try, I need to try. Answer me, God, please. Say something. Do something, please. I'll love it all again, all the bullshit, the crap. I'll love the whole damn world."

He raised his hands up towards the sky like a child reaching for its mother.

The sea was still and wide.

After sunset, the sky drained of color. Owen drifted in and out of consciousness, unable to bear the psychic weight of his fate. The chill of the ocean was impossible to escape, and adrenaline had only kept him warm so long. Even if a boat could find him now, was it already too late? Would hypothermia kill him before he could drown?

Even this fear, and the fear of unseeable shadows, could not sustain him forever.

His eyes opened to see a small gray trawler floating relatively close by him, maybe three quarters of a mile out, the small antenna guidelight blinking out a cutting red hole in the world. Though he could barely speak, he cried out to them for help.

"Help me! Help! PLEASE!"

But the boat did not turn towards him. On its deck, three figures stood silhouetted by the dim glow of the deck lamps, either watching him writhe about on his river tube like statues or fully oblivious to his presence. He could not see what way they were facing. The sickening weight of realization grew in him as the ship bobbed steadily on the black water. If these figures saw him, they chose to leave him to the sea.

Once he had lost the will for shouting, the boat tacked starboard, disappearing into the void, and Owen understood at last he was truly going to die.

Hours passed. The waning moon was a cold and vicious blade, threading the unending fog. Owen's mind wandered to a day in his youth when he and his brother went sledding down a large hill alone off the interstate a few miles from his home. He had hit a drift-buried rock and went barreling into a sturdy old tree. Sprawled out in the snow, dazed and confused, his skin burning from the chill of snow beneath his clothing, he laid there a while and wondered what would happen if the snow buried him alive. He wasn't scared of the thought, but death was still so foreign back then, just some light-switch dream state and not the unconquerable silence he understood it to be now.

He felt his breath getting shallower, his heart and lungs beginning to shutter towards stillness. Sleep, or death? Did it even matter?

He almost didn't feel the ocean shudder from somewhere far below. He looked around for signs of a ship passing through the darkness, but he saw nothing. Felt nothing. But then it shook again. A low seismic groan rippled upwards from the black abyss, and all the surface water quivered in response. Owen did not understand what his half-frozen extremities were sensing, but his brain knew enough to panic.

The waves began to crest and fall as if a great storm was brewing, but there were no signs of storm clouds in any direction. Owen wondered if he were about to witness the birth of a hurricane or a tsunami, if the tectonic plates beneath the earth had cracked open at this, the worst and final moment of his life.

The water broke open and spilled out like a waterfall before him. It seemed too large to be a shark or a whale or even a submarine. The black waters of the deep Atlantic rose and crashed, canyons of water carved with shearing white foam. In the fog, a looming and incredible shadow grew tall and wide. Owen cried out, gripping his inner tube for dear life, his dry bag and bucket hat slipping into the chaos below.

The mountainous silhouette now blotted out the moon. In its place there were two wide reflective surfaces catching what little light remained. Those are eyes, Owen thought, before his inner tube descended quickly down a foamy ridge, hurtling to the brackish underside of a looming wave.

He lost his grip and fell into the water, churning in the icy black. The pressure slammed the air from his lungs as it spun him about, untethering him from gravity. From above him, his eyes could see the silhouette looming ever closer. Owen swore it was no shark, no whale, but the pale face of a man, alien yet human, growing in immensity until it was larger than the world.

He saw a cavernous vacuum of a mouth open before it slammed into the water. Owen had no air to scream with, no sanity to reason with. He tumbled into the ravenous darkness of the beast, towards total annihilation, thinking of his brother.

He missed him very much.

IV. Throat Catch

In the swallowed sea water, Owen felt nothing but the rapid churn. He knew he was falling, descending into greater darkness, but there was no direction to ground himself, no air to breathe. The pressure was a crushing, maddening swirl, shredding him down to an event horizon of fear and pain, until all at once his body jerked to a stop, arrested in the air as the water continued its descent past him. Further below. Though his eyes could barely open, he could breathe again. He watched out a torrent of water falling from above him, raining down what appeared to be a snaking tunnel of flesh leading up to an undulating ring of muscle, dilating wide enough for a school bus to pass through unclipped.

How had he stopped? His skin was so cold he could not feel anything, but by some strange dim light he could see the dark netting suspended from wall to wall. He had been caught, a fly on a spider's web suspended over oblivion.

A harsh, seasoned voice of a man cried out from somewhere nearby. "We got a live one, mates! Hop to it!"

Stirrings of shadows flickered in the light. Owen wondered what final dream this must be to see light and hear voices now. Soon dark figures loomed above him, lifting him up and off the net towards the far wall. The figures passed over some wooden posts and, Owen in tow, crawled into a small tunnel of flesh straight through into a widening polyp the size of a nicer office cubicle. Inside, the light of covered torches glowed, casting thicker shadows than before.

Owen felt himself laid to rest on a warm, muscular floor and felt immediately sick to his stomach. Seawater, brackish and flush, bubbled up and out of him and onto the writhing floor.

As his eyes began to adjust, three ragged men adorned in burlap sacks suspended by rope stood before him. They looked wet and weary as if accustomed to an unending storm. The eldest of the three, stocky with deep age lines carving shadows on his face, bent down to his knee and rested his large hand on Owen's shoulder.

"You must have many questions."

Owen laughed vacantly, still coughing up foam and shivering fiercely.

"Call me Gabriel." The old man rose up to his feet, gesturing to the men on either side of him. "This here with me is Hans and Serge, good men, loyal and true. They're the first you'll meet but far from the last. Like you, we were all adrift at sea for one reason or another and eaten by the beast. By God's providence alone, we survived. There are more of us, aye, but it was us assigned today to throat catch, so it's nice to meet you."

The man on the left with a substantial wiry mustache that trailed upwards into sideburns cleared his throat. "None of us asked for this life, sure. They say the first of us lived in constant anguish and misery, succumbed to their fate of scrounging in the dark like worms, but we've laid down infrastructure now. Things are pleasant enough."

The opposite man, gaunt with dark hair and deep-set eyes, tutted in response. "Let's not oversell it, Hans. It's a living hell the man's woken up in. All we can still do is prolong the inevitable and survive another day."

"Enough, lads," barked Gabriel. "Granted, this is a dark and hostile environment we find ourselves in, but come now. Think back to the lives you knew before the terrible whale swallowed you whole. The sun and stars were ever brilliant but the world laid below them was no less brutal. Death was a constant there! Death, blood, sickness, robbery, infidelity… 'Twere no Eden."

"Aye," the men replied, reflecting somberly on his words.

"Let's leave philosophizing for another day, gentlemen. We've a new crewmate to orient! Hans, do you believe there's an available cavity for Mr…?"

"Owen."

Gabriel smiled. "Mr. Owen, then."

Serge spoke. "I have a free cot in mine, sir."

"Fantastic. We must be sure to add our new arrival to the Ledger in due time. Mr. Owen, if you've any questions, look to Serge. A finer soldier and friend you'll never know. Now then, I must return to my post. Fare thee well!"

With that, Gabriel and Hans were off, ducking back through the low tunnel and back out to the throat of the massive beast. Only Serge remained beside Owen in the quivering polyp. Owen felt raw and delirious, instinctively resisting his senses as if he could reason his way out of this new reality.

"You know, he's right," Serge said quietly. "Once you get used to it, it's not so bad."

Owen did not mean to glare at Serge, but his body insisted. It needed an outlet for its shock and rage. A lightning rod to suffer the storm.

Serge ignored him and carried on. "I bet I can hazard a guess as to your thinking. You're thinkin', *this ain't no whale.* And you'd be right."

Owen remembered his last moments at sea. The parting water, the shivering moonlight. The two great black eyes and pallid flesh the size of a mountain. "What I saw-"

"An unfathomably large man? A Titan? The sort they say the Olympians bested before the Age of Man, adrift in open waters where any passing vessel might see? Perhaps even some Leviathan of God's design?"

Hearing it aloud itched the insides of Owen's bones.

"I saw the same. And if you're at all familiar with anatomy, you no doubt noticed that the throat was nothing like a whale's. No, this great body we inhabit is designed in the manner of man, some way or the other. Explore the rest of it and you'll see the same play out. But don't hold that truth against Gabriel! He's been inside longer than any man or woman alive. For whatever reason, he sees this place as the innards of a whale. Refuses to speak of it otherwise. We think it makes it easier for him somehow, so we don't press him. Patience with the elderly is its own reward."

Owen gripped his pounding skull and grit his teeth hard to block out his thoughts with pressure. He could listen no further, accept no grimmer turn of fate. He was at its end.

"I don't understand!" he shouted. "What is this place, really?! We can't be alive, can we?! Where are we?"

Serge was unshaken by the outburst. He leaned up against the tissue of the polyp to lay it out plain. "One of two places, friend. We're either floating at the bottom of the sea inside a wrathful god of old, trapped forever to scavenge and rot and be consumed entirely, or we're in Hell. A cruel and specific hell for sinners and bastards, a level all its own, disconnected to the others, meant to sustain this communal delusion of the greater flesh."

He continued, his expression softening. "You must be filled with this horrible need to escape, but don't worry. In a week or two, after you've woken up and found a new rhythm to live by, you'll realize that the answer doesn't matter. It's just your life. And you'll make your peace with it or you'll kill yourself. Many do. But I'll tell you something. I've seen countless souls perish trying one way or the other to get out, but it's only the peaceful that ever escape."

Serge extended his hand. Owen did not want to take it. It felt like a surrender to the terms of this hell, some unspoken contract with the great unknowable architect of suffering, but he was too tired, too broken to stand alone. He took Serge's hand and was startled by the dry warmth of it. Whatever this place was, at least he wasn't alone in the moving dark, dwelling on the fading memory of the teeth and eyes of his new home.

V. Gut Check

According to the Ledger Man it was Thursday, though there was no sun, moon or exterior world inside the Leviathan, making the exact transition of days, weeks, months and seasons a mystery to those counting. There had been a contentious argument many years ago about the clock and calendar system used all across the interior society. There were no working mechanical, satellite or atomic clocks, and of course no sundials, and so some argued for a complete cancellation of observed time inside the beast. Those in favor of cancellation argued that imaginary, unprovable time was an insult to life, a torture mechanism used to enslave minds and enforce violence. This attracted vicious rebuttals from Gabriel and his closest captains, who argued convincingly to the masses that time as a construct is essential to the function of a healthy society and serves to regulate the flow of human behavior, commerce, and culture. After a healthy debate and reeducation period for the most vocal and disruptive of calendar agnostics, order was restored and time resumed its unbidden, unstandardized march onwards.

To Owen, however, it was Monday. Unlike most people in Levi (what Owen learned most of the devoured called their corpulent home) his body could remember the warm embrace of sunlight and it was deep in the throes of withdrawal. His first few days in Levi were spent in a damp hammock tucked into a dark crevice occupied by Serge, sweating out a shuddering fever, as much of the mind as of the body. It wasn't simply sunlight he was craving. It was clear water, fire-cooked meals and the feeling of the wind on the small hairs of his neck. He missed trees, quesadillas, jeans, ice cream, the sound of traffic and above all things, more than anyone or anything, he missed the Internet.

After his fever broke, Owen was assigned to a work schedule, part of the natural order all residents of Levi agreed to. His partner for the day was Hans, the man with sideburns standing guard at the throat-catch with Gabriel and Serge when Owen had first arrived.

Hans did not remember the Internet. He had been swallowed by Levi in the mid-sixties, before that having been a tuna man all his life. The revolutionary development of information technology had barely been a flash on the horizon when, one dark day on the Norwegian sea, his ship was capsized in a storm. Before help or heaven could find him, the Leviathan had. And so his new life began.

As the two of them scraped the upper intestinal tubing for build-up, pushing weathered mops through the waist-high villi that rippled like stalks in a grassland, Owen artfully committed to describing the best cat videos he had ever seen.

"I can't believe how long you've been in here for," Owen pondered. "You must be close to a hundred years old."

Hans chuckled heartily, beating his chest with his mop handle. "My boy, I have the body of a forty-seven year old upholsterer, or perhaps a thirty-nine year teamster! Maybe I have missed many beautiful things in the old world, but mark my words, Levi sustains us. He's not so bad, you'll see. Out there beneath the hateful sun, we mortal men suffer and rot like bananas on a shelf. But here, in service of our precious boy, we are pickled into long, rich lives!"

After a few minutes of painfully thorough tales of the evolution of life inside the Leviathan, Owen gave up trying to convince him otherwise.

Once work was completed for the day, Hans escorted Owen back to his chambers. The area of the titanic body where Owen's "room" was situated was called The Heartlands, the inhabitants' name for the vast thoracic cavity outside the major organs of Levi where many lived, worked and slept. Since he had arrived, he had spoken only briefly with Serge, his new friendly-yet-depressive roommate, even during his brutal fever. Serge had come and gone from their small cot composed of flotsam and sails in silence, leaving Owen to his solitary delirium for what might have been days or weeks on end. Owen had found the silence confusing and hurtful, given Serge's paradoxical display of initial kindness, and after spending a shift with the talkative Hans, that dissonance was more distracting than ever.

That night, his body was weak from scrubbing, legs raw and tender from hours of wading through the shallow creek of acidic juice that ran down the intestines and across the steep inclines of tissue and bone that made travel through Levi such an arduous affair. Though he was beginning to adjust in some ways, even becoming somewhat curious about the human activity he saw coming and going in unmarked tunnels all across the Heartlands, he wasn't yet ready to meet new people. To try to join what passed as society inside Leviathan. He wanted to rest.

In a long row of cots, tents and lean-tos snaking up alongside the second to lowest right rib of Levi, Owen came at last to the miniscule cavity he had begun to accept as his home, a world apart thanks to generous and full-bodied entrance curtains. Inside, he found Serge hard at work mixing out a bowl of Levi's wax to refine into candles and torchlight.

"Evening, friend. How was work?" Serge asked, eyes fixed fully on his labor, the circles around his eyes like lunar craters reflecting the sun in the glow of the flickering wax light.

"Hey. Thanks. It was fine, mostly. You?"

"Oh you know. Another day of double duty, but it all

pays off in the end."

"It does? There's a benefit to working more than you're assigned?" Owen asked.

Serge spared an upwards glance volleyed by indignation. "Sure there is. You can move somewhere nicer, close to the heart. Then there's the bartering, of course. Supply enough candles and you might get a raincoat or even some work boots made of ship-rope. That's worth a few sleepless nights, eh?"

He chuckled to himself as he dipped three fingers and a line of twine into the wax, curling it into a tall spiral candle designed to burn for months on end.

Owen laid down in his hammock, suspended between bare shelves of exposed cartilage. He tried to ignore the sound of the wax being slapped and patted into shape enough to get some sleep and face whatever tomorrow might hold.

The next day (when the mass of the Leviathan's survivors began to shuffle out of bed, the silence of agreed upon night fading like the tide) Owen had no major responsibilities, so he decided to brave a journey to the stomach. He'd heard from Serge and Hans that the gastropool was the place to be, the epicenter of life inside the body. Owen struggled to accept that the most common job in Levi was that of controlled baths in the digestive acid, but Hans had sworn up and down it was the easiest job of all, that it was a mild burning sensation at most, and that once Owen relaxed about it and followed the guidelines, he'd be lining up for the duty all the time like everyone else.

The gastropool was ringed with several layers of wide wooden platforms and arched ledges, stitched together from the broken flooring of ancient ships and whatever other sturdy flotsam had fallen into Levi over the centuries.

Makeshift chairs and tables, rudimentary desks and booths ringed these platforms, used with joyous intensity by the people who congregated around the acid, stepping in and out of the caustic brine as if in a sauna, wrapping their tattered rags around their neck to keep from dissolving. The stomach had a strange, pallid yellow glow from the acid reflecting off the slick mucus of the stomach walls. Coupled with the soft torchlights burning wax suspended safely around the chamber, the space seemed to glow with a warmth not unlike a hearthlight.

It was a sick realization, Owen thought, to immediately feel as if he had escaped the harshness of his new life conditions by traveling here. Almost nothing was kinder or more dignified here than out in the dim labyrinth of the chest cavity. Despite this, he felt the moth in all human souls flitter within him, drawn madly to the light, with every step he took.

On a large platform close to what the eye might recognize as ground level, a crowd was forming rapidly. As Owen approached them, he could begin to make out that there had been an accident. Four workers had been doing a patrol of the left calf when Levi had scuffled up against a large rock and gashed its skin open. One of the men had died instantly, sucked out into the abyss by the sudden change in pressure. Another was apparently in grave condition, battered by the cold weight of the floodwaters. He had been lucky enough to make it up and out of the leg to signal for help. The other two patrolmen were, at this hour, still missing in action.

For the time being, travel to the leg was off-limits, and word had been sent to the Ledger Man to see if there were any signs that Levi might return to warmer waters.

"But what if Levi stays down here and dies from shock? If Levi dies, won't we all die as well?"

This whipped the crowd into a panic until at last a thunderous stomp rang across the panelboards and silenced the rancor.

"Enough of this!" cried Gabriel, damp with frigid seawater, clutching a dull blade aloft so that it caught the light of nearby torches, shimmering above the mass around him. "If it's truly Levi's time, then so be it! We shall die with dignity and pride, knowing we have lived for so long against the odds and fought so very hard. But, my friends, all is not yet lost! The wound will heal! Levi, like all living things, can feel his own body cry out. It speaks to him and he shall listen. He knows what is required to survive, so must we be like him! We must risk the danger of the day to hang on for tomorrow. We must go and blockade the leg and minimize flooding to preserve the core and keep the fire of our humanity burning in the darkest of nights! Who is with me?"

A great cheer rang out, bright and true. Owen was awed at the power Gabriel held, the love the people held for him. A party of daring volunteers quickly congregated around him, ready to risk themselves for the cause. In a blur, they departed from the gastropool, headlong towards the wounded leg, and the nervous remainder dispersed, muttering quiet prayers to a God that none believed was listening.

Owen watched them go in silence. He wanted nothing to do with this, wanted to risk nothing of the scrap of life he clung to since the Leviathan had swallowed him whole. Still, he envied the crowd and their confidence in Gabriel. Part of him wished he could let go of his fear like that. It must have been built up over decades. What would life be in Levi without a man like Gabriel to lean on? And how, Owen wondered most of all, did Gabriel find the strength to be the Gabriel they all needed?

"Madness," said a voice behind Owen.

Owen whipped about, startled. Standing not far from his shoulder was a bald woman clad in a burlap toga. She was thin, medium height with smooth skin that gleamed in the acidglow. In her hand, a wooden cup sloshed with a dark orange red liquid. *Wine?* Owen gulped despite himself. He'd kill for a drink.

"Sorry?" was all he could work out.

"What they're doing. It's madness. Rushing about as if any of us are in genuine danger."

"You don't think we could drown in here?"

The woman chuckled. "Have you ever seen a whale drown from a harpoon wound?"

"I've never seen a whale."

"And it shows, dear."

Another woman with thick black hair came rushing up from the other side of the gastropool, cradling a bundle of fabric. "Janice, I need you to take Sean back. You've been avoiding me all day and enough's enough."

Janice, the woman with the drink, winced. "Oh, but he loves you, Nina. I don't know what I'd do without you."

"Janice."

"Oh, *fine*." Janice grabbed the bundled baby from the woman's arms. As if on cue, the baby began to squirm and cry. Janice fired a passing glance of irritation at Owen before chugging what remained of her drink, rhythmically bouncing the apoplectic bundle in her arms and disappearing behind a scaffold.

Owen wasn't sure what to say.

"You must be new," the other woman, Nina, said.

He nodded.

"Nina. Nice to meet you." They shook hands.

"Owen."

A silence passed between them.

"You have questions."

Owen nodded. "The baby, yes. Also the wine."

"Oh, they keep wine up there on the upper patio. They ration it out very slowly, though, so I doubt you'll get drunk. Janice gets a little extra because everyone feels sorry for her. On account of the baby, obviously."

"Did she have it in Levi?"

Nina touched her stomach from nausea. "No, god, no. They were swallowed together a few days after Sean was born. Still horrible."

A deep chill ran up Owen's spine. "Wait, when did they-"

"Ask her sometime. She still has the ticket. Keeps it on her person constantly like it's worth something. Funny part is, if we ever get out of here, it will be."

The fluorescent acid of the gastropool hissed and bubbled as the two new acquaintances stood in silence. The now-distant cry of baby Sean clawed at the fractured part of Owen's psyche still trying to assert a baseline, contextual normal.

"So," Nina began, "did I hear correctly that Gabriel's trying to play triage in the left leg?"

Owen nodded.

"That's going to go wonderfully."

"It confuses me, too, yeah."

"He doesn't know the first thing about aquatic skin coagulation," Nina said bitterly. "He's a hundred plus year old sailor, he barely remembers fucking electricity."

"Do you know about aquatic skin coagulation?"

"Before Levi swallowed me twenty miles east of Bermuda, I was a marine biologist. Obviously I didn't study giant sea-people, but it's not nothing."

"Does Gabriel know that? Should you help them out?"

She glared at Owen for a moment with a flash of visible distrust and turned away. The pause in the conversation grew long and Owen felt increasingly uncomfortable for having asked that question. He tried to think of something else, something light and witty and relieving to say, but nothing came to him. He just felt dumb and sick.

Just then, a series of distressed voices blared out from some distance below. The crew that had gone down to the leg were now rushing back to the stomach, their numbers thinned and ever more frantic.

The cries intensified, echoing through the gastropool. "Move aside! Hurry!"

Three men came bursting into view carrying the horizontal body of Gabriel, his pale and bony figure trembling and silver-blue.

"We need to get him warm!"

"Lay him in the pool!" someone shouted.

The men nodded, lifted him up above the gastropool and dipped him in. He floated in peace for precious seconds before howling in pain, clawing with locked hands at his dippers like an emaciated wolf clamped in iron jaws.

Panicking, they hoisted him up and out of the acid. His hypothermic skin looked boiled thinner, little more than raw and pulsating matter. His eyes, only hours before carved keenly out from beneath a strong and stony brow, were as round now as baby moons, so lost to trauma and shock they were gasping for light.

The crowd grew closer as the frantic crew called out for help. Everyone knew there was no help to be found in Levi; but the call was echoed again and again, whether out of sympathy or senseless mimicry. "Bandages! Blankets! We're losing him!"

Owen watched as Serge, his tentmate, thrust out of the crowd in a frantic rush. He swooped in and lifted what was left of Gabriel off the flotsam patio, cradling him in his arms.

"Gabriel, we need you! You're our captain, our king! We can't go on without you!"

Gabriel's stiff and blackened hands rose up to graze the tears cascading down Serge's cheek.

"You must. Stay together. Stay human."

His hand dropped lifelessly onto Serge's lap. Serge began to scream.

From the other side of the maddening crowd, Owen noticed that Nina had returned, her gaze fixed keenly on him. Their eyes made contact as the chaos in the gastropool reached boiling point. She looked close to laughing, but she soon faded to the background, thronged by grief and panic.

Gabriel had perished. Nothing could ever be the same.

VI. Fractured

It took some time for any semblance of order to return to the gastropool. Cries of fear and sorrow rang out in all directions, spreading into the tendrilous dark, bearing the black wings of Gabriel's passing to all who drew breath inside the Leviathan. It was impossible to stem the tide, and no one tried. To fight the impulse would be as vain an effort as to crawl up and out the mouth of the Leviathan itself and swim to shore.

A great mass had gathered, enough to fill up all the standing room inside the stomach, each galleyway and platform packed with weary, weeping folk. It became quickly apparent that Gabriel would require a swift funeral if anything like normalcy was to be reasserted. His closest lieutenants, Hans and Serge among them, cleared space around Gabriel's body. Fabric was called for to dress him as his limbs were folded into a state of eternal repose.

An aged woman named Patricia, a full-time acid soaker and cultural institution inside the Gastropool, was the first to arrive with canvas in her arms. She brought her forest green wool sleeping blanket, a personal luxury she had been swallowed with decades before. She laid it down above Gabriel gingerly, as if tucking in a child and stepped aside to let the others do their work.

Gabriel was wrapped from head to toe in the wool and bound in it by loose strips of netting from a nearby workstation. His body, now clean and composed, was left to rest as the lieutenants sized up the situation, scanning the levels of the stomach and the quiet, desperate congregation.

Owen watched from above. He wanted to feel something, some kind of loss, but he couldn't. This was all too new, too chaotic a development to register as tragedy. He was still mourning his own death, or rather grim turn of fate. Gabriel had been kind to Owen in his way but Owen felt hollow at the memory of it. He knew better than to show his complicated feelings, at very least. This moment wasn't for him. He was still a guest. A stranger here.

Hans stood up, his tall cheekbones wet with tears. "Friends, the worst has come to pass." He cleared his throat and wiped his face, pushing the subtle tremor out of mind and throat. "We've lost our Gabriel. A man of unquestionable honor and integrity, long-toothed and storied, a strong and loving father for us all in the dark pits of Levi. But were he here with us now, he would tell us to gather close to one another and carry on with our great labor. We must survive! We must continue. It was his wish, his heart's lantern-light that gathered and guided us all together. So let us honor him in his passing and sing for his immortal soul, which may yet one day escape this place and fly up to bright, billowy heaven, where we may one day join him, Lord be willing."

The crowded stomach was silent. Patricia rose from her seat, assisted by two other women Owen did not know flanking her on either side. The trio stepped up to the central podium, where for over a century Gabriel gave his fiery speeches to all who would listen. Patricia whispered in the ears of her guardians, who listened closely and nodded. One woman shuffled over to Hans and whispered in his ears, at which he began to tear up once again. He hid his face from the crowd, nodding lightly, and turned to Gabriel's hooded form.

When the third woman returned to Patricia's side, they each shared a glance with the other and faced the crowd before beginning to sing. Patricia's voice broke high and bright, shocking Owen from his seat on the higher rungs. It bounced against the quivering membrane, against the glow of the acid before the other woman joined in harmony. It took Owen a moment, but he recognized the hymn from his youth. Summer days, yellow Sunday light through stained glass, heavy time he never owned.

Hail, Queen of Heaven, the ocean Star,

Guide of the wanderer here below,

Thrown on life's surge, we claim thy care:

Save us from peril and from woe.

Mother of Christ, star of the sea,

Pray for the wanderer, pray for me.

Some of the witnessing mass joined in on the song. Hans and Serge, along with some large man Owen had not met before, lifted Gabriel's body up from its resting place. They stepped into the acid, wading slowly towards the ever-dilating pyloric antrum. Once their grip was assured, they lowered Gabriel's body down to soak and float on down the line.

O gentle, chaste and spotless Maid,

From sin's domain God kept thee free,

Plead with thy Son, for He has paid

The price of our iniquity.

Virgin most pure, star of the sea,

Pray for the sinner, pray for me.

Serge led a military salute, right hand up and flat, facing forward. He too had begun to cry. Owen hadn't realized Serge was ex-military. He'd have to ask him about that when the time was right. Owen wished he was closer to the funeral. Maybe it would all be easier to take if he didn't feel quite so removed from it all. The sound of the singing had become unpleasant where he was seated, as if the driftwood choir was choking up all the oxygen in the room. He figured it was time he stepped away. As much as the body he now resided in horrified him, his instinct in moments of discomfort had always been to go for a walk.

And while to Him who reigns above,

In Godhead One, in Persons Three,

The source of life, of grace and love,

Homage we pay on bended knee.

Mother and Queen, star of the sea,

Pray for thy children, pray for me.

The music faded with the light. Owen wandered up and out of the stomach, following the wooden walkways towards the Heartland residences opposite his own. With the majority of Heartlanders attending the funeral, the normally bustling paths were quiet and still enough that Owen could make out the sound of the Leviathan's lungs rising and falling above. He could even see the flesh of the torso contract and expand, shifting its weight ever so slightly as it floated through some unknown sea.

Owen thought of one bright still morning he laid in bed with Ciara. They were both naked and coiled up in each other half below the sheets. Owen's head was resting on her chest as her fingers ran through his hair and he listened to her silky breath mingle with the dust floating above them in a sunbeam.

He couldn't help but wonder if she had learned what had happened to him. *Lost at sea on a river tube meant for two.* Would she cry remembering the small moments already surrendered to the past? Would she miss him? He knew he'd miss her. As long as he could remember her face, her laugh, the feeling of her skin, he'd miss her like the wind.

Owen's tears fell onto the warm and writhing meat below him, absorbing each bit of moisture like thirsty desert sand. Soon enough, he lost the will to give up another drop and sat in silence, head nested low in his arms, surrendering himself to a place of unthinking stasis, a negative, apocalyptic zen.

Time passed. Owen tried to center himself. In and out, Inhale, exhale, the machinery of the world of flesh like a clocktower citadel commanding attention.

Two voices passed by on a pathway some distance below. Owen could barely make out what they said at first, but as they circled by the quiet of the evening allowed him the clarity to hear as follows:

"Do you think he'll return this time?" One man asked.

"No, I don't think so," another replied. Neither voice was known to him. "This time seems different."

"But you said he's come back before, yeah?"

"I believe so, but I can't say for certain. He'd disappear for days or weeks at a time and come back stronger. A little younger looking, they'd say. Once he was gone for a year. But ask anybody in charge and they'll just say he was sleeping. Part of getting that old. That's the line they give and nothing will make them drop it."

"Fascinatin'."

"Remember: not a word to anyone, okay?"

"Right, right, loud and clear."

The conversation passed even further below, well out of audible range, leaving him once more with nothing but the heaving dark.

That night, Owen swung restlessly in his hammock. Every part of him needed rest, needed the blissful forget of sleep, yet that sleep came only in fits and spurts. His mind raced with questions he had no idea who to ask, or how. *How many others have died inside Leviathan? How many others were swallowed throughout the years, who still live here? How old was Gabriel when he died? How old was the Leviathan, really, and where the hell did it come from?*

He wanted to ask Serge, who he was most comfortable with normally, but a new fear kept him away. Serge, in shock and grief after Gabriel's passing and summary funeral, had been huddled in the corner of their shared tent-space for what felt like hours. Owen had tried to comfort him after Gabriel had died but to no avail. Serge had gone dim behind the eyes, a vacant dusty vacation house of a human body with one light left on through the autumn. Nothing would be heard.

Owen watched over Serge, offering him water and keeping away visitors until he had run out of energy. He curled up in his hammock and closed his eyes, hearing again the subtle pressure of the ocean on his inner ears that haunted him at the end of every night. He struggled to accept the thought that they really were underwater, likely too deep to survive a swim up to the surface. He thought of the Leviathan swimming in the waters of Key West watching the Cape Canaveral launches, in the black sludge-sea around London. *Why does it need to eat us? Why does it care who we are?*

He had almost drifted off completely when a queer noise caught his ear. The sound of hot metal letting off a bit of steam, a bit-down grunt. He peeked out from the edges of his hammock to see Serge awake and clutching a hot knife over a cooking-fire, cutting lightly into his forearm as he muttered bloody words of prayer.

"In Everything does the Heavenly Lord lay down His Immutable Design. Do so now in me, O Lord. Make me your canvas, make me your tool."

Owen sprang up in a panic. "What are you doing, Serge?"

The steam of the knife rose up from Serge's arm and passed before his unmoving gaze as he carved further into his skin, the wounds shaping into runes and circles. Meaningless sigils.

"Give me that knife!" Owen cried, pouncing forward. Serge, with the instincts of a wild dog, bit Owen's left hand with considerable force. Owen cried out in pain, reacting with a forceful slap of his right hand. The hit stunned Serge into releasing the grip of his jaw, sending the knife flying into the corner of the tent. The hot knife stuck in the floor of flesh. A tremorous boom shook the tent, shook the Heartlands whole. In the far distance, the shouts of the throat-catch shift rang out warnings to the people below.

"What the hell, dude? What the fuck is wrong with you?" Owen yelled.

Denizens across the body had sprung to life to investigate the bodyquake. Serge's feral gaze looked out at the stampede outside the tent. Owen clutched his bitten hand, wet with his own freshly drawn blood. Serge rose with a hunched jerk and gripped the dagger, yanking it free with slick certainty. The flesh ground began to bubble with fresh, black blood.

Owen froze. He was afraid of his only friend.

"What happened to peace, do you remember that? You told me it was the only way out!"

Serge stepped forward, red knife glimmering.

"Remember what Gabriel said!"

Serge froze. That reached him. His hands began to shake.

The flap to the tent flew open. It was Nina.

"Are you two alright in here? I heard shouting."

They both turned to face her, painting a violent scene. Nina noticed the knife at once. Without a word she left. Serge looked at Owen again, his manner changed completely. He looked fearful, manic, but the grip on his knife stayed firm despite the blood pooling down his forearm.

"...He said stay human," he mumbled. "But is this human? Is this humanity? Are we still fucking human?!"

Owen said nothing. Serge grew angry at the lack of response and the sound of approaching footsteps. His body tensed in feral readiness. With a grunt, he dashed out of the tent, pushing through the approaching crowd. Nina returned, followed by an entourage. They surrounded Owen, asking him question after question about what had happened, what Serge had said, where he had gone, as if Owen knew, as if he himself had not gone somewhere far away.

VII. Community Backbone

Morning came, supposedly. After the night's long commotion, life had finally settled down into a muted shade of normalcy. Hans stopped by the cot to see how Owen was holding up after the attack. He shared the news that Serge had disappeared somewhere inside Levi. Every search party sent out had been unable to spot a trace of him, and personnel were needed elsewhere throughout the body. He told Owen not to worry about his assigned duties for the day, that everyone understood how difficult Serge's break must have been for him. A small break was well within reason.

"Isn't there something I can do to be useful?" he asked. The idea of sitting around, stuck in his thoughts, watching the pulsing nooks and crannies of the Leviathan for signs of his feral roommate filled him with dread.

"Y'know, there might just be. You met the Ledger Man yet?"

"I've heard of him, but met him, no."

"Odd fellow, that one. He's in charge of records, calendars, marking the passage of time, things of that nature. Keeps to himself most always. 'Course that's always been for the best. Man's a bit of a nutter. He'd just get in the way down here."

Owen *mmm*ed knowingly.

"Anyway! Listen, in all the commotion, what with Gabriel… passing and Serge, y'know, going rogue, there hasn't really been a good time to let the old guy know everything that's happened. It'd be a good chance for you to meet him, get acquainted, while the rest of us see to things. Sound moxy?"

"Sounds moxy." They shook hands, and Hans was off. Owen watched in silence as he left, trying to imagine the kind of person the Ledger Man must be to stand out inside Levi. By the time he realized that Hans had never given him directions, there was no chance of tracking him down.

Owen was unsure where to begin, but there was little to do but move forward. Despite the jelly feeling in his legs, he set out in the vague direction of the throat, the highest point of Levi he had any directional awareness to find. As he snaked his way around the narrow wooden walkways of the Heartlands, he found himself stopping and looking out at the cavernous enormity of the monster's torso. Great canyons of bones and flesh, tissue and nerve. The expanse of viscera felt more like a castle or a grand demonic palace than any living thing.

He remembered again the shape of Levi breaching the dark water, great black pearls for eyes on a body of impossible size. Had it truly been this gargantuan then? Somehow the proportions felt wrong, as if the interior of the beast was larger than its exterior boundaries, piercing the deep sea like the hammer of a vengeful God.

Owen gripped the fleshy wall beside him as he felt himself lose his footing. Deep breaths, he reminded himself. In and out. It did him no good to question how.

"Feeling dizzy there?" called a voice from the walkway. Owen turned to see Janice, the woman he had met days before, her arms swinging freely by her sides.

Owen did his best to laugh. "A bit of vertigo, yeah."

"It never gets any easier. Oh mercy, especially when the thing gets hungry! You'll feel that soon enough, I'm sure."

Owen nodded. He didn't need that part explained.

"So, where were you headed on this beautiful day?"

Janice asked.

Owen laughed, despite himself. “Hans asked if I could head up to the Ledger Man, let him know about Gabriel.”

“Oh!” Janice clapped with approval. “What providence. Heading there myself, getting a little time away from the gumdrop, you understand. Care to accompany me?”

“That'd be awesome, actually. Hans, uh, didn’t actually tell me how to get there.”

“What a lovely stroke of luck. Each of us helping the other in the very spirit of seamanship. How droll.”

“How am I helping you, exactly?” Owen asked.

“Word is there’s a killer about! A girl can’t be too careful in times like these.”

Serge. “Right.” Sorrow returned like a weight as he remembered the night before after briefly, pleasurably putting it out of mind. He felt like he had made the wrong choices. Had he failed his new friend? It hurt to think it. But he barely knew Serge, let alone how to talk him down from his madness. No one could have talked him down then. *No one but Gabriel.*

“Dreadful business, all that,” Janice tutted, her disaffected eyes flickering in the torchlight. “Well then, shall we?”

Owen nodded, doing his best to put the grief once more behind him. The pair set off together, climbing the walkway of ship parts and hooks that spiraled around the endless torso of the impossible beast.

For some time, they followed the path in silence, passing around the perimeter of the gut and heading towards the upper back. After passing the intestinal periphery and slipping into the curtain of muscles contracting and expanding like mighty pistons or veiled suspension cables on a bridge, they had at last arrived at the great and towering spine, writhing like a snake between the folds of sinew and skin.

At their level, a small ropeway ran alongside the spine for some distance. At its end, it unraveled into a thin wooden bridge suspended above a gap between spine and flesh that led to a vertebrae that seemed much wider and deeper than the rest. On its surface was a circular door made of shipwood with a portcullis in its center, emanating a warm yellow light.

"Is this where he lives?" Owen asked, short of breath from the journey.

"Oh yes. Raffaele's got one of the nicest rooms in Levi. Figures he would, given how long he's lived here and all."

Janice crossed the rickety bridge and rapped her knuckles hard into the plank of the door. From within there was a muffled cry of shock and the sound of something heavy falling to the ground. Owen looked at Janice with concern, but she shook her head, smirking.

Two bulbous white eyes peeped up from the bottom rim of the portcullis, dipping out of view in a flash.

"Come in!" came a raspy voice. With a loud click, the heavy door popped open, letting more light spill out into the dark corner of Levi. "Quickly now!"

Owen's eyes were immediately strained by the density of light in The Ledger Man's chamber. Since his arrival, the light he'd become accustomed to was the greenish luminescence of the gastropool or the small lanterns and cooking pits casting deep shadows on the interior dark, but here was the light of a hearth. A strong, hearty fire. *The only hearth in Levi, and for one man?*

The room was narrow and deep, built into the meeting place of spine and rib, composed almost entirely of reused ship parts. Alongside the long walls were rows and rows of bookshelves crammed with books of many shapes and sizes, age and binding. Owen felt stunned at the sight of them. He realized he hadn't seen a single book since he'd arrived.

"Is that a new face I see? Please, come and have a seat," spoke the Ledger Man from his chair by a desk in the center of the room. The desk was sturdy and imposing, etchings of laurels and vines on its columned edges, a true relic of pre-modern opulence, with a large book with dry and leathery pages sprawled open on its surface. Behind these objects, The Ledger Man himself seemed much smaller, almost immaterial. His bony arms, peeking out from beneath a burlap sack of a robe, were covered in darkened bindings. The wrinkles of his face were deep as stone, which certainly tracked if the rumors were true and he had been here earlier than anyone else (save possibly Gabriel).

"Raffaele, you're looking fabulous," Janice shut the door behind her. As she did, Owen took note of how dry and smokey the air was inside the Ledger Man's room. *Must be incense or smoke to help keep the books from getting moist.* Janice slinked over to a modest wooden seat in the far corner and got comfortable, throwing her legs over the right arm and lounging like a cat on a windowsill.

"Thank you, my dear," the old man chuckled, pulling his ragged sleeves towards his wrists. "Now, it would appear we have a new resident!" He slapped his dry hands together and turned a page in the broad tome on the desk in the center of the room. "You must tell me everything there is to know about you."

"Me? Everything?" Owen asked.

There was a twinkle of light in The Ledger Man's eye. He nodded.

Owen, left with little option, did his best to share everything. He started with his name, city of birth, and a summary of his childhood interests and memories, the details of which Raffaele took particular interest in. They moved on to his adolescence, overcoming his social anxiety, his first loves. Janice had already snuck off to the back of the room and came back with a cup filled with an orange liquid, sipping it between quiet chuckles as Owen opened up with greater detail than he'd intended. All the while, Raffaele's quill was flying, spilling ink from a wide-topped bottle onto the heavy pages. He seemed to write small, conserving as much of the ink as he could with every stroke.

"Oh! The quill is dry. Just a moment." The Ledger Man rose, taking up the dark-stained bottle and walked over to the fire. He set the bottle down, reached over and took a small knife from a hook. Daintily, he laid the knife down on top of the burning logs, watched it for a moment, then began the slow act of unraveling the bandages on his left arm. Then another knife from a hook. Owen's hands gripped the arms of his chair. *Just like Serge.* The Ledger Man's bare arms were red, raw and mangled flesh wetly stuck to the glaze of the bandage. He cut into the arm without a wince or gasp of pain. The blood pooled down his arm and dripped into the jar, drop by drop. When the blood began to thin, he reached into the fire for the cauterizing knife.

Owen looked over at Janice, to see if she knew what Raffaele was doing, only to discover her in a delirium of her own, pupils missing in her open eyes. She was laughing and talking as if at a dinner party and not sprawled out, legs waving off a chair, inside the body of a beast of ancient myth. Owen was surprised by the pang of envy he felt. She was the first person he had seen smile like that since he arrived, even if it was in some sort of seizure, but still. It was a smile, a smile of peace.

The Ledger Man returned to the table, his arms rewrapped (bits of steam escaping from loose bandage) and holding the refilled bottle. "Now then, where were we?"

"Is all your ink made of blood?" Owen asked quietly.

"Most. I have been quite lucky over the years and received several octupi from the lads in throat-catch. For as long as I can keep them here and living, I've used their discharge as ink. But this body is just a tool to carry on my work, and in lean seasons a spot of blood will do nicely."

Owen looked at the dark, thick pages of the Ledger Man's book and back at the man's thin arms. He decided against his next question.

"I'd almost forgotten. I came here to tell you. There… was an accident. Gabriel has died."

The Ledger Man closed his eyes. "Thank you, but I am already well aware."

"You are?"

He nodded. "I felt him pass last night. He is an old, dear friend. We are bound together tightly, he and I. There will be a great struggle now without his leadership. It is inevitable."

"How did you-"

Suddenly, the wooden cup Janice had been drinking from slipped from her fingers and bounced against the flooring. The contents spilled out and stained the aging panels, causing the Ledger Man to laugh.

"I must fetch her a blanket," he said, rising to his feet to do so. Owen rose, too.

"What happened to her? What was she drinking? How did you know about Gabriel? Why does no one seem to care that someone died in here? Aren't you scared?!" His voice had risen more than he had realized.

The Ledger Man looked deep into Owen's eyes, as if watching the emotions dart back and forth inside his mind. Without a word, he walked over to the back of his room, into the shadowy corner the light but poorly reached.

He returned, a new cup in his hands, and set it down on the table without sitting.

"I was once very afraid. Afraid to be in here, afraid to die. Desperate for answers and meaning. But in time, I came to realize the many ways we are, inside the Leviathan and in the open world, intrinsically connected. Gabriel has not truly left us here, nor are we ourselves gone from the world that we remember. It is all more fascinating and strange than that."

He pushed the cup towards Owen. "Drink, if you wish to understand."

Owen looked at the small barrel of a cup with trepidation. He looked to Janice, giggling in a stupor in the corner. *Did she know more than she pretended to? What exactly was she going through?*

Raffaele returned to Janice's side with a blanket and laid it over her with a smile. Owen lifted the cup and looked inside at the amber liquid floating within.

"What is this?"

"It is the nectar of the gods, boy. Drink it and your eyes will open to the truth of this world, as I have. As Gabriel did."

"What about the others? Hans? Serge? Joanna?"

"None of them have made that choice to date."

"Why?"

"Because it was not offered."

"Is there a downside?"

"Wisdom always has its cost. But so too, its value." The Ledger Man laughed. "You won't die. Janice here drinks some every week or so."

Owen looked into the fire at the end of the room. His eyes were drawn to it, to the sheer brilliance of its light. He realized how violently sick of the darkness he had become. He was already becoming lesser inside Levi. Telling Raffaele of his past, it had felt like the story of another person's life, just a dream he had appropriated as his own. He thought of Serge, out there somewhere, already a shadow of his former self from the weight of this life.

What was there, really, to fear in a cup inside the belly of an evil god? Would he see visions of hell? Would he awake to find himself broken, unable to face his daily existence?

The drink could do nothing but set him free.

With a shout, he knocked the whole cup back like a beer at a frat party, taking Raffaele by surprise.

"My goodness, you drank that quickly. I was expecting you to take a sip or two at first. You should sit down before-"

VIII. Sea Eggs

Seagulls. The taste of sand. A beach.

Grey skies, jagged cliffs. Dry, white wind cutting as it blows. He stands. Something is missing in the feeling. No salt sitting on the lips. No warmth or chill on the skin. He rubs his hands together, fingers strangers to palms.

Below, by the water, a woman by a wooden booth. The sign reads **SEA EGGS**.

He scales down the rocks. Trips. No pain.

The woman waves.

He crosses the shore. Waves back.

She lifts up a basket and sets it on the booth. Inside it, a large red egg. She rubs her thumb and index finger together with one hand, extending the other.

He frowns, naked and pocketless. He asks her what she means by sea eggs.

She frowns. *Cheapskate.*

She points to the sea. She says, *Eggs from there.*

He doesn't understand.

She shakes her head. From her booth, she reaches down and grabs a whistle. She walks to the water and blows.

Nothing happens. He is unsure what to do in response.

Again, the whistle. The note held high and long. He walks over and touches the egg. It glows somewhat. He removes his hand.

Something snapping. A large wave rises and falls. Water flows out onto the beach, reaching the stand.

A guttural chirp. Before the woman, a great sea turtle rises from the wave.

She motions to the turtle. *Get on*, her eyes suggest.

He does.

She kicks the side of the turtle. It yawps and pushes itself back into the water.

He holds on to its neck, expecting it to dive. It doesn't.

He looks back at the shore. The woman waves farewell. He waves back. She flips him off and walks back to her booth.

The turtle is already far out to sea.

In the sky above, the sun and moon start moving. Day turns to night to day at a rapid pace in a starless firmament.

The turtle begins to sing.

Around them, bobbing in the waves, sea eggs. Thousands of them, ruby red and gleaming.

An island rises into view, large and draped in steep walls of stone. At its center, reaching high into the sky is a colossal tree of bone, segmented and writhing in the windless horizon. Its branches sway like fraying nerves weighted by heavy fruit. A single of its crystal seeds drops into the water and rises, red and egg-like, joining the rest.

On the shore, a figure stands, waving the turtle toward them.

It seems to recognize them.

IX. Open Waters

Owen's eyes opened. His skin was clammy and damp and felt like a stranger's. He could barely move, barely think. It was as if he had gone down into the shell of his body and was only now emerging. His extremities received the message of movement from his brain, but they did not yet belong to him again. His body twitched slightly, testing its functions.

"Oh, you're awake," came a startled, familiar voice. Peering overhead, the face of Nina appeared. "It's about time."

Owen blinked. He wanted to say "About time? Have I been asleep long?" But instead his lips limply slapped together and a raspy little moan came out.

Nina laughed. "Thirsty, huh?"

She drew a waterskin and put it to his lips. With every gulp of crisp, clear water, Owen felt the spring of life bound up and flow like dawnlight through his stony veins. With what strength he had, he lifted himself slightly from the bed.

"About time? Have I been asleep long?"

She nodded. "Janice brought you down here yesterday morning. You've been asleep like this the whole time. Every now and then, your eyes would open and look around, but you were completely unresponsive. It was unsettling, to be honest."

Owen's mind went to the steep climb of the walkways heading up to the Ledger Man's cabin. Had she really carried him down on her own? She'd acted like she needed protection, or so it had seemed at the time when they crossed paths. Thinking back on it now, however, made him realize the obfuscation and control in everything that Janice said. After all, she drank that liquid once a week, the Ledger Man had said? And Owen was only-

"A lot's happened, Owen," Nina said somberly.

He blinked. "What?"

"Since you left. A lot's happened. You should know about it."

She started explaining what she could. Only a few short hours after Owen had left for the Ledger Man's, a call had rang out from the throat-catch. Levi had swallowed a living human again, the first arrival since Owen himself, the first arrival not to be met by the stern and loving guidance of Gabriel.

"Needless to say, people were worked up," Nina noted.

Crowds gathered in the gastropool to meet the new arrival. Hans, sensing the disarray, reminded everyone present to stay calm and to remember to treat the digestive immigrant with the respect and support they had all been extended after finding themselves in such shocking and horrible conditions. But he had barely begun assuaging the crowd when a second cry went out, this time accompanied by the emergency bell.

"Emergency bell?" Owen asked.

"Right, you wouldn't know," she replied. "There's a lever system in the throat that connects to a cathedral bell Levi swallowed from a collapsing seaside church. This was long before my time. A few other places in Levi are also wired up to it, but it's meant to be used only in dire circumstances to call for immediate aid."

"Well what was the situation, then? What justified using the bell?" he asked.

Nina rubbed her face in grief. "It turns out our new neighbor is a killer."

Owen's stomach turned. "Oh."

"When the rush of swallow-water had passed, the throat-catch workers found themselves looking over the bodies of two men coiled in the nets. But, as they called out to the new arrivals, it became increasingly apparent that only one of the men was moving. They sent out a warning, recognizing the danger of a still body in the nets. Right as they reached out hooks to draw the bodies in, it happened. One rose and drew a gun."

"Wait, a gun?" Owen asked.

Nina nodded. "They said it's the first gun to be swallowed by Levi since the end of the second World War."

She continued. The story went that the throat-catchers froze in place, unsure of what to do. The man with the gun took aim at everyone he could make out around him. He was confused, agitated. All too common a reaction, made that much more dangerous by the weapon he had been swallowed with. They did their best to let him know he was in no danger, that they were there to help him. After some time, the man seemed to calm down, but he refused to hand over his weapon. He held tightly to the steel grip, ready to fire at a moment's notice.

The catch-hands tried asking him what had happened to the other man, who increasingly appeared to be no longer living. The man said he was not sure. He spoke poor English, so he was hard to understand for those working that particular shift. The workers offered to take him to the gastropool and provide what medical assistance they could, as was procedure and the man relented, letting them lead him down to safety.

“Do you remember the throat-catch Jack?” Nina asked.

“Vaguely, yeah,” Owen replied. He did not.

“He’s the one who rang the bell. He did it on their way down, thinking it might help warn us here in the gastropool, but I don’t know how they could have prepared us for what would happen.” She paused. “Do you think you can stand?”

Owen checked the feeling in his toes. “I might be able to, yeah. Why?”

“It’s best I take you to Hans and you see for yourself what’s going on,” she muttered.

After a few moments, Owen found he could stand and move around, albeit slowly. He adjusted his patchwork robes and fixed his hair and they were off. The Heartlands were buzzing with motion, people running headlong, peeking out nervously from the walls of their cot. In the distance, coming from the tunnels leading to the gastropool came a new, eerie glow and the sounds of many people speaking at once.

Owen looked to Nina, who met his eyes. She nodded, one eyebrow lifted, as if to say *You ain’t seen nothing yet.*

As they passed into the central chamber of the gastropool, Owen’s eyes strained under the new light. Rather than the normal low-green luminescence of the acid, the wide chamber of the central stomach was bathed in a pale, cold brilliance. Nina took Owen by the wrist and led him onwards, up the shipwreck scaffolding and closer to the sound of the chanting.

On the center platform, halfway up the total height of the stomach a crowd of thirty people were gathered, looking upwards towards the roof of the stomach. Despite the newness of the light, the harshness of it on his eyes so well-adjusted to shadow, Owen too looked up. Above them, floating as if in deep water was the source of the alien light: A still, laid out human body.

A gruff voice came rising from the crowd. "Nina, Owen! You've made it. Thank the devil." It was Hans.

"I just got him up a few minutes ago," Nina replied loudly, the assembly paying them no mind. "He knows about the newcomers but not all this."

Owen squinted at the floating person, mesmerized by this strange new development. He couldn't make out how it was the body was floating in the air or how the brilliant light flowed forth from its frame. It wasn't coming from the open eyes and mouth of the body. It just *shone.*

Hans gripped Owen on the shoulder like an uncle might, half-lovingly, turning him back in towards the conversation. "I'll give you the skinny, boy. I could tell that Russian boy was nervous about being near the stiff for too long. Figured he'd been the one who killed the fellow, out at sea to dump his body when ol' Levi decided on a snack. Now, we don't have any protocol for things like this. Most bodies in throat-catch come living, whole or, well, chewed up, as is the bugger's way. Just how it is."

Owen shivered. *So Levi really doesn't swallow everyone whole.*

Hans continued. "By the time we've ascertained this fellow here was dead as a doornail, the Russian can tell we're none too eager to discuss the matter. Nina mention the gun yet?"

Nina nodded.

"Since I got here, I ain't never seen a working firearm in Levi. Gabriel used to say a gun or two had ended up inside a bit of ship, 'longside a body of course, but wet and rusted things, gussied scrap. So none of us felt too worried about this one until we'd gathered around him, ready to pounce. Figured he was as much a harm to himself as to the rest of us. Sharp eyes on this Slav, though. Worked out the plan. It was Lee who lunged out first, going for a sweep of the legs over the netting. That's when he fired."

Hans motioned over to the edge of the platform, where Lee lay, a dark wet rag covering his face.

Han's eyes were dewey with tears. "Lee was a good man, one we sorely needed after Gabriel left us. He deserved better."

Nina shook her head. "It was a stupid goddamn plan."

Hans went red on a dime, incensed at Nina's insubordination, but his eyes drifted over to Lee and the fury calcified into bitter regret. "Aye, it was."

Nina stared at him a moment before clearing her throat. "You were explaining the glowing."

"It was pandemonium. The moment the bullet hit Lee, that dead fellow started to shout. Threw everybody off, *especially* the Russian. Stiff screamed this deep, low howl and the air all 'round him started to blow at us like a seastorm gale. Then the bastard started floating, glowin' just like this a moment after. By the time we acclimated to the dead man's weather show, the other was gone, shouting something or other in his mother tongue."

Behind them, the onlookers in the gastropool lobbed ropes up into the air, trying to bind the floating corpse and bring it back to the rickety platform, gasping in frustration as the ropes slid tensionless off its radiant, dangling limbs.

"So, the Russian is just... gone?" Owen asked.

"Do we have people out looking for him?" Nina asked.

"Aye, but few. We're still getting our grounding since Gabriel died and the leg flooded, which we've done well to handle, I'd say. The old badger ran a smooth ship but he never passed on any administrative tips or well-worn notes of encouragement to us. Keeping Levi in order is a tall ask these days, I'm not happy to tell you."

Owen felt cold sweat on his neck. It was hard to think things could get worse here than normal, but it had. What little security Owen had adjusted to on his arrival was gone. Every shadow, every orifice was a threat now until the problem was addressed. No safety, no comfort in the belly of the beast.

Nina stomped firmly, snapping herself into action through a flare of will. "Has anyone checked The Pits?"

Hans blinked. "N-no, but that's-"

"Not safe for most of us, no. But Owen and I could pass through mostly unnoticed. We're no obvious targets."

Owen felt nervous at the thought of wandering outside the safe perimeters. "What about Serge? He's still out there, somewhere."

"It's not Serge that's our greatest worry anymore," Nina replied. "This gunman threatens everything. At any moment, he could kill Levi with a well-placed shot and leave us all dead in the water. He needs to be found. Stopped."

Hans nodded grimly. His eyes bore keenly into Nina, judging her posture and conviction as if in search of something. "Are you sure you're up to this, Nina? The Pits are outside our boundaries. Now more than ever. We can't reach you if there's an emergency."

"In and out. We find them, we bring news back."

Hans grabbed Nina by the forearm. "No playing hero."

She broke his grip and dusted off her shoulders. She wasn't going to let herself be diminished like this any longer. She had her pride, and she knew the risks better than Hans ever could. "Have some faith in me. In us, Hans."

A rope-pulling Heartlander fell from the scaffolding, dangling above the deep centerpoint of the acid. Hans, ever the steady sailor, whipped around and lept to action with a lion's roar, grabbing the man's forearm.

"With me, men! Heave! Heave!"

Putting their all into it, Hans and two other groaning men lifted the rope-master from the edge of the platform and safely away from the thirty foot drop into the acid below.

Hans rose and turned back to Nina and Owen. The sweat-licked lines of his face had changed since Gabriel died, grown deeper, becoming canyon ridges, the creases book-ending his grim smile carved the deepest.

"Godspeed, you beautiful bastards. Smoke that Slav gopher out his hidey hole."

X. The Pits

It had been a long time since Nina had stepped foot in the Pits. Years, if years were years anymore. Long periods of dark. It's not that she hadn't wanted to, she had, but wanted it the way a person who's leaned too far away from bitter truth learns to crave their comeuppance.

Leaving the gastropool with Owen barely registered as an experience. Her mind was elsewhere, caught up in the distant past. With minimal effort, she could close her eyes, relax her muscles and all at once be back again in the open ocean, floating in a scuba suit in the eye of a cuttlefish tornado. The memory of laughter bubbled up in her throat, hollow pressure imitating joy. She could almost still feel the ticklish churning embrace of the school's movements reflected in the water from that precious moment.

Growing up, she'd laid beneath the sheets come bedtime and dreamed of the warm and colorful world beneath the sea. The secret parade of life and light below the gray wastes of dry, continental society. She had not dreamed of the dark of the Leviathan. Not that shadow from the deep. Not that hellish absolution. But dreams could only carry so far.

"Hey Nina?" Owen asked, bringing her back to her surroundings.

"Yeah?"

Owen seemed afraid to ask what he wanted to know, looking down at his hands like something was written on them. Nina found herself appreciating that hesitation. Many of the men living inside Levi were too sure of themselves, too demeaning, the cruel or unexamined hearts of sailors and patriarchs, but that was nothing new. Nina had run up against that long before she was eaten by the beast.

"The way you two were talking about the Pits..." Owen started.

"That they're not safe for Heartlanders? Yeah. A bit of an exaggeration on Hans's part, but not completely wrong."

"Hans said 'outside our boundaries.'"

Nina felt that pit in her heart fill with bitter ash. "Gabriel's doing. You got here just to catch the tailend of the status quo, but the image Gabriel painted of solidarity for all us survivors was built on top of a foundation of shit."

They headed down alongside the snaking intestinal mass, weaving between the odd passerby.

"Where are we going?" Owen asked.

"There's an equipment station ahead. We'll need to be ready."

They continued in silence, Nina leading the way, Owen following close behind. Nestled into a barren corner was a wooden shack. Fragmentary shoots of dim light peeked through slits in repurposed panel walls as the smell of something stale and rotted tainted the air.

"This is it," Nina mumbled. "The Armory."

She walked up to the front door and rapped on it with the back of her fist three times in quick succession. A pause. Then twice more.

The stiff silence lingered in the air. Nina looked at Owen, her confusion turning to anger.

A nervous voice behind the door called out. "Who goes-"

"It's Nina, you twat! Open the door!"

The door flung open. A small, stocky man with a

hefty wart on the left side of his chin and a patchy beard looked at Nina with great displeasure, harrumphed, and moved aside. His hooded eyelids hid two white embers that flickered on and off in the shadows outside the Armory.

Owen couldn't help but smile at Nina after her sudden outburst. "Was that a British accent just now?"

Nina sighed, frustrated at having been caught. "I grew up in London. I didn't stay, though. It only comes out in bursts."

"That's cool. I've never been to Britain. Did you like it there as a kid?"

Nina shook her head. The last thing she wanted to talk about was her parents, or the life of a young black girl in London decades ago. She had made so many choices and lived so many lives since those days. She preferred to avoid sharing anything of her past anymore. It served no good inside Levi to keep old identities and cling to flags and empires. They all served under one ruler now, and old lives were nothing more than weights that left unchecked sent you sinking down into the cold abyss. This is what called her to the sea in the first place. To be free of these petty narratives she had never decided for herself.

"So what are we grabbing here?" Owen asked, sheepishly standing inside the Armory. Nina realized she had been glaring at the door guard, who had lost his composure entirely under pressure and was squirming to the far side of the shack to escape her gaze.

"Right, right." She stepped inside the shack, grabbing two cloaks off rusty nails beaten into the soggy side-panels of the makeshift storehouse. "Put this on. We need ropes, a lantern. Tools to navigate and blend in as much as we're able."

Nina watched Owen fumble his way through putting

on the cloak, struggling to get his arms through the raggedy armholes. He really was kind of pathetic. With a quiet laugh, she grabbed two shivs, fastening one to her waist-rope and holding the other out towards the hole where Owen's head would pop out of the cloak.

He emerged, gasping at the blade in his face and falling backwards into the haybed the guards used to rest in between and during shifts. Outside, the doorguard also gasped, clearly startled by the sudden noise and fearing the worst.

Nina laughed vigorously. "You'll need this, too. Can you protect yourself?"

Owen frowned and quickly grabbed the knife. "Yeah, I can." He hooked the knife to his own rope belt by the hook nailed into the end of its hilt.

"I'm sorry. You're just easy to abuse, like a cat."

"I almost got stabbed a few days ago, forgive me for being a little knife-shy." Owen's eyes registered how Nina's mood had lightened, and his frustration sublimated into simple embarrassment.

"You know, it's good to be a cat," Nina offered, finishing up gathering the last of their essentials before they exited the Armory and the doddering doorman returned to his peaceful isolation. "With nine lives you might actually outlive us all in here."

What the Heartlanders call "The Pits" is really best understood as the lower half of the Leviathan. Anything below the upper intestines, from the gluteal hills, calves, knees and below qualified. From the anatomical center, life extended in every conceivable direction with diminishing returns, fighting against the inevitable and carving out cancerous pockets of normalcy contained within the walls of flesh of the great devourer.

In the world of the Pits, most of that normalcy could be found in the area of the Leviathan's groin. It was here the people of the Pits could benefit from the most residual body heat of the creator's core. People made the most of the Strip, the long band of space between the skyscraper-like thighs, turning it into a labyrinthine construction of ropeways and patchwork bungalow huts and tents that brimmed with activity at almost all times of the interior 'day'. Life in the Pits required resources like fabrics and repair materials at a far greater rate than the Heartlanders, with far less access to intake. This led to competition, brutality, crime (as Heartlanders would still refer to it, a word that Pitters would laugh away as vestigial noise of the old world) and always, for those at the bottom who had not already surrendered to their fate, it left the climb.

The Strip was busier than normal, or at least as Nina remembered normal to be. People rushed along the plankways, bartering with merchants dangling from stalls and open windows. Courageous souls rappelled on taut ropes down to the inner thighs, strapped tight with buckets of boiled seawater to bring back down below. Life was moving at a breakneck pace, which struck Nina as all the more disturbing. Pitters knew better than to waste their energy unnecessarily. Down here, it was the most precious resource of all.

Nina and Owen watched the commercial strip from inside a currently vacant lean-to just off the main thoroughfare of the Strip. "This is incredible," Owen whispered.

Nina nodded. "People work hard down here. Harder than the Heartlanders. They've got no choice in the matter."

As they sat and watched, Owen noticed the entirety of the Strip teeter back and forth from the undulations of the

Leviathan. "I thought it was disorientating back in the stomach, but this is... Gravity feels different."

Nina said nothing, but Owen's observation stuck with her. Long ago, she had turned her analytical mind off to the physical conditions of life inside the Leviathan. It was a defense mechanism, a way to accept the disgusting, incomprehensible reality of extended life inside a man-like hypergiant. In order to survive, to press on without succumbing to madness, there was much she had needed to not see. To forget. But Owen was right. Gravity felt "realer," more earth-like in the torso, no matter what way the titan oriented itself in the water. *How?* she wondered again, despite herself. How could anything defy so many common laws of physics, so many obvious impossibilities?

All Nina had ever found in that line of questioning was this: Truth, science, natural law, the body's senses, everything concrete, everything Nina once took cold comfort in, it was all a lie. A comfortable illusion. Or Hell, in its abyssal dominion, abided by no rules but the rule of the beast.

"We need to focus," Nina said, gritting her teeth. "We have a job to do."

Owen nodded. "So where do we start?"

"You go ask around. You're too new to be recognized. Act the part. Say you heard a rumor someone has a gun in the Pits, ask if they've heard anything. If they offer the barest glimmer of a response, look to someone else for approval, make any visible signal, you get the hell out of there and make your way back here."

Owen sighed, the risks they were committing to vividly dancing on his face. "What're you gonna do?"

"Try to keep an eye on you, and while I'm at it stay on the lookout for signs of suspicious activity. There's a good chance there's something going on beneath the surface. There's a new tension in the air. An excitement. Excitement is normally the first thing that dies in the Pit."

"Okay, gotcha," Owen said, readying himself to leave. Nina, panged with anxiety, reached out and clutched his forearm.

"Nothing reckless," she insisted. "In and out."

Owen smiled, a little relieved to be reminded. "In and out."

He passed out the lean-to and into the thoroughfare. With the trained awareness of a city boy, Owen quickly faded into the crowd of passerby. It seemed he knew without being told to take a wide lap before stopping and drawing any attention to himself. Nina sighed with relief. This wasn't quite as hopeless as she feared. From her spot in the shadows, she watched Owen move down the ropeway and disappear from view before turning her attention back again to the street ahead.

It hurt, in some quiet way, to look hard. It hurt to be reminded how many Pitters were disabled, from before or after they had fallen into the sea and into Levi's thrashing maw. Unlike the Heartlanders, they were older, sicker, bundled up in the cold with the ones Gabriel didn't trust to work or maintain order. The label of 'outcast' felt all the harsher when you looked close at who was bundled and discarded together beneath its shadow. Nina knew all too well it wasn't the smart, the good or even the strong who were saved. It was the able and complaint. The permissive. The weak. Once, it had been her.

Just outside the lean-to, Nina could make out fragments of a passing conversation.

"Heard old Gabe died recently!"

"Bloody hope so. Rat bastard."

"Wouldn't they have told us by now? Made some 'proclamation'?"

"What good would it do them fuckers to tell us anything? Might as well tell the family dog you took a shit at work, or the milkman-"

So not everyone knows. Nina kept her eyes trained on the ones doing business, shaking hands, whispering into each other's ears. Unlike the gastropool, where people often spoke and reacted in large groups, accustomed to the psychic safety and abandon of the group mentality, there was little to gain from sharing knowledge. Nina remembered life down here as an economy of secrets, a web of give and take. It kept power in the hands of the powerless and evened the playing field, though it also made things dangerous for the careless.

How was she going to learn more? She'd been confident before this was the right path, but revisiting the Strip had keenly reminded her of its difficulties. Still, there was no one better suited in the Heartlands to this task. Anyone else might have come with force and fury and kicked up a hornet's nest. She needed to prove to the others and to herself that there was a place for her. There was yet a purpose to her days. There was a reason to keep on moving.

On the ropeway, Nina could make out the silhouette of Owen's cloak bobbing closer, moving a pace or two too quick. She reached to her waist and drew the dagger, hiding like a heavy shadow by the creaking door, readying the taut muscles in her arm to strike.

With a huff, Owen tucked in around the corner and hid against the wall. Their eyes made contact and she read danger in his gaze, darting back and forth from Nina to the direction he came. Followers. Nina flashed a sliver of steel at an upward angle so he understood the plan. He held out two fingers, mouthed "*slow*."

Like cobras suspended on a jungle branch, cold-blooded and sure, they waited.

A figure quickly passed them by, then several more just behind. None had a hunter's awareness, just unconditioned momentum. The static blur of A to B. Owen's eyes widened. He could feel his pursuers getting closer, hear their footsteps ring heavy and slow on sodden planks.

They held their breath. The two figures crossed into view a short distance from the doorway. One tall, missing most of his right shoulder. The other, shorter, wiry. They inched forward, scanning the Strip as if they were unsure where exactly Owen had gone. The shorter one stepped closer to the lean-to sniffing like a pug. Despite the imminent danger, Owen stifled a laugh. Nina looked at him with furious confusion, her weapon arm still prepared to strike. She mouthed *SHUT UP SHUT UP* and Owen bit his tongue.

The wiry man turned to face the doorway where they lay in wait.

A vicious *SNAP* slashed the air. A taut pulley rope split in half just above the main level of the Strip. A woman, suspended on the line, screamed with horror as she plummeted below, into the dark space of crushing muscle where thigh meets torso and becomes a moving ravine. A few cries of panic and concern, countered with an equivalent smattering of cynical laughter filled the vacuum of silence left in her wake. A crowd quickly massed together on the edges of the ropeway, as if one might be able to spot where she had fallen, and the two men were swept up in the madness and away from the bungalow door frame.

There was no time to hesitate. Nina grabbed Owen by the collar and pulled him out of the hut, keeping low, going against the pedestrian tide.

"Where are we going?" Owen asked, crowd-whispering.

Nina had known from the beginning she would have to see him again, no matter how much it would hurt. It was even clearer now that there was no other option.

"To see a friend."

ტ

After a few moments of panicked creeping, Nina and Owen had slipped through the ill-defined boundaries of the Strip and its decentralized patrols. As soon as they had passed into the meat of the upper leg, the small tunnel spaces bore into tectonic plates of supple muscle fiber, things got dark and cold. The faint and haunting suggestion of warmth hung on, emanating from the flesh of the beast, but away from the human frictions the true cold of the sea seeped in and claimed dominion over the Leviathan's distant extremities. Those that bore this bleak and hellish night unending were never proud or powerful. They were but hollow figures, shades of their original life. Bundles of rags shuffling about on bony hooks, clutching to well-weathered canes for help with their footing on the chill and slippery meat.

"Is this the leg that was cut open?" Owen whispered.

Nina nodded. "It's still so cold, it must be. Who knows how many were left to die of frostbite or drowned down here in the frigid floodwater without being brought topside to thaw."

Ever since Gabriel's passing, she had been terrified. She had fought the urge to check, to ask others to be sure. It would have been easier to look away, to let what happened happen without dwelling too hard on the brutal truth. That was the choice she had made, wasn't it? That was who she was. Nina knew there was a good chance her friend was gone. He could have died by now. Likely should have. But maybe not. Maybe he had left of his own accord, become a Pitter proper. Started over.

She weaved between strands of contracting muscle, following the unspoken compass in her bones to the last place she had seen him. Each step came slower than the last, knowing her answer was before her, neither possibility a fulfilling one. Was he still waiting, or no? Was he dead or alive?

A voice like a paper howl rose up from the dark. “Hello, Nina.”

Nina froze in her tracks, causing Owen to walk into her back and fall back slightly. She looked around for a familiar silhouette, for the presence of weight that would tell her where the man she had once loved was hiding.

“Here,” came the voice again, and all at once she understood. Against the wall of flesh, inside it, was the face of Mannfred, set like an ornamental mask, his features placid, eyes distantly deep. The rest of his body was gone from view, as if he were floating beneath the water and breaching just to breathe, buried in the ever-writhing soil of meat.

Nina bit her tongue, the shock like a cannon to the gut. “Dr. Steinhagen,” she just barely made out.

“Doctor,” he croaked, his sheet-thin voice breaking into a raspy laugh. “Such respect.”

“What… What happened?”

His downward gaze hid a light smile. “I had nowhere to go, Nina.”

“And no one helped you move?” she asked, hating the words she was speaking, feeling their bitter condemnation like a hot knife buried in the ribs.

Again, he laughed. “No. But now… I am less cold. So

it is fine. What brings you back to me, Nina? Why now, so very close to the end? Apart from irony."

Her footing grew weak as she sought the words.

"We were sent to search for two dangerous men," Owen spoke up, startling Nina. "There's reason to believe a man with a working firearm has retreated to the Pits."

Mannfred's snake-like smirk was unchanged, his gaze placidly locked on Nina's slumped shoulders. "I see… You put yourself in danger to protect your fellow man. Commendable."

Owen looked at Nina for a signal. It was clear he was unsure of his decision to speak up, but he knew nothing of Mannfred, nothing of Nina, really. He was in over his head, learning of the endless dark of Levi's shadow, where even the narrative of survival he had been fed upon arrival rang hollow and sank deeply, as if without all meaning.

"Gabriel is dead, Mannfred," Nina announced, reaching for authority in a moment of great discomfort.

Mannfred's eyes lowered. His smirk grew. "A great rush of water. The screaming of men. A call rings out: *'Hark! Pull him aft! His skin is ice, warm him! To the belly, damn the rest!'* Then another: *'No… we finish the deed. It is required of us, men, above all else. Who is with me?'* A long pause, pregnant with meaning. Again: *'Then I go alone!'*"

Owen and Nina were both astonished. "No one helped Gabriel that day?" Owen asked.

Mannfred hummed an uncertain tone. "So it would seem. But what authority can the dead claim among the ones who walk above them? Heed me but little."

Nina sighed, salt cascading down her cheek, the taste of blood and iron on her tongue. "Mannfred… I'm sorry. I thought… this was what you wanted. For me to leave. To keep hoping for some way out. I just couldn't face you. I could barely move. Even now, I don't know what brought me here. I hate these Heartlanders, Mannfred. I hate this life! I want to go back to Bermuda. To our days, you and I, beneath the sun, on open waters. I want us to go back one day, somehow. I want… I want..."

Mannfred's death mask face began to soften, a flush of life rushing below his pale cheeks and brow. Though his wrinkles were smoothed out or sanded down and his expression stayed all but steady, even in the dark a change could be seen. "Sweet Nina, waste no tears on me. We are both dead, you and I. We died in blue Bermuda. Nina should have aged by now, you see. Hair all streaked with gray, creases framing her almond eyes, an expert in her field, a life well lived. You… You are a dream of a woman of Earth, a living thing, here to torment me away from that last fading step into my final slumber. I am long dead, Nina. You could not hurt me. You never could."

His eyelids limply closed, his mouth slightly agape. Nina cried, collapsing to her knees. Owen laid his hand upon her shoulder. She could not bring herself to take it but let it linger there.

Mannfred was right. She was a ghost, a shell of herself. And yet, her shell still kept moving, kept chasing this impossible quest: To survive. Escape. To revenge her dead soul and that of Mannfred's on the Leviathan who had damned them all.

"Mannfred...Have you heard anything of the man with the gun?" Nina asked, her voice raw and quivering.

Mannfred's eyes did not open. His lips were still. A moment of quiet passed between them all, before:

"The Perennial. A mass is gathering. Seek it."

Nina wiped her eyes, stepping forward. She placed her hand upon his cheek, as much as she was able.

“Sleep, Mannfred. Become the sea.” She kissed his brow. It felt like winter. She steeled herself and turned to Owen watching her with care. “Let’s go.”

ዕ

The Perennial, nestled in the valley center of the groin between two great walls of flesh and bone, was the chief watering hole of the Pits. It was a fortress of flotsam, the sturdiest construction in Levi outside the broad shelves of detritus in the gastropool. The flickering glow of hearthlight seeped through the windows and cracks in the paneling, a lodestone for the weary Pitter in need of respite from their sorry lot. People hung from the balcony ropes, clamoring up and around the building like partygoers at a stranger’s house, forming clusters of manic activity above the steady buzz of the general crowd.

By the main entrances, several imposing figures stood about, chatting amongst themselves, just as Nina had expected. They didn’t need to get into the building, not today. Just stick close to the commotion. Take in what they could. She knew just the way to do so. In the back of the structure, a small windowed alcove leading straight into flesh was the perfect place to hide, wait and bear witness.

Nina rested up against the bar’s exterior wall, taking a moment to center the typhoon inside her heart. She had known this expedition would test her, that it would cut her down to the marrow. After all, why else would she have taken the lead? Why else throw herself back into the valley of wolves if she was not, in some strange manner, desperate to be eaten?

Owen, looking in from the window sill, tapped her

on the shoulder. "Look!"

From their vantage point, they could make out the mass of Pitters sitting about the feast hall, glowing in the warm light from the central hearth. They were largely encircled around the bar. Owen was shocked to see the Perennial was better stocked than the Heartlands, pointing at the wall with stunned awe, but Nina remembered the brewing scene down here was as cutthroat as it was profitable. So many bottles and barrels, so much flowing alcohol to drink and sell and kill over, and yet the secret of the alcohol itself, what it was and where it came from, was as guarded a secret as anything topside.

Seated at the bar, distinguished by a shock of bleach blonde hair slicked back, emphasizing his pale skin and darkened eyes, was him. The Russian. The tattoos on his face and arms were already losing some of their permanence and shape inside the Leviathan, as if the enzymes that clung to every surface were eating through his skin. He stuck out like a sore thumb, but no one seemed to be looking his way.

No, it was the woman with one foot up on a stool, her red naval coat fluttering behind her, her left eye wrapped in fabric beneath a roam of onyx locks that commanded the room. Nina knew her well. She was the current owner of the Perennial, setting up roost after being devoured in the Spanish Civil War. A firebrand who cast out towards the revolution of her time and found only damnation on the path.

"Carmela," she whispered.

"My people!" Carmela sang out, each syllable pouring forth like fire. "Gather around, drink deep and be merry. On this dark night in Satan's ass do we drink to the death of Gabriel!"

The people cheered. "Fuck the stiff! Death to Gabriel!"

"Few in the Beast have done more to perpetuate the suffering, the hardship of our people! Few have deserved as pathetic a fate as his, crying in pain, frozen and burned alike in his own bathhouse of inequity!"

Another cheer.

Carmela's laughter fell like a bawdy waterfall, her cup of schadenfreude runneth over. "News of his death has been confirmed through several sources, but none so interesting as our new friend here, the most recent arrival to Levi, Ivan of Russia. Give him a Perennial's greeting, my people!"

Ivan raised his cup to toast their boisterous welcome.

"Ivan speaks little English, as many of our number do. Allow me to tell you the tale, my bastards! Drink freely and listen well!"

"She is *electrifying*," Owen whispered.

Nina scoffed, unwilling to openly agree.

Inside, Carmela downed a swig of mead and slammed her foot into the counter. With a graceful leap, she came down into the center of the crowd, her arms swirling like a vortex to lure in the attention of the audience as the embers of her eyes shimmered with a mummer's conviction.

"As Ivan tells the tale, the Russia of today is a land of blood running beneath the cobblestone. For those born into high status, life is beautiful, the sweet summer air kissed by the breath of the Black Sea. But in the shadows of the light many such as us, such as Ivan, are born. An alcoholic father drowned in his sin, a mother a destitute and hardened rose. What fate, as ever, awaits a child so damned by circumstance? We all know!"

The crowd, battered and rehearsed, calls back: "The Beast! The Beast awaits!"

Carmela laughs and nods in a half-pirouette. "And it found him at sea! A man of Sochi, a living tool of death, a mafioso! You would think he would be greeted like a king in the Heartlands, but no! For his story was from its very conception an act of Fate, a series of impossibilities that struck our world and reached us here in hell as if to spark a heavenly fire! The people must understand why and how, so tell them all! Why were you at sea, good Ivan?" Carmela asked, wheeling her theater back to the subject of her production, to the killer with white hair.

Ivan barely moved from his seat in the chair. He looked up at Carmela, his eyes wet with admiration, embarrassment, hatred and pain, to hear his life performed, put outside himself and thus transformed by this woman's powerful telling.

"To kill my brother," he spoke. The room went quiet.

"And why did you seek to kill your brother, Ivan?"

"My boss, Sergei. He says... Dimitri cheats him. All of us. It was him, or my family. My mother. Two sisters. And it must be me."

Carmela's hand graced his chin, sliding one soft thumb on the curve of an imaginary tear. "So you took him to sea."

Ivan nodded.

"And you brought with you a gun, with which to commit your ordered fratricide."

He nodded again, pupils black. But then, after a moment's hesitation, his head shook violently to each side. "No. I could not. It… it was poison."

"Yes. Because you could not shoot your brother. Because you are no monster, Ivan, but a man, trapped in pain, ordered to suffer and to make suffer. Instead, you fed your brother the poison at sea."

"We had dreamed of sailing the world as boys. It was a gift. For us both. I gave him wine."

"And as your brother drank the wine, as you looked out on the sun setting on the lolling waves of the Black Sea, a shadow passed beneath you. The shadow of a whale and a man in one. The waves roared open and your ship cracked in twain. In an instant you felt yourself slip into the sea and pulled beneath, all the world a storm, everything pointless and cruel and suddenly black."

The crowd was silent, looking down into their cups, each and every soul reliving their last moments with the sea and sky. Nina wondered, in the freeing pause, just how the Leviathan had crossed into the Black Sea from the Atlantic. How was it that no world power, no portsman of Istanbul knew of the god-beast that swam below them? Or was it somehow else that the Beast could travel where it may, bending space and time in order to swim free?

She thought to run it by Owen and turned to do so only to discover him lost, eyes transfixed on the scene in the bar, tears rolling down his face. He was being pulled in, she realized. And though it pained her to realize, why would he not be? If this was true, if Ivan really was innocent, what was it they had truly volunteered to do?

Camela continued her performance. "So it was Ivan joined us in the Beast, strung up in the throat-catch net, poisoned brother by his side. The topsiders, led by Hans, could not speak to Ivan, could do nothing but suspect, detain! And in this moment of confusion, this fearful hellish scene, two miracles at once transpired!" Carmela turned to face the crowd, her inner fire summoned back to its fullest. "The first: Ivan's gun went off!"

The room became a barrel of pandemonic awe. Some

moved forward, gripping each other to stay standing. Chairs and tables, glasses and wooden legs were thrown about the room. Carmela climbed back onto the bar.

"I know that you all know what this fact means! It warms my heart to see the tremor pass through each and every one of you. The terror! The confusion! And yes, the *hope*! But there is more, my brothers and sisters, my demons of the deep, for you see there was a second miracle! On the border of life and death, as if responding to this all important revelation, our own dead Dimitri awoke!"

The crowd ran forward, taking hold of Carmela and Ivan, tugging at the fabrics of their clothes, begging to know more, so shook by the story that they had lost all faculty for reason.

"They say he is floating in the ceiling of the gastropool, emitting holy fire! Whatever Ivan's brother was in life, he has become something altogether different. He is a comet! A prophet! A harbinger of the Norsemen's Ragnarok!"

They cheered, bloodlust and hope on their tongues, risen to the call and surrendered to abandon.

"For too long have we suffered an unjust system, believing in our hearts that this was our deserved fate, that we were always meant in some grim way to take hold of Satan's mainsheet and steer his corporeal craft through endless water. But Ivan and Dimitri come as bringers of the dawn! The bastard Gabriel drowned in acid! This is our time!"

Another furious, cathartic shout.

"Soon we must rise! Cast off the oppression of the Heartlanders and their systems of above and below! We will not wither away in the cold and the dark! We will rise! Rise! Rise!!"

The barroom of the Perennial exploded in revelry. Cries of joy, bouts of dancing and sailor songs, a fist fight spilling out into the darkness with drunken bouts of laughter trailing just behind. Nina felt her stomach tighten into knots.

She had no idea what to do. Since the day she had been swallowed in the Leviathan, she had fought to stay alive. To do what she must to keep her hope alive. The hope of escape, of meaning. Of something close to peace. She left the crippled Mannfred to his final rest. Mannfred, the man who once fought to fund her research, the man in soft love and wisdom who brought her to Bermuda to study the migration patterns of cuttlefish, who smiled with all the light of the atmosphere from their small ship as she drifted joyously below. She left him to rest and let him die. *What was up and what was down?* she asked and asked again.

Owen, also overwhelmed, noted she was lost in thought and spoke up softly. “What should we do? Should we leave?”

Nina looked at him, then back into the crowded room through the scuffed windowpane. “I…” *What should they say when they return? What was their duty here, and to whom?*

Her eyes met Ivan’s and time came to a standstill. They’d been too obvious. Amid the flowing ragged crowd, his pale thin body stood out, his movements crisp and slow. By the time she noticed the gun’s slick sheen it was too late.

Her ears rang bright and her vision faded. She fell back from the window, clutching at her head in pain. Before her, Owen was already collapsed on the sloping wall of flesh behind the Perennial, blood gushing from his throat. His eyes were white, hands clawing at the hole in his esophagus.

Nina, head still swimming, crawled over to him. She had no idea what to do. Her body felt the urge to run, to escape the thunderous judgment of the only gun in the Leviathan, but this was Owen, her sweet, dumb, innocent new friend. This was him in terrible fear. Dying. Between harsh gasps, he let out jagged little weeps of feral, dehumanizing pain.

The Leviathan's flesh began to move. Tentacular sinews quickly began to coil around Owen. Tendrils came up like new growth through his neck wound and stretched up and outwards over his chin. Nina fought back a wave of nausea at the sight of it. She gripped Owen's hand to pull him away from the clamoring growth, feeling the resistance of the sinews harden around his upper half.

BANG. Another bullet had fired. Nina looked around for it until at last she noticed that her own ring finger (and half of Owen's palm) lay in splattered bits all around them.

Shocked beyond pain, she looked back at the Perennial. Ivan peered outwards from the light of the window, a silhouette as dense as space.

Nina ran.

Ivan, unmoving, let her go. His deep-set eyes were fixed on the sight of Owen and his convulsing body being swallowed up by flesh. He was entombed in the pulsing, swollen red for just a moment before the space that he had taken up was empty and the sloping wall looked as it always had, as if it were not also alive.

XI. The Frozen Sea

It had been a long time since Janice had dreamed of her husband. Normally, she preferred it that way. Wilbur had always been a dullard of a man, a retired British colonel nearly twenty years her senior. Not the sort of gentleman a young and handsome woman at the prime of her abilities, contentedly at play in the throes of the New York social scene, should have wound up with. But her marriage, like almost all the conditions of her life, had been assigned to her. It was a duty. Wilbur was a duty, and so too was Sean, her newborn son, quiet for the first time since the *Empress of Ireland* had cast off from Quebec City.

The air was still in their private cabin, as if the sea were sleeping. The sun had rolled down out of view of the porthole window, the soft afterglow of early summer dusk reflecting on the churning water of the Saint Lawrence. Since they had come aboard, Wilbur had taken to sipping at ararat from a snifter he had brought with him back to North America after his grand tour abroad. He spoke little, seeming almost as unenthused as Janice at the prospect of married life, though he was not overtly cruel or violent. Janice's father Edmund had told her his countenance was a product of the war, the campaign into Somaliland that kept him half-apart from his surroundings. Edmund had met Wilbur at some social club gathering where they "had become fast friends, bound by fellow purpose," as Janice was told the day she learned of his existence, the very day she learned they were to marry.

"Why is it you show me nothing of the man who so impressed my father?" Janice would come to ask him time and again, receiving only quiet sighs as a response. Such was the lot of the fourth daughter of seven. Her dreams of romance, of life in the storm's eye of the new world had been taken from her, and for what? A dull alliance of aging men, the true value and purpose of which she was not privy to learn. A child she already resented.

As if on cue, Sean pulled harshly at the loose curls of her hair, causing her to yelp with pain and grab the baby's arms fiercely. The child's strength was strangely overwhelming to her. Everything she knew of babies before her marriage had led her to believe they were soft and inoffensive creatures. But then, she had always been apart from children. Really, apart from everyone but her governess, maids and on the rare occasion, her own parents, returned for a season from abroad.

Sean pulled her hair again, cooing softly as he viciously tore at her scalp. Fed up, Janice stormed over to Wilbur and snatched up his glass, downing the ararat with scurrilous glee. A flush wave of rage flashed across Wilbur's stoic face, his dry reddish hands curling into swollen fists.

"I am sorry, Janice, that I am so poorly to your liking. In time, I hope-" he started, before some other thought struck him, his aspect and voice trailing off into a deflated murmur. He took back his snifter again and drank of it, disappearing into himself.

"Acknowledge me, you miserable bastard!" Janice yelled. Sean flinched in her arms with a panicked cry. Pushed to the brink, she tossed the polished glass bottle of ararat at the freshly paneled cabin wall. It struck clean and shattered into a rain of fragmentary glass and yet made no audible sound. All at once, a wave of silent, force-like pressure rippled through all the present matter in the room, sustaining itself, deepening as it rolled through Janice and Sean like slow thunder.

Ahhhh, some inner voice released. Janice knew now what she could not know. A lock in the fabric of the dream had slipped open.

The nature of the cabin light transmuted, the flickering lamp-light straining to reach the corners of the room. Sean's crying was now a distant howl on canyon wind, the cabin portholes devoid of any glimmer of the exterior world. Wilbur shifted in his seat, averting his gaze, as if he too could feel the changing.

"Here again," Janice laughed bitterly, prowling gingerly towards the armchair Wilbur sat upon. Sean pulled again at her dangling curls which came loose between his fingers and fall away. "It has been too long, dear husband."

Wilbur's thick hands quivered around the empty snifter. "Too long? Your words are senseless. What is this folly?"

"How precious. How droll. You still pretend. Tell me, while I have you here. Did you know? What am I saying, of course you did. What truly matters is, how *much* did you know?"

"You are distressed, Janice, but this gross manner you have adopted is unfitting for a lady. For my wife! Now enough of this, I command you. Think of our son!"

He was reacting to her as if this moment were the present truth and not a waking dream, a fairground she had tread time and time again. His skin was pallid and slick with sweat. He was truly afraid. The great abyss lay just below the fragile ice.

"You owe us answers, husband, a thousand answers and more for what you've done, but there is no point in asking. I see that now. You love us both so little your lips are sealed forever. You married your secrets and took me on like cattle. Sleep, as you did. Dream of Ogaden, of all your hellish failures, and leave us be. I would go elsewhere."

"You did this to us, you know," he responded in a petulant mutter, a giant child denied his toys. "You broke the vow, your sacred role. You came to me a whore. There is nothing to save, nothing to remember."

Wilbur rose slowly from the upholstered armchair, leaving the glass on the plantation cherry pedestal carved in the shape of a lilypad. He laid down on the crimson sheets, his skin a bloated, pallid shade of blue, and climbed beneath the covers, whispering another language, one Janice could not understand. His voice fell into a disembodied choir, rising as if from the skeleton of the Empress itself. The incantation was as distant and ever-present as Sean's crying as he clutched at strand after strand of Janice's soft copper hair.

It was time again to venture out the cabin door, earlier than ever before. Earlier than the true night, all those many years ago. This should have been impossible for her to do within the dream, or so she had once believed, but each time she found herself within its strange conditions, she was stronger. More able to bend the firmament to her will. At first, she could not open the door a moment early. It had been incontestably barred. She could not walk out into the hall, could not escape the stifling weight of her cabin until the water had leaked in from the door. Until after the sudden, heavy crash that Wilbur never heard. But here she was.

Behind the cabin door, the night's fog was seeping in. Janice had never noticed it inside the *Empress* before, not in life or any of her dreams, but there it was, thick rolling storm clouds churning like high tide over the carpeted halls. It passed over her with a whisper, rippling cooly on her skin like ice fingers in a velvet glove.

Janice wondered how far this newfound power might go. She tested each doorknob in the hall for a bit of give on the lock. None were barred to her. She hesitated. What dire consequence might befall her should she stray too far into the dark corridors of the dream? The Ledger Man often told her to keep out of the shadow and the sea when wandering. *There are times it is better to not know, but we cannot know when until we have already learned too much*. The costs are not always apparent, but they are real.

Still, she thinks. She must know. She opened the nearest door and stepped inside.

In the room four adult figures stand about a wooden table wearing cloaks of a rare pearlescent white, their faces featureless as virgin canvas. They held up silver goblets studded with beveled crimson gems and cheered, lipless mouths intoning in a lost undying language, a tongue that sounded like the one Wilbur had fallen into. These figures did not seem to notice Janice nor hear her child's discontented wailing.

At the center of the room's sole table, eyes wide and slowly blinking, was another child no older than twelve. His hands and feet were bound to the legs of the table, held in place with heavy iron nails and yet he was not screaming. He turned towards the hall as if he could see Janice, peering in her direction soundlessly and calm as a hook-curved dagger pierced the center of his chest.

She shuts the door. The sound of the tide and the chanting is rising, the fog thickening in the *Empress*' hull. Her head balds at the pace of rain, her autumn strands shriveling and dancing as they fall. Water begins to fill the hall. Janice runs. This time, this strange incarnation of the eternal dream, she hopes to make it to the captain's quarters. She wishes to see the fool who veered this ship of lambs into the path of the *Storstead*. To understand, as if that might mean anything at all.

The omnidirectional chant grew louder. All the doors of the hall flung open, one shortly after the other. Janice did not slow down to venture into any room, but from the periphery of her vision she could make out more cloaked figures standing still as if abandoned statues waiting for the encroaching tide. In other rooms, oblivious passengers lay about in beds or slumped over like burlap sacks in their fine wooden chairs. A rare few move about in clear panic, clamoring towards the deck like Janice, but these are but shadows. They are immaterial fragments or echoes of souls recalled by Janice and by the dream. She has come to recognize the lack of weight in their silhouette, in their gaze. The water rushes down the stairwell in a briny wave, causing the echoes to holler out tin can screams and fade away into the water.

It happened so fast, Janice remembers, *the flooding*. There was enough water already to cover most of her body, to drown her, yet she did not lose her footing nor choke from lack of air. She was long since a sunken thing. How could the memory alone harm her now?

Janice realized Sean's cries had disappeared, and so had he. He was gone, swept away with the echoes. Janice felt true fear for the first time in this dream, a guttural panic, but the great inner voice reminds her: *That was not Sean. It was a dream of Sean, a memory as much as all the others. Press on!*

She trudged on through the water and up the tall and flooded staircase. She recalled another staircase from another lifetime, standing beside Rosamund and Mary on the grand steps of Waldorf Hotel. It had been her debutante ball. The instructional book the girls had all been given said simply "Be Good, and Cultivate Charm." As if either command were ever quite so simple.

Week after week, the girls' tutors ran them through drills to master the higher graces. How to carry yourself with an aristocratic bearing, how to turn and smile with intent. Every step and gesture was measured, channeled and signed off on by their betters like a soldier's rifle. Janice was, like her peers, a crop, a chaff of luscious wheat flowing beside her sisters in the spring breeze, perennially awaiting the joyful, clockwork glimmer of the shear.

She could not help but revisit that sweet rebellious night with Adelai the stablehand and the simmering tension of summer that preceded it. Playful stares held firmly as she rode by on the family carriage. Glances, smiles, salutations. Even, once or twice, a touch upon the arm or brow. How the unspoken courtship reached its breaking point one sweltering August night when her parents were away. Janice remembered the way the wind felt on her hair as she chased him across the grounds of the family estate, pressing his blushing figure down into the hay and straddling his cock, of claiming him, fool of a boy, as her own. She had never thought it might have gone so far, her one small act of rebellion. Her solitary conquest. But in the lamplight of her heart, below a hundred years of pain from the tormentous fate she was allotted, she could never bring herself to regret it. No pressure would crush her. Not death. Not motherhood. Not hell. Not even the sea.

She rose from the sunken stairwell and pushed open the half-shut doors leading to the deck. Topside, the fog was thick and all-consuming. *The Empress*, in the hazy darkness, was tilting sidewards, taking in heavy sums of water with frightening speed. Passing out of sight, moving along at a lulling pace was the Norwegian freighter *Storsad*, the ship that struck the Empress and damned it. It was as if they knew and did not care what fate awaited the other vessel. Their voyage came first. On the deck stood a multitude of half-present shades, calling out to the *Storsad*, clamoring for lifeboats, unmoored from time, ebbing and flowing, freezing and becoming dust. They passed through Janice as if she were the vision, the echo of substance. A shiver ran through her heart as she felt the cold touch of long abandoned life.

She would not linger long in this harsh scene. She headed across the length of the deck, towards the captain's quarters, a solitary light above it elevated in the fog like a northern star.

Behind her came the sound of footsteps, full with human gravity. Rising from below deck, the cloaked figures walked in a ritual procession. Every fifth member held aloft a fresh-claimed human heart, red blood staining their billowing milky sleeves. Others swung about silver thuribles, their thick and bitter scent mixing with the smell of the sea.

"Sweet little bird," called a voice from the crowd. Emerging from a white cloak stepping closer was the face of Janice's father. "Why have you returned to this horrid night? What good has all this pushing done you?"

Janice wanted to feel surprised, sick, but the interior voice, that marrow call that guided her sturdied her where she stood. *There is no time for pain. The window is open. Reach out.* "Were you here too, Father? On the *Empress*?"

The ship, great steel yawning with the weight of water, began to tilt starboard into the sea. The shades of the passengers screamed. From behind, some cloaked figures lost their footing as the port bent upwards. Janice's father, solitary, was unswayed, steady on the angled hull.

"Not originally, no." His smile was cold, his eyes blacker than the sea.

"Did you know?" She asked him, struggling to keep her footing. "Did you desire this sort of end for me?"

"Want" is a funny word, kitty kat. I have always loved you, and I always will." He stepped forward, walking steadily on an almost horizontal angle, the ship moments from complete submerging. Above, the stars screamed out vibrant light, burning an entire night's worth of brilliance in this one swirling moment. "But you must understand. The Order asks of us all to give up what we love. The Labor demands us to be free of all that chains us to the lesser world."

"The Order?"

He stood right before her. At this distance, she recognized how much his face had changed. He looked quite different from their last encounter, when she and Wilbur bid farewell before heading to the northern border to catch their ferry home. His hair had lightened into a brilliant white, his wrinkles sanded away by time. It is as if he had become a painted statue of himself, vibrantly unliving, timelessly vital. The pupils of his eyes were unmoving, passive pools of darkness watching playfully as the two fell into the water.

For the first time, Janice felt moved about by the water. She was ripped from her place on the deck, from her unmoving father. Despite the abyssal darkness of the sea she could gaze out and make out shapes and movement for a considerable distance. As the Empress sank, body after body floated from the great crack down the center of the hull. These people, as if enchanted, never woke to notice their drowning. Carelessly, soulessly, they lingered in the water, waiting for the end.

Janice knew the dream was ending. She looked down towards the ocean floor, past the veil of everdark. She could feel it there, approaching. The silhouette of a gargantuan head filled her vision, bulbous eyes like galaxies piercing the deep. Its wide mouth smiled before opening, pulling everything above it downwards like gravity, the nearest bodies sucked down into its reach.

It bit down, dark blood rushing, swirling in the frozen sea. Janice remembers. All her dreams end this way. No matter where she goes, where the visions take her, it finds her. Bite by bite, it feasts on countless bodies. It is inevitable, all-consuming. Like the hollow horn of the underworld arose a noise akin to laughing as it claimed its mortal feast.

A light flickered in the water. Janice squinted her eyes against the weight of the water to see it clearer. It was an oval light, glowing with an amber warmth. Like some sort of egg or seed, it pulsed with the spark of life. She reached out to it. Inside its membrane cradled baby Sean, eyes open and unfeeling. He floated into her open arms, his glow enveloping her.

Janice did not feel the Leviathan approach, its pearl boulder teeth passing wholesale around her, swallowing them whole. Sean laughed, bright and clear as babies do. Janice laughed too.

She was awake. Senses returned little by little: the smell of the Ledger Man's fireplace, the musk of his books, filled the room. She was here again, in the original dream. Root reality, or as close as she got. She rose from the makeshift cot Raffaele prepared for her in the corner of the room, feeling out her limbs, encouraging the blood to travel and flow. This was second nature to her now, the readjustment period after a dreaming.

"I went deeper this time, Raffaele. I changed things. I can change things!"

Janice realized, despite waking, that she could still smell blood in the room. She heard the sound of a knife severing flesh and tendon, bouncing against brittle bone.

From behind Raffaele's large chair, the familiar face of Serge emerged into view. He stepped out, bloody knife in hand glowing with hearthlight. In the other, the head of Raffaele, mouth lifelessly agape, dangled by balding strands of hair coiled in his killer's fingers.

"Fascinating. Tell me how."

XII. Regret

The waxing moon rolled silver over the abyssal horizon of the bay. On a bench surrounded by gangly reeds billowing in the sea breeze, a young man nursed a bottle of peach whiskey alone. He sat in silence, watching the water crest and recede, fed by the adjacent river as if waiting for something he knew would never arrive.

This solitary trip had become a nightly ritual for him since the day he lost his job. A man had floated out to sea on his watch. It was the unforgivable sin of lifeguarding. Not loss itself but unnecessary, negligent loss. Weeks later and the man's body hadn't been recovered. The family was kind enough not to press charges but the damage was done. Patrick's old life had died along with that man and he had no one to blame but himself.

His phone lit up in his hoodie pocket. Reflexively, the muscles in his hand twitched as if to grab it. His body craved the chemical satisfaction of someone reaching out, making a fun little joke just to him, but the craving gave out quick to bubbling revulsion. It had been his job to protect innocent people and a moment's weakness, a single stupid selfish impulse led him to look away.

He didn't deserve the serotonin. What he deserved, he believed, was to look out at the long dark of the sea and remember the man his carelessness had killed, becoming like a lighthouse of grief for the poor man's soul, as if regret could be a light that would guide him home to rest.

His mind resisted. It argued: "*Why was there only one lifeguard on duty? Why wasn't there a net in place further down to catch someone in case of incidents like this? Why was this placed so heavily on my shoulders while fucking Wally washed his hands of culpability?*" But what were arguments weighed against a human life lost forever? His heart knew better than let that line of thinking win.

He liked his bodies warm. Patrick got up from the swinging bench, walked across the strip of sand to the water's edge and threw his cellphone as far into the void as it could reach. He couldn't see or hear it fall into the water, but the feeling was enough. He sat down, hugging his knees to his chest. He was too much of a coward to hurt himself, too angry to accept the selfishness of suicide. But what should he do next? What could he do from here to make amends? Could there be a path forward for someone like him? He wished he had someone, anyone in his life he felt comfortable enough to ask.

A frigid wind blew. In the distance, a solitary figure emerged from the murky reeded dunes between shore and mainland. Beneath a new moon it would be impossible to make out against the darkness, yet under the night's soft silver glimmer Pat could see them ambling slowly towards the water. He wondered who else might feel compelled to visit the bay at night alone and why. The train of thought quickly became impossible to ignore. He couldn't risk another soul going missing on his watch.

He decided to move closer, just out of sight, to make certain that this person was no danger to themselves. He rose from his seat slowly, creeping over the icy sand alongside the outer boundary of the reeds. The figure stood now at the edge of the tide, dressed in some loose billowing fabric. A dim crimson light was being cast before them. It was nothing like the pale familiar glow of LED or even candlelight, but try as he might, Patrick could not make out its source.

Something stirred in the water, catching the light. A deep-timbered voice carried upwards on the wind in some language Patrick could not recognize. Here and there in its droning intonation he could register some subterranean understanding, as if his body had learned and forgotten the tongue long before he was born. He felt drawn in by the sourceless voice, by the language without meaning, and so he drew closer to the shore, as close as he felt he could without attracting attention.

There again shone the gleaming light floating in the sea. Thick scales curling in a lull between waves, swimming in range of the red light. It was huge, more like a snake than a fish, with a deep hole bored into the center of its head.

A sturgeon, Patrick recognized. But here? And this large?

The robed figure extended their arms, holding out from its core a glowing stone. This was the source of the light, pulsing unbidden in the palms of their hands. From the water, in communion with the stone, the sturgeon surfaced, its body all but fully visible. It was three times the length of a man, curving in place on the edge of the tide, staring keenly at the orb. With a sudden jerk of its head, the hole on its face began to spew forth a heavy white mist that flowed outwards onto the beach. Despite the evening's breeze, the mist gathered and clung to itself and the shoreline, gathering strength and volume with each passing moment, flowing like the slow birth of a tornado, twirling up in height until it matched that of the hooded figure in shape and form. It was becoming a man, or the image of one.

The first figure kneeled as the foggy visitor materialized before them, still connected by strands of formless mist to its source.

"I thank you for your visit, Herald Separ," the kneeler spoke. It was a man's voice.

The Herald, now a cloaked figure identical to their supplicant, cupped its silver hands in recognition.

The kneeler continued. "I pray you bring good tidings."

"Yes." The voice of The Herald was hollow yet sharp, even from a distance. "Your Offering was Accepted."

The kneeler removed the hood of his cloak, though from a distance Patrick could not make out his features.

"Then my brother is dead."

The Herald laughed. "Consumed. Consolidated. Welcomed."

"Of course. Yes. You are right, Herald."

"You do not regret The Compact? Not now, surely?"

"No, I assure you. Mother and I understand the Tenants. This… was the best use of him."

The Herald did not nod so much as flow with light approval. "Banish these lingering regrets, or you shall find no place in The Labor."

"Y-yes, my lord."

"I am no lord. You have but one, and he awaits you both at the Festival of Souls."

The kneeler bowed with understanding. "On the full moon we shall perform the ritual, as was instructed."

"Good. Tend to the witness before you go."

"The witness?"

The Herald pointed past the supplicant to the exact spot Patrick crouched in silence. A piercing chill ran through him. In that instant, Patrick finally understood this was no dream, no dark vision but a terrible mistake and a threat to his life. Whatever he had seen that night was not meant to be seen.

The figure whirled about and started sprinting, a

flash of steel emerging from his cloak. Patrick could not help but scream. He took off into the reeds, as fast as he could make it. Though the figure was determined, frantic even, he was no athlete like Patrick. Even drunk and dehydrated, he was a varsity swimmer. He had a body at the height of its power and he would put every ounce of it to use in surviving this hellish night. The distance between them began to widen with every heavy step on the thick sand.

The silver mist was now flowing loosely on the wind, rolling past Patrick on either side. As if whispered in the nape of his neck, a sunken laugh caught up to him and crawled into his ears. Each laugh felt more solid and sharp inside his head until the pain set in. The sound was cutting the flesh of his inner ear. He reached to cover them and felt the heavy mist coil around his hands with real pressure. His ears were bleeding out into his fingers.

Without a sense of balance, a full-tilt sprint across the beach is a challenging act. Almost impossible.

Patrick did not feel himself fall. When he realized he had collapsed, he tried at once to stand, adrenaline pushing him to keep going, but his arms and legs gave out beneath him. The mist and its laughter was all around him now. It was holding him down.

The cloaked figure had caught up to him now, looming overhead. The dark hood had blown off him in the pursuit and he was panting. Patrick recognized him. He looked nearly identical to the man who had drifted out to sea on the river tube. He had stared at that picture a thousand times in the days since. Those same almond eyes and wide cheeks, that same nose.

"You," the cloaked man panted. "The lifeguard."

"You died," Patrick said. "I killed you."

In his hands the hooded man held a gleaming dagger, curved and serrated along its back edge, the handle a cool and polished bone. It shivered in his uneasy grip.

Do not falter again, commanded the hollow sturgeon's whisper, seeping through the fog. *There is no room for weakness here.*

The man's eyes were wide and restless with panic. "I'm sorry. I have to. I'm sorry."

The dagger lifted up into the waxing moonlight and sunk like the tide.

XIII. 1995

Owen doesn't want to be here. It's summer, after all. He wants to be with his friends or playing video games, something *meaningful*, but his family paid good money for these tickets and so the whole family was going. Besides, it wasn't often the whole family got together, all the aunts and uncles and cousins normally too busy with the needs of regular life to gather en masse for a trip. Even Pop-Pop, fresh from his court case, was coming along for the ride.

Owen looked over at Alan sitting beside the other car window, busy whittling a stick with the pocket knife Dad gave him for his birthday last winter. Alan had always been handy, craftier than Owen by far. Joining the Scouts had only accelerated that trend (though it had also made him fall in love with starting fires and tying knots, dangerous trades for a young boy, new to the wider world, to be adept in.) There was something vicious in these gifts, Owen felt, though he did not want to look too deeply. He still loved his brother, even if he was a little afraid of him.

"You boys excited to go river tubing?" Mom asked from the passenger seat, her head gently hanging out the open window. Owen saw her reflection in the rear view mirror, how her big bug-eyed sunglasses hid any clue to her expression. Dad, driving, said nothing at all.

"Yes, Mom," they both replied.

The family caravan arrived at Wally's and claimed the furthest corner of the wide gravel lot. Under the sweltering July sun, the lot of stones burned like coals on Owen's bare feet. He'd forgotten to bring shoes, or at least made the semiconscious decision to do without. Whenever possible, Owen liked going about barefoot around the confines of his neighborhood, in the backyard. A particular favorite was the neighborhood creek. He liked to stand in it and grasp at wet stones with his toes, feeling the water and soil flow over and past him. It made the distance between his thoughts and his senses seem smaller. Almost nonexistent. Like he was also the world.

Mom talked with her brothers, Uncles Ben and Victor, who were fetching a blue and white cooler of cheap beer and fruit juice out of Victor's 1989 GMC Vandura van. Alan had gone over to help carry things, his shoulders stiff and head hung low. Mom rested her hand in his scruffy hair, as much for comfort as control. Dad had walked away from the others towards the reeds on the side of the lot that fed into the river. From what Owen could tell, there wasn't anything there, no booths or rafts. He didn't understand what was going through his father's head, or anyone's really. They all felt miles away.

Owen followed unevenly behind his father, skipping from stone to stone between the shadows of the automobiles. At the weedy edge of the lot he saw the parted green of his father's path and jumped into it with gusto, expecting the fluff of soft grass beneath him. Instead a sharp twig laid in wait, slashing open the flesh of his big toe in a lunar arc, leaving a loose peel of dead white flesh hanging from the meat. He crumpled down into himself and lay there for a moment, holding back the urge to cry.

An odd, hard sound like a tree falling from deeper in the green distracted him from his pain. Owen remembered his mission. His father was acting strangely and he wanted to know why. The pain was secondary to that curiosity and fear. In fact, it already felt like a memory, a story that'd been told to him. Slowly on hands and knees he rose, carrying on through the foliage with a middling limp.

He came down a small wide hill that led to a quiet

tributary ribbed with murky silt. Like some pagan pillar piercing the low and shallow rapids, Owen's father stood and watched the clouds above flow and break apart.

"Dad," Owen called out, "I got cut! My foot is bleeding!"

Dad didn't turn around. "Stand in the water, then."

Owen did as he was told. The silt felt good on his cut, like it sucked up all the painful air and left him cool and well-supported. As he got in deeper, he could make out a flow of blood leaking out and break down into lesser elements in the cleansing water. A crowd of cormorants laughed haughtily from a calcified windthrow further down the bend.

Owen wanted to ask what his father was looking at. He was normally so dynamic, so animated. Here, he seemed so silent. Fragmentary. The light warped around him like he was a hole in the sky.

"Have you seen it, son?"

"Seen what?"

Dad turned around. His eyes were empty sockets of absolute dark.

"The Shore."

Owen fell backwards into the water in horror at the void that shared his father's face.

"Have you seen The Shore? The White Tree?"

A wave of soundless pressure rippled through Owen, sustaining itself, deepening. He had seen it. He had been there. He knew this.

His father stepped forward, unraveling.

"Go to it."

He lifted Owen up from the suctioning mud and water by the neck. Owen clutched at his father's arms in panic and felt nothing like skin. His father's grip was severe. The abyss of his eyes siphoned the light of the day and the air between them.

"Go to the island. Never return here."

There was no anger in his voice.

Owen, vision darkening, nodded, though he did not understand how he could. His father dropped him and he crashed back into the cool water, submerging into the muddy green shallows. When he emerged, gasping for breath and clutching his taut neck for support, the silhouette of his father was gone.

He looked back the way he'd come, past the ferns and saw that it was gone. The world that was. And the water was rising.

Owen got up and ran forward, following the river. The rapids swelled and crested higher and higher, reaching his legs, becoming the horizon. The sky had collapsed into the yawning void of his father's eyes. All that was left now was water and absence devouring the rest. He saw a figure rise before him from the enveloping rapids. It was The Ledger Man. His eyes and neck were weeping blood but he was smiling.

"Good," he spoke, "You have awoken. It is time you understood the Mysteries."

XIV. A Parley

A small fire had been started by the newly fortified barricades overlooking the pyloric sphincter, just atop the rope and stone dam constructed many years ago to control the flow of acid and refuse into the lower intestine. This had been done for many reasons, chiefly to ensure the safety of any workers who descended down to clean the fleshy tunnels. In time, strategic tunnels had been carved in the intestines allowing it to function as a highway of sorts to the lower torso of the Leviathan. It was the primary trade route between the Heartlanders and the Pitters, the one true highway of Levi society. As such, it had quickly become the first theater of war.

"I haven't heard 'nothin in hours," groaned Fernando, one of the Heartlander guards.

"Me neither," echoed Parker, his comrade-in-arms, "but you just know these slippery leeches will poke through and gut us at a moment's notice if we look away."

Fernando peered down the open tunnel and into the looming dark. Since the war began, all the tunnel lights had gone out. The innards of the Leviathan were as dark as they had ever been.

"You think they'll come round this way again?"

"Sure fucking hope not, but I'm no great thinker and neither are you."

A long silence passed between them.

"What was your favorite thing about life?" Fernando asked.

"We're not dead yet, you loon, come on now."

"You know what I mean! From before!"

"Ah. Yeah." Parker thought for a moment. "Liked working with dogs. There was a summer or two I helped my aunt Peggy with her sheep farm in Donegal. She was always cold with me, something to do with me da, but that didn't bother me none. Anyway, she had this sheepdog. Moss. Black collie, eyes like little buttons. God I loved her. We were thick as thieves. We worked out some great routines, she and I. Flips and jumps, things like that. Tried to get old Peg to let me compete with her but she wouldn't have any of it."

Fernando stroked his chin. "Yeah, that sounds nice. Pleasant, even."

Parker scoffed. "Some response. What about you, then?"

"Sex, mainly."

"Right. Fair answer."

"Also eating."

"You're a simple man."

Fernando shrugged. "Always have been."

"Oi!" came a shout from above. Coming down the main rappel chain in the rickety patio trolley was Hans with two others, the light of the Holy Corpse silhouetting them on their descent. Hans was dressed in wartime regalia, plucked off a privateer's corpse and preserved with care against the corrosive elements of the gut of the Leviathan. His soggy feathered tricorne made him look a few inches taller than he really was.

Behind him, pale and hooded was Nina, her right hand in a white glove, its ring finger dangling unfilled. On his left was a broad shouldered man half extra the height of Hans. He carried a broadsword, another artifact of the

Heartlanders, and wore steel armor half-rusted by time and its brief yet distant submerging.

Parker and Fernando assumed a military salute, straightening their spines and spears. Hans paced around them, inspecting the grounds of the sphincter dam. His large, buggy eyes gleamed with what little light illuminated their post. "Report, soldiers."

"All clear here, sir," said Parker. "No sign of enemy movement since the last skirmish."

Hans grimaced. "Good."

"Do you bring any news, sir?" Fernando asked. Parker slapped his arm for his impudence.

Unbothered, Hans stroked his mutton chops and looked out towards the sphincter. "None. Upper patio fortifications are going well. Most of the Cavity has been evacuated, but it isn't safe yet to make searches for those who haven't yet reported in. For all we know the Pitters are already collecting hostages or lying in wait to launch an ambush. And we're sure not ready for that, are we boys?"

"What's the status of the Holy Corpse?"

"Still floating, shining," muttered Nina. "We can't rope him down. For some reason he's stationary up there. A fixed point."

Looming behind her, the broad knight grunted. "A problem."

Hans laughed throatily, his teeth and gums desperate for tobacco to chew. "Damn straight. If he wasn't already dead I'd say we try killing him to get it over with."

"A problem?" Parker asked despite himself. "He's really just an unusual lamp at this point, right?"

"A lamp you can't turn off, maybe!" Hans roared. "A

lamp that's damaging the circadian rhythm of your people in the middle of open *war*, perhaps! A lamp that some weak souls pray to as if it will protect them better than the men to the right and left of them!"

"Of course, sir. Sorry, sir."

Hans sighed, leaning against the wooden railing for support.

"Sir was my father's name, soldier. Gabriel's. Me? I'm just a tired old sailor trying to get this ship to port. Why'd this all have to happen this way?"

Nina watched him bitterly from the dim corner of the patio, holding her wounded hand with her strong. She found his wistful attitude difficult to endure. It rang hollow.

Just then, a shrill noise broke out of the lower darkness. It was the blare of a horn, high and bright. Fernando fell back from his post by the railing as the rest of the patio guard fell to their knees or leaned against a sturdy wall.

Hans clutched his cap in his hands and turned to the others. "It's a damn raid!"

The large gentlemen in the knight's armor stepped forward, drawing the large sword from his back and leaning up against the railing, his eyes trained on the sphincter and the impenetrable shadow beyond its aperture. "Behind me," he said.

"Good man, Edmund," Hans muttered, patting him on the back from his defensive squat.

The grim horn belted out again. The dull light of torchfire built up slowly on the walls of the intestinal tunnel, the clamoring of footsteps and agitated voices echoing upwards. Fernando and Parker held their spears aloft and angled upwards on either side of the knight as if they might repel assaulting cavalry.

"Come no further!" yelled out Parker, voice quivering.

"My god, there's so many of them," Hans muttered, watching the general din of the torchlights split into a multitude of source points against the curling wall of tubing. He darted over to Nina, keeping his head low, and grabbed her forearm. "Signal the trolley!"

Once more did the horn herald the coming crowd. A voice as strong and full of passion as the horn called upwards to the patio guard. "Parley! Parley!"

Nina recognized that voice immediately. It was as unmistakable as fire itself. *Carmela.*

"And we should believe the likes of you?" Fernando called out in response to the parley. "Two steps forward and I'll parley this spear into your fuckin' gullet!"

The Pitters groused furiously at that. The torchlight seemed to bob and flicker brighter, the nearest sources drawing ever closer to the sphincter dam. They might truly seek to seize it if this continued as it was, Nina realized. A fight here, on Heartland ground, would be the beginning of the end for them all.

She took a deep breath before sealing her own fate. "I'll go."

Hans, Parker and Fernando were flabbergasted, Hans still clutching her forearm tightly in disbelief.

"Are you mental? There's dozens of them!" Parker whispered. "It's an obvious trap!"

Hans, grip tight, peered inquisitively into the pools of her eyes. Since she had returned from her scouting mission to the Pits alone, she had been mostly silent, nursing the stub where her finger had been. The loss of Owen had clearly, visibly worn heavy on her, but the knowledge she'd brought back had given the Heartlanders a chance to fortify themselves against ambush. She had saved lives on both sides, or so she believed. But, she could not help but wonder, did the others see it that way? Did Hans? Or did he still doubt where her loyalties lay?

"Go," Hans said, surprising Edmund and the guards as much as Nina. "But don't die out there."

Nina nodded and walked towards the rail, bellowing downwards: "I shall meet your parley!"

From a distance, Carmela laughed. "Wonderful!"

From behind the pyloric sphincter, a grappling hook launched upwards, coiling around the load-bearing wooden beam of the makeshift intestinal dam. Carmela quickly ascended up the rope, swinging forward and back to build up the momentum necessary for her to clear the first barrier. With a flourish, she jack-knifed her way through the dilating flesh door and up and over the barrier, landing on the ropeway on the other side. She gazed upwards at the paltry defenders, the devil's grin and embers in her eye.

Fernando gasped and applauded before Parker sensibly shoved him quiet. Nina descended from the central patio to the forward battlements where Carmela awaited her. Carmela's thick curls of black seemed darker than the unlit shadows of the Leviathan, backlit by the warm glow of the unseeable army standing ready beyond the dam.

"Good to see you in one piece, Nina," Carmela said.

Nina held down the bile in her throat and offered a polite, if minor, bow of the head.

"So little courtesy for a fellow Pitter? My, how the Heartlanders have changed you."

"Enough of this mockery. You called for a parley, Carmela. What is it you want?"

Her smile unfaltering, Carmela took three steps closer, her large bright eyes flitting upwards to the men on the banister above before returning to meet Nina's.

"Yes, I did," she said, her husky voice that much softer, less projected. "And I am truly thankful that you and you alone were here to meet me."

"Is that right?"

"Do you truly wish for war, Nina?"

"Do I wish for war?"

"That is what I asked you, yes. Do you?"

"You sheltered Ivan. You worked up the Pitters. You killed… You killed my friend. An innocent, whose last words were in awe of your flowery speech about justice and freedom. He might have wanted to join your cause and now he's nothing but Leviathan food. And you dare ask me what I want?"

Carmela's shoulders dropped slightly, her body tilting to the side, turning inwards. "I do regret the death of the boy. It has complicated matters."

Nina, furious, shoved Carmela back against the barrier wall, the ropeway shivering beneath them. "Complicated?!"

"Yes! Complicated! We should never have been enemies, Nina. Most Pitters see you as a traitor, a worm to catch and crush between their fingers. But what have you betrayed, really? The Pit is not a true culture. It is a container of Gabriel's design, a prison colony for those who cannot or will not serve the eldest of the devoured. All you did is what your Mannfred wanted: You fought to survive. I may resent the Heartlanders for their oppressive, callous ways, but I have never believed you to be a hopeless cause. Or rather, I have left room in my heart to hope otherwise."

Nina turned away, unable to stomach Carmela's words head-on.

Carmela continued. "My scouts tell me you have been watched, day and night, since your return to the Heartlands. The stain of your roots, of your Pitness, is all they see. After everything you sacrificed to appease them. Even now, the audience of Heartlanders watch us converse and wonder what secrets you spill."

"Is that what you want from me? To sublimate my rage and return to the fold, another good little soldier or spy for your ranks?"

Carmela laughed heartily. "I had no knowledge you were here when I called parley. Though I would welcome you with open arms and a loving and tender embrace."

"What do you want? What is this meeting actually for?"

"I am no queen, Nina. I am the voice of the people. All I do is speak for the downtrodden strewn about the feet of giants."

"Then what do the downtrodden say?"

"They offer an armistice before the last night comes. Before we all draw blood and die inside the beast like rotted worms."

"And their demands?"

"Simple: a swap. The Pitters take the Heartland and vice versa."

It was Nina's time to laugh. "You think they would accept this?"

"Build your battlements, man the porous holes that mark your footpaths. The gun is ours, and with it comes the passion. Pitters have little fear of death. They will swarm the barricades for a chance to harm as they have been harmed, to bleed as they have bled."

Nina grabbed Carmela by the collar, panic and pain pushing her forward. She began to bleed from her finger wound, staining Carmela's well-worn burlap dress. "And all the Pitters and Heartlanders alike who would die, would they enjoy their victory? Would it mean anything at all?"

Carmela drew herself close to Nina's ears and whispered with a vicious sting. "Wake up. Look around you. What is the meaning? Where is the life?"

Nina shoved her away, insulted by the proximity.

"I do not want to surrender hope, Nina. I never have. Like you, I still wish to go on. I feel the warmth of others on my skin, my heart beats proud, my lungs draw breath deeply. I believe, despite everything, in the small glimmer of hope that one day we shall escape this beast and feel the sun at our backs once more. But the ones behind me? The blowers of the horn? The fire starters? They have surrendered to their pain. They are lost to the tide."

Nina felt eyes boring into the back of her neck. Too much longer, too much closer and she would be seen as a traitor to the Heartlanders. If she wanted to return, to have any chance at stopping the bloodshed, she knew she must end this mummer's farce at once.

"You never told me what *you* wanted, Carmela. Do you really want this bloodshed? Do you think it's necessary?"

Carmela laughed again, but from a hollow place. "When the beast found me, I was at sea, on my way to fight in a distant war. I believed it to be a noble calling. I never made it to the front, to the war that I believed in. All these long years, that same fire has burned in my breast. It has never faltered. But was it lit to burn the vile or warm the frigid victims? I don't know. I've never found an answer."

Nina knew her time was up.

"I will pass on your message, Carmela. This I vow."

Carmela composed herself, adjusting her patchwork tunic and taking in a deep and jagged breath. "Very well. Shall we meet again in two days?"

"Someone will be here with something to say."

Carmela laughed. "Of course."

As Carmela swung herself back into the shadow, Nina made her way towards the others. The guardsmen stood huddled tight together, watching her ascend the rope-way to eye level. They said nothing. She did her best to hide her creeping fear.

The horn of the Pitters rang loud in the tunnel below as the lamplight flickered away.

XV. Orientation

It had been sixteen hours since Emily had last heard from her son. She was beginning to get nervous, deeply nervous, that for whatever reason he was going to be late for orientation. This was unacceptable. She had always thought of him as the responsible son, the capable child, and the facts of his life had borne out that observation. He had done quite well at school, never missed a dentist appointment and showed up to parties at a respectable time. He would always notify others when there were emergencies or issues that created an obstacle before him. This was not a meeting they could afford him to miss. Getting to this moment, to this afternoon's meeting, had cost the single greatest expense of Emily's life, and her son's tardiness suggested he still did not, after everything, grasp the weight of its importance.

She pecked at a cigarette and looked out the driver's side-view mirror of her new convertible, a status gift from her new husband, at the mostly vacant parking lot's unassuming entranceway. It was all she could do to steady her hands, though she had to be careful not to get any ashes on her clothes. The robe was new and pearlescent white and any stains would be obvious at first glance.

She tried calling his cell phone again. It rang. Rang. Rang again.

Nothing but the click.

"Fuck," she muttered, kicking the space between her car's accelerator and brake, causing the car to shudder forward. She realized immediately the car was idling in place with her foot on the brake and turned the ignition off.

A knock on the passenger side window. It was a security guard for the nondescript office building where the orientation was set to commence. He seemed to want something.

She lowered the window. "Good evening, officer."

The guard, a man in his sixties with graying roots and warm cheeks, gave a thumbs up, beady eyes bouncing placidly between her robe and the ivory mask in the passenger seat.

"See you're here for the meeting this afternoon."

Emily nodded. "That's right."

"There's refreshments being served in the meeting room, if no one told you."

She feigned a smile. "Wonderful news. I'm just waiting for my son to arrive before we head in together."

The guard chuckled knowingly. "Sons, right? Can always count on 'em to waste your time, bless their little hearts."

Emily laughed as was expected of her, putting her cigarette out on the left side door. "Truer words were never spoken."

The guard faced the sun hiding behind the thick post-morning rain clouds. "Got three of them myself, between two wives. Well, ex-wives, obviously." He held up a ringless right hand and wiggled it a bit. "No secret kids on this old family tree! The first ex has two of them living with her in Fort Collins. Don't get to see them much these days. Old enough to go to college and make holiday plans with their little girlfriends but not old enough to realize their old man's not gonna be around forever. But hey, that's all alright. I never really did that right by them, you know? Sure I tried, everybody tries, but that's not how you get Father of the Year mugs for Christmas. No participation trophies here! Nobody likes saying it, but most people aren't ready to be good parents right out the gate. For some of us blockheads it takes a lot of time, lotta trial and error. Even then, you never really know if what you're doin' is what you should be doing. You just… do it, and hope it all works out. Or doesn't. Not that big a deal. It's all a lot of nonsense, anyway."

Emily had no idea what to say.

The man laughed at something and patted the car door gently. "Enjoy your meeting, miss. Been a pleasure."

"L-likewise."

With that he sauntered towards the office building, humming off-key what sounded vaguely like "Best of My Love" by The Emotions. When he was out of view, Emily let out a shudder and looked down at her wrinkled hands, flattening out the folds in her robe.

Ten minutes passed.

Out of the corner of her eye, she saw it. *It's him.* Alan's car, a modest cherry red Honda Civic (a horrid status symbol for such an accomplished young surgeon exploring his nascent political options) swerved into the lot and settled into a corner spot close to the thin industrial park treeline. Emily watched him park. There was no sign of movement in the car, no opening doors. She turned the ignition and drove slowly across the lot towards her son, parking in the same row four spaces down. She got out of her car and walked over, every step slower than the last.

She could see him, hands firmly at ten and two on the steering wheel, staring straight ahead. His hands were caked in blood. Emily opened the passenger door. The smell of dried blood, that unmistakable oxidizing tinge filled the chilled conditioned air. In the backseat a damp, darkened wool blanket covered an unmoving figure.

Emily sat down in the passenger seat. Alan did not

move his head.

"You're late," she noted.

"Yes."

Emily sighed. "Why didn't you answer my calls?"

A single tear rolled down his cheek. "I don't need this shit right now, Mother."

Emily watched him for a moment, looking for something in particular from her son's expression. He would not turn to meet her gaze. She was mildly annoyed at that.

"You know there are grave consequences if we're late to this orientation. I know you know this. It's not a matter of punishing you."

Alan's head fell onto the dark stained steering wheel. "I am aware."

Emily leaned back in her seat to face the back and lifted up the soaked blanket. "This is…"

"The lifeguard. From Wally's," Alan admitted, hot tears cascading soundlessly in rapid fire.

"He wasn't at fault, Alan. You know that."

"He *saw me*, Mother! With the Herald! He was… He was there. I don't know why. I think he was drinking."

Emily ahhed.

"I had to, Mother. I had no choice. There was this-this mist, it-"

"Yes. You had to. That's correct."

Emily lowered the passenger window and lit up a cigarette. Alan watched her, a red-faced child again, petty disbelief and rage roiling visibly within him.

"*Now*?" he asked.

"You want one?"

Alan seemed about to burst, gripping the wheel tight enough to cut his circulation. The fury built up to a head, plateaued, then dissipated.

"Sure," he said.

They smoked together in silence. Alan was not a frequent smoker. Between drags, he tried not to cough, but it was difficult for him. Emily found it endearing but kept that to herself.

"We made our choice, Alan. When we sent your brother to Wally's, we were in agreement. It was a terrible thing to do, a painful, terrible thing. But we both understand that choices like this must sometimes be made. That, to do great things in the world, to become great people, we must sacrifice. We must do the impossible."

"I know, Mother."

"When we go inside, we'll tell someone there was a witness to the Herald. The Order will clean this up for you. We're as much of their number now as anyone. No one else will know."

"I know."

Emily thought about what the security guard had overshared. She thought of Owen, her other son, as he was when he was young: Loud, needy. His eyes had looked exactly like his father's, that same painful darkness round the edges nothing could hide. He had always been helpless. It was only a matter of time until the world had broken him, too.

It was better this way. Now, he had amounted to something. He had helped his brother to do more than survive. He had helped him to live.

"The meeting is starting soon, son. We need to get you into a fresh set of robes."

Alan sighed and nodded, retreating inwards. His careful, skillful hands had stained the steering wheel with flakes of blood.

Emily reached into her purse and drew out wet wipes and a bottle of spring water.

"Come here."

She took his hands in hers and wiped him clean. As clean as he could get, anyway. Another heavy tear formed on the cliffside of his cheekbone. She dabbed it off with her wrist, letting her hand run soft and cool through his curly hair.

"My sweet boy."

She knew it sounded hollow, but she meant it.

The meeting was in an ordinary conference room with a projector screen and a desk and chair in front and center. The dull fluorescent lights hummed like dead bugs above a soft charcoal checkerboard carpet that ate all the shadows in the room. Behind the four rows of plastic chairs there was a catered snack bar with an assortment of donuts, pastries, French press coffee and more.

A small mass of people was milling around in white robes and matching expressionless masks, careful not to spill anything on themselves as they indulged. Only two people in the room looked any different: The man in the front of the room, sitting at the podium and fiddling with the output cables of the computer casting blue onto the pull-down projector screen, and the security guard from earlier helping himself joyously to the complimentary snack spread.

"Don't mind me, just grabbing a bite before y'all start!" he chuckled as Emily and Alan moved past him, heading for seats. His eyes flashed with recognition as he somehow recognized Emily beneath the mask. "Ah, your son made it in time, that's wonderful news."

Alan looked inquisitively at his mother, who turned away and said nothing in reply.

"Listen, young man," the guard continued. "You got a lovely mother figure in your life. Not every man can say as much. Try and do right by her and show up to your obligations on time, alright? It's just good manners. Listen to me go on! Anyway, have fun, you two." He grabbed one last Danish before nodding politely and walking out the room.

"I thought this was supposed to be a secret society," Alan whispered.

The man at the front of the room cleared his throat performatively and the other initiates began filing into seats. Within two minutes, the room had fallen quiet save the sound of coffee sips and the gentle sighs of older attendees settling into place. The speaker reached into the podium and drew out a small remote, using it to dim the overhead bulbs to a quarter of their original luminance.

"If everyone is ready, let's begin."

The blue projector light changed to the title slide of a PowerPoint presentation. The slide had clip art of tranquil forests and blue lakes and read **INTERSTICE ORIENTATION**.

"I'd like to start today's orientation by taking a moment to thank everyone for being on time today, as well as to congratulate you all for reaching this point in your Initiation. I know each and every one of you have to make some big choices to get to this point and you all deserve a round of applause."

The speaker started a soft, polite clap that quickly spread across the room.

"Just excellent. The Order is lucky to have Initiates like you all who are dedicated to The Labor and excited to contribute to its grand fruition."

The speaker took a light sip of water from a paper cup.

"Now I'm sure many of you are wondering exactly why you're sitting here in this office building watching a presentation before you join one of the oldest and most powerful organizations in human history. Trust me, when we started doing this, we got a lot of feedback saying just that, so don't feel too alarmed if that's how you're feeling."

An awkward, uneven laugh played out.

"Now, everyone here is at Initiation level one. That means you've made your first Offering, you've confirmed it with a higher member, maybe even a Herald! You've had to do a lot with minimal answers for the sake of vague promises and are probably feeling a little insecure. That's an entirely natural feeling at this stage in your orientation."

Alan shifted in his seat, panic and disgust bubbling inside his throat, until the cool, dry hand of his mother rested on his own. From behind her mask she watched his every twitching gesture of discomfort. He understood what she meant and did his best to calm himself. The time for this had passed.

The speaker continued. "Recently, those of us at Acolyte level were tasked by our superiors with updating our Initiation rituals to better suit today's society. In the 21st Century, people are increasingly secular, cynical and plain-spoken, and are accustomed to unprecedented levels of autonomy and self-determination, offering up demands and questioning authority in any and all social situations. These are all fine traits for day-to-day life, but before the Festival of Souls, it's best if we drop some of the mystique and tell you as much as you're authorized to know at this stage to avoid unnecessary complications. It's important that you all feel completely secure in what's expected of you before the big day, because the Festival is a solemn and ancient ritual and deserves the utmost respect and sanctity from all participants."

"This next rule is critical: if you should question or interrupt the Festival in any way, shape, or form as it transpires, you will be killed on the spot."

"...Killed?"

"Yes. Also, a friendly reminder: Should you share anything you learn today with anyone not in this room, expect a similar fate. But this shouldn't be difficult to grasp. After all, you're here today, right?"

The speaker clicked his remote to proceed to the next slide. It spelled out: **CORE TRAITS OF AN INITIATIVE: DISCRETION. INTENTION. SINCERITY. CAPABILITY. OPENNESS.**

The speaker laughed, looking out at the still stunned crowd of junior cultists. "Spells out 'disco'. Isn't that fun?"

Some tried to laugh. The presenter continued to the next slide. **UNDERSTANDING THE MYSTERIES.**

"Quiz time! I'd love it if some volunteers would raise their hands and tell me what they know about the Order, its history, and The Great Labor. Don't worry, there's no way to fail. Can anyone get us started?"

One initiate raised their hand. They were a petite older gentleman with a firm beer belly jutting up from beneath his robe seated close to the front. "The Order is an ancient and powerful society with members around the globe who indirectly control modern society!"

The speaker laughed, the loose hairs of his small, tight ponytail dancing on the back of his scalp. "Somewhat true, yes! Thanks for your enthusiasm. Now, the Order does have members around the world, many of whom do hold positions of power and influence in governments, militaries and more, but it's a bit of a misconception to say our goal is to *control* the populace. There are approximately eight billion people on this planet, all with wills and potential of their very own. It'd certainly be a headache to try and make all of them do what we'd like. The Order encourages its members to live their lives to the fullest and influence the world however they like. It has only a few core 'in-house' goals it seeks to accomplish. If you're looking for a more traditional hegemony of control, we'd highly suggest seeking membership with the Freemasons or the Illuminati!"

This got a bigger laugh from the room, from mostly the older voices.

The Initiate with the beer belly shifted uncomfortably in his seat. "Wait, the Illuminati *do* control society?"

"No, my friend, that was a joke. I'll make this as clear as I can. The vast majority of narratives about power and control you hear in polite society are just that: *narratives*. Power, as it exists here on earth, is nebulous. The winds of erosion whittle away at all our structures, laws and bloodlines. We collapse, rebuild, collapse, rebuild. Secret societies are no different: prone to decay, failure and restructuring. On the surface world, we live and we die like rats, and no amount of political influence or cultural cache changes that. That is what makes human existence so tragic and so terrifying. Nothing we make lasts on this Earth, save, of course, for The Labor."

Another initiate raised their hand. It was a woman younger than the norm in the room, somewhere in her late 30's maybe, with a high and husky voice like Sissy Spacek. "So the Order supports us like the Herald promised as long as we follow all the Tenants?"

The speaker quickly took another sip from his water before continuing. "That's right. You'll all be eligible for entrepreneurial, financial, and political support from our other members so long as you remain in good standing. World's your oyster. Achieve your dreams! Blame, blackmail, rape, murder, oppress, control, claim and conquer! Just don't contradict The Labor."

The woman spoke up again. "I'm sure you'll get to this in your presentation, but what really is The Labor? The Herald I spoke to was vague on what that was, exactly. They just said it was the most worthwhile endeavor humanity has ever known, and I thought that sounded nice."

The speaker wagged his finger at her with a fox-like grin.

"I like you! Openness. Intention. You'll do just fine."

The next slide hit the screen. It read: **THE LABOR: FEED THE BEAST. POPULATE ATLANTIS. ACHIEVE IMMORTALITY.**

"Let's break this one down nice and slow."

XVI. Suspended

Janice's head was throbbing. She roused herself from another fitful slumber, the same piss-poor sleep she'd grown accustomed to since she found Serge decapitating Raffaele in the warmth of her old friend's hearth. She was bound tightly to this wooden chair. Expertly, too, she noted. Serge had clearly lost his mind, and yet his days as a French soldier had not left him entirely behind. Her throat was dry, her lips chapped and raw. She knew from painful, distant experience that she could not die of thirst or hunger, but it would ache just as bad as if she could until she found some manner of relief.

The fire had long since gone out. The once cozy ship captain's cabin of the Ledger Man, a refuge for Janice during her many years inside Levi, now felt like a cold and stifled tomb. It had become one, after all. What dim light poured in through the scuffed portcullis window fell upon the severed head of Raffaele, resting as if in peaceful slumber on the surface of his writing desk.

She still had so many questions to ask him. For all their conversations over the years, all the many secrets and truths that he had shared with patience and care for what her soul could handle, there had always been more below the surface she had wished desperately to reach.

For one, she had never believed the story of his arrival. He had told her he was shipwrecked on a small isle in the Atlantic in the late 1700's. He had been a privateer, he'd said, abandoning the minor pauper's life he had been entrusted by his domineering father. He took a job documenting trade corridors and transactions, charting the passage of goods as well as the lives and tidings of those who sailed behind him. He had always been an observer, a passive eye.

Inside the Leviathan, he kept on as he had. A creature of habit till his last.

Nonsense, she thought. When he was finally comfortable around her after years of visits, when the performance he committed to dropped away as Janice became someone realer than the masses he avoided, she saw him differently. His body would fall still for days and weeks at a time and yet his eyes would flicker with life. He was not some feckless quill, some wayward clerk in hell's damp pit, but something closer to a doctor. A healer. Maybe even a wizard, if those existed. *But many things exist, don't they?* She had seen the truth of the world in her dreams. He had given her that gift.

Her dry throat ached for water. For booze. For the amber spinal fluid of the beast that sent her spirit into the astral sea. She wanted to be gone from here forever, to be a dolphin, a swordfish piercing the wind. The face of baby Sean appeared before her, laughing, unaware of the harshness of his world. Forever a seed, forever observing, waiting to sprout.

If one day the Leviathan should die, and from the bloated cavities should crawl out mother and child, would he begin to grow? Would his features finally mature? Would he understand how impossibly long he had been a weak and fragile weight in her arms? What would he say to her?

"Mother, you held on so very long. Thank you for carrying me through the shadow."

With sudden rage she tried again the tensile strength of her ropes. They did not budge, sickly digging deeper grooves into her skin.

Janice screamed.

"Now, dear. It will be alright."

She turned to the door, reflexively panicking that Serge had returned, but it had remained closed. She looked to the portcullis, to the corners of the room but there no solemn figure stood. At last, when nothing else made sense, when nothing else could be accepted did she look again at the head of Raffaele.

Its glassy eyes were open and moving, the frozen lips curled into a warmly animated smile.

"Are you hurt? Are you well?" it asked.

She blinked, as she could not rub her eyes. It blinked in return.

"You have suffered so very much because of me, young Janice. My sincere apologies."

"Are you…"

"Your old friend Raffaele? Yes," he chuckled, offering a genial wink. "Though I suppose I've lost a bit of weight."

"H-how?"

"I should have explained this to you long ago. This body is, well, *was*, not like yours. It never has been."

Janice remembered the bloody stumps of Raffaele's forearms as he drained them for his ink, his thin ribs jutting boldly underneath the leathery skin buried in his ancient tunic. He had always seemed to be strung together from spare parts, a patchwork doll of an elderly man, but she had chalked that up to his age and the horrors of centuries below the sea, waiting about in the abyssal locker of a foul god's heart.

"I have died several times before this one, little dove. I expect to die once or twice more, before my final end."

Her mind raced with questions, with confusion, but above all a sense of relief. She long ago abandoned mortal wisdom in order to escape the Leviathan. If anything, this painful episode emboldened her. There was more still for her to understand, more for her to master. The road ahead continued on in darkness.

She fought back tears. Her body could barely afford them. "Why did you wait this damn long? I'm fucking parched, Raf."

Raffaele's head wobbled forward on the desk, drawing closer to the edge nearest to her chair, leaving behind a thick trail of semi-dried blood in his wake.

"Well, there has been much elsewhere for me to do. And besides, I would have you know that reanimating flesh is no simple task. Finding the severed thread and bonding to it tight requires great fortitude and willpower. I would like to think this attempt to come and check on you is a personal record," he grumbled. "If I could make use of my body again, I would check my archive to see."

Janice laughed. It really was her old geezer.

Raffaele's eyes lit up, humored by her uplifted spirits. "So then, where has the boy tyrant gone? Did he say?"

"I'll admit, I wasn't really all there when he left."

There was a shuffling from the corner, the sound of creaking boards. "Good morning to you both," yawned Serge, rising from the makeshift cot Janice often used to stay the night. "It's good to see you've finished hiding what you are, Ledger Man."

Serge, covered in a thick tarp cloak, was barely visible from the shadows, save the gleaming knife so bonded to his twitching hand it hung like a raptor's talon.

The head of Raffaele sighed bitterly. "Very well. It cannot be avoided any longer. I do not trust you, Serge, and I had hoped to not share any secrets with you, but if it is time to barter, then so it is."

Serge paced the room like a jungle cat, laughing with a bright and chalky manic pitch. "Clever as always, but I have to ask: What is it about me you hate so badly? I murder somebody you love? You're still kicking, no? So my hands are clean. Virginal, even."

Raffaele said nothing.

"Exactly. You have nothing and you know it. For decades upon decades, I served with true eagerness. I love my fellow man. Whatever Gabriel asked of me, I did, without hesitation! I was born a soldier. I lived as a soldier and died as one, ending up here. Inside the Leviathan. Again and again, I climbed up from the brink of self-annihilation, because it was my task and lot in life, because Gabriel promised me a light to follow in the dark. No one could take that from me. Only now… my captain has left us behind! Now, we have no order, no clarity! We are abandoned to bicker and feast upon each other like feral dogs between the trenches with nobody but God to answer to, and God, in all his wisdom and cruelty, will not answer me! I call to him from the shadows, I cry out. But nothing! No voice fills the space, no purpose! Nothing!!"

Serge held his hands upwards in supplication and rage, as if he was once again beneath cathedral glass, remembering the gold forgiveness of the sun.

Janice chuckled. "Did you play Hamlet in primary school? What a *performance*."

Serge turned and kicked Janice's chair so that it tipped backwards and crashed onto the floor. As Janice struck the floor, the air came out her lungs in a heavy gasp.

"Enough!" yelled Raffaele, surprising them both. Janice had never heard him raise his voice before. Also, he had no throat or lungs to shout from. Serge looked down at Janice at the floor, glancing for a moment at the screaming head, before lifting her chair back upright.

"Sure like Janice, don't you?" he muttered.

"You can gallivant around all you'd like, cut this body of mine up into ribbons, but Janice must be kept safe, if all of this is to mean anything at all!"

Serge walked up to Raffaele's head and lifted it off the table, holding him at eye level. "Elaborate."

"Answer me this first. Where is the true source of your rage, Serge? Is it with me, or Janice? Is it with Gabriel? The Pitters or Heartlanders below? Is it with God? Where does its true origin lay?"

Serge's upper lip began to sweat. He tried to hold his anger, his focus, but the question dug inside him like a ravenous worm. Eventually, the weight made his eyes flicker downwards, unable to stand equal to the head that he had severed.

"It's the Leviathan."

Raffaele smiled wistfully, the way a grandfather does watching a child stand on its own two feet for the first time. "Close enough."

Serge set Raffaele's head back down upon the table, his eyes darting between the dim corners of the room. Some fragile foundation had broken in him.

"Would you kill it, if you could?" Raffaele asked.

Serge laughed despondently and nodded, facing the far wall and rubbing his hands over the back of his neck.

"Even if it was the death of everyone still living within?"

He said nothing for a long time, contemplating the

enormity of what that question meant to the man he used to be. "Yes."

"And you, Janice? Answer me, dear. Speak true."

Janice's first thought was *Yes, of course, you buffoon. But we can't. It isn't mortal. It isn't something that can die. I know better than anyone. I've seen-*

It hit her. What Raffaele had meant. Why he cared so much, why he had made a home for her. It was affection, sure, but it had always been more. There had been a purpose to his initial acts of kindness, to letting her step foot inside his lonely chambers. She'd known that since the beginning. Once, she thought that he had wanted sex, like most other men, but the long years passed without a gesture of the kind. But the spinal fluid. The dream dives. The talks. All this time, they'd been training.

"It's not the Beast itself that needs to die, is it?"

Serge's face was filled with the terror of curiosity, of knowing at last how little he knew.

Raffaele laughed. "Sharp as ever. Then what must come to pass, if the future is to change?"

Janice remembered what she saw most frequently in her dreams, when she did not sink into the past, most often from a distant shore. The tree of bone, the island. Beneath it, the gleaming white city, as if the walls were pearl or polished bone.

"It's there. The island. But I don't know how to get there and stay conscious. I've never made it all the way."

Raffaele looked at Serge, who had slumped inwards in his confusion, a tremoring cicada shell of the mad soldier he'd become. "Untie her. There is much to explain and more to do. The Interstice is coming."

XVII. Rally

The mood in the gastropool was tense since news of the parley spread. The impending sense of battle, of the missed opportunity to avoid bloodshed and all its associated anxieties and indignities had torn asunder any remaining sense of stability in the Heartlanders. These were people who craved peace at any cost, who found ways to enjoy day-to-day life soaking in stomach acid inside a giant beast. To be pushed to this grim place, this creeping inability to settle the mind, was a new and irreversible tipping point. Below the fragile nest of normality lay a dark abyss where thoughts and actions that man may never otherwise entertain first take root.

From the driftwood holding cage they had locked her in, Nina watched the change blossom like a rot in the faces that passed her by. She did not want to believe her imprisonment two hours after her return had been Hans's idea, but as the legitimacy crisis born of Gabriel's death grew into full-scale civil war, he had become a singular authority to the Heartlanders. It had changed him, made him colder, stiffer, but he had not run from his new place of power. If he truly believed in Nina, he could have pushed back. He could have vouched for her, talked about entrusting her and Owen with the scouting mission to the Pits, but it was clear. He himself was full of doubt and fear of betrayal.

Nina, since she was young, had become used to that look, the one in all the Heartlanders' eyes. The look of the 'other'. Sharp, psychic fences jutting up around the heart. A cold and total absence of light.

A familiar voice began to cry.

From a nearby tent, a Heartlander, Miranda, approached the cage, holding in her hands the wailing baby Sean. Miranda looked exhausted, shaking. She was too tired to fear, too frantic to judge. She stood limply by the cage, unable to verbalize the obvious, needy pleading in her body language.

"Give him here," Nina said.

Miranda, weeping, passed baby Sean between the wooden bars. "I'm sorry, I-"

Nina shushed her with her hand. She didn't want to hear it. There was the baby to deal with. Plus, whatever Miranda had to say would probably just annoy her.

Sean recognized a familiar warmth and opened his eyes, dark pupiless pools of spirit. Nina had been afraid of them at first all those years ago, a terrifying consequence of life inside Levi, but over time, she came to see it: In Sean's dark eyes, what little light before him seemed to come alive. In his innocence, he reflected echoes of a kind of joy and love that no one else could muster.

Nina had always been unsure around children. She had never wanted to be a mother herself. She was a scientist, an adventurer. She craved novelty, freedom, exploration. But in a world as dark and small as this one, there was an escape of sorts in Sean's company. Against unspoken terrors he was a flickering candle in the unending night.

Miranda had left without saying a word. Nina tried not to laugh. Even caged she knew she was freer than most.

"Attention!" cried Hans. From her cage's location higher up the stomach lining, Nina had a premium view of the core chamber of the gastropool with all its makeshift tents and chattering crowds. It had been days now since the leaders had called all Heartlanders together. Nina had forgotten just how many people constituted the crowds of the

Heartlands. A hundred and fifty, maybe more. Most, she now realized, hid themselves in their preferred crevices and holes, doing little to pitch in to the communal survival efforts but staying conscious and comfortable as best they can. But how much of what was done in the name of survival was truly necessary? None died of hunger or thirst. It was the busy work, the semblance of order that the Heartlander society fought so desperately to maintain.

"I need your attention, one and all!" Hans called out again. The crowd sprang to life, the mumbles and commotion rising to a cacophonous level.

"Silence!" screamed Edmund sternly, armor shimmering in the light of the central fire. The crowd fell silent in short order.

Hans climbed up the rope ladder to the central stage, the elevated podium that Gabriel had often used to address the Heartlanders. He readied himself like a senator, gazing out at everyone and no one in the crowd, projecting what he clearly believed was an authoritative, paternal energy.

"Now, I know there's been a lot of confusion and fear, and those of us trying to sort it all out have heard your fears and worries, believe you me! We all know these are uniquely concerning times we find ourselves in. T'were only a few days ago, a few dark sleeps and panicked days, that we were still blessed with the company and courage of Gabriel. He was our leader, our captain, and our friend, and in his absence all of us are hurting. But even in states of pain and fear we must continue to face our fate and carve out our own path by the choices we make together. Choices for the betterment of some and the detriment of others. Choices of peace, and war. Violence and surrender. Power and charity. No one is equipped to make these choices, least of all me. But choose, we must!"

This played quite well with the crowd, though in the space between their cheers there was a visceral undercurrent of fear. The discontented murmurs were too loud, too decentralized to ignore.

"After speaking with our community leaders, we have come to a consensus of sorts regarding the terms of the Pitters. They have demanded, as I imagine all of you already know, that we trade places with them or risk full-out war. Their claims are especially concerning, as we all know they harbor the fugitive Russian, armed with the first working firearm in Levi since the days of the last World War. Those few of you who were present for those black hours should recall the horror and the violence that spilled out to every corner of the world. Are we truly ready for this? Do we have the courage to stand up to these bullies, to say '*This is our home, you will not take it from us!*' Do we, I ask you?!"

The proudest Heartlanders roared in the affirmative. Others cried out and gasped, contemplating for the first time what they stood ready to lose in this fantasy of war. Some fell silent and watched, filled with feeling or blank as canvas inside, all alike.

Hans nodded knowingly from his place at the podium like he was listening intently to each and every person in the crowd. "As I'd expect. Now, I'm nothing but an old sailor. You all know me well enough. Wish I were a more interesting man, but a bit late for that! Now, you don't get to be an old sailor without learning to read the signs. God, in his mischievous wisdom, is always speaking to us, even now. He lays his patterns down and calls on us to *look*. And what better sign, what better message than the Corpse?"

The luminous cadaver, rotted son of the sun, hung above the hypnotized crowd. They had grown numb to its strangeness until now. A bony woman, half-dissolved, raised her hands up to it and others followed suit, their outstretched limbs limp with affected supplication, desperate for faith in anything and all its imagined rewards.

Hans continued. "I'll admit, I thought little of it at first. A strange bit of business in a place accustomed to oddity. But this past night, lost in thought and prayer, thinking of you all, thinking of damnation and goodness, it came to me. The Corpse don't move. It sits there, in the centered air, glowing with nothing less than heavenly light, telling us this message: '*This is the center, the source of the fire.*' It's not just a bit of shine, it's a miracle! In its shadow we stand as one, and we are promised to survive! O, I see it clear now, brothers and sisters! We must stand strong! Damn the Pitters, damn their gun! We are the lightbearers! We are the chosen, the blessed, the righteous and strong! Who stands with me? Who will stand against the shadow?!"

Everyone cheered, stomping their feet and calling out to the Holy Corpse. Hans laughed and waved his dominant arm, basking in the approval of his authority, the visceral response to his bold gambit. Nina could see the naked truth, even from a distance. He didn't mean what he said at all. Whatever his true feelings were, whatever motivated this decision to speak, it was crystal clear to her that this was all a choice. A performance.

Suddenly, there was a voice. It was close, like a whisper coming from somewhere inside her inner ear.

Hey, Nina.

Nina convulsed. She wheeled around, panicking, but saw no one close enough to be the source. Baby Sean, despite the commotion in the gastropool, had fallen asleep in her arms.

Sorry to scare you.

Tears began to well up in her eyes as the voice came

through clear enough to place. "...Owen?"

Yeah. You holding up okay?

"Are you fucking for real?"

Stupid question, I know. But at least you still sound like you. That's a relief.

"You're one to talk. You're dead. I watched you-"

Only sort of. It's a lot to explain.

"Are you really talking to me right now? You sound so clear, like you're here in this cage with me. This isn't me going insane. This is real."

Yeah. I'm talking to you through the Corpse.

"What?"

Gabriel calls it a 'liminal engine'. We think Sean's the same, but less extreme of an example. Or maybe more.

"Gabriel? Gabriel's not dead, either?!"

He's as not dead as I am. We're in the same room on the Island, but he says I should keep explanations to a minimum. It's hard to tell how long we have to talk. This is the important part: We're breaking you out.

Nina, delirious, felt a pang of hope rise up in her like pink and yellow dawn over cool lake water. "Really?"

Really. Listen, I gotta go. It's about to get really bright in there. Look for Serge and cover your eyes as much as you can.

Every node of animal instinct in Nina wanted to ask "Serge?!" like it was the insane, unsafe development that it clearly was, but she understood time was of the essence. She decided to shelve her discomfort and need for answers for later. "Owen… I don't get it, any of it, but I'm glad you're okay."

I'm glad you're okay, too. Good luck. The buzzing pressure in her head slowed down to a soft ringing that faded slowly out of perceptible range. Across from her, at near eye level to her cage, the Holy Corpse radiated a steady light, barely dampened by the heavy cloth sheets and ropes draped and tethered to its form by the Heartlanders.

Nina stared keenly forward, waiting for any sign that the voice had not been a flash of madness, that the tides were truly changing. The Corpse did not stir, did not twitch, and she began to doubt her hope. She held a hand up to her ear in order to cradle that ringing closer to her just a moment longer.

The ropes quivered. The sheets rippled, and a soft pulse of new light flowed out of its confinement. Nina began to laugh. With a sound akin to a choir holding a high note, the Holy Corpse exploded in brilliant light. The sheets flew off, blown about by heavy solar winds, allowing the body's radiance to magnify rapidly to every corner of the gastropool.

From down below, cries rang out. "A sign! Another heavenly sign!"

They cheered and screamed, one and all, in awe and terror. Even Hans, the cynic pontificating on stage, must have wondered what it was he saw, but Nina could not see him. The light consumed almost everything, even the shadows. It started to hurt, burn even, like looking head-on at the sun. She held Sean close to her chest. He did not cry at all.

A silhouette appeared before the makeshift gate. With precision, a knife cut through the rusty chains holding the door of the cage locked shut. It was Serge.

"We must go."

Nina rose and left behind her cage. The two made

their way across the rope-way to a barricaded exit, the unconscious, bound body of a guard underfoot, turned to face away from the source of the light. She let her eyes relax. It was, more than anything, the feeling of touch that guided her now. The holy winds at her back, the weight of her body pressing onwards. Each foot struck flesh and carried on.

XVIII. The Interstice

"Did you get through alright?" Gabriel asked, drinking from a goblet as he looked out the thin lancet window of his study into the early morning. Laid out on the wooden floor by the edge of the fire, Owen stirred slowly. His body was weak and distant from the seat of his senses, or so it felt, but he had done it. He had crossed back into the Leviathan and spoken to his friends. For the first time since Ivan shot him in the throat, he felt like smiling.

"I did."

Gabriel took another sip and cleared his throat. "Excellent. You've adapted quickly. You should be proud of your progress."

Owen got up off the floor and did some rudimentary yoga poses that Ciara had taught him several years ago. Gabriel watched him with confused interest for a spell before returning his attention back to his drink. Owen's blood and muscles felt different than before, changed somehow, but he struggled to understand just how to interpret the change. There was still stiffness and pliancy, a flowing of energy, but the movements, the little sensory details of body habitship all felt unfamiliar, artificial even. He tried not to dwell on it too long.

"What's next for us, Gabriel?" He was ready to leave this study. Gorgeous as it was, furnished like a lush parlor of a well-supported academic in the posh fashion of the 17th century, he had been unable to go anywhere physically since they arrived and had grown sick of looking at the same stone shelves and ornamentals. "Will we be going back to Raffaele's cabin to meet up with the others?"

Gabriel chuckled as he stroked his beard, whiter here

than the dull gray he sported in the Leviathan. "He talks as if it's some minor fuss, forming a body. No. The effort is not worth it at this juncture. The Insterstice begins tonight. We are needed here."

Owen nodded. Raffaele and Gabriel both had mentioned the Interstice since they found Owen in the astral sea and brought him into their plans. It seemed to be a preoccupation of theirs, something of pivotal importance, but every time he asked for clarification, he was ignored, talked over or offered vague platitudes about the weight of knowledge and the importance of pacing it out sensibly for those who seek to follow its path. His gratitude had kept him from pressing the issue before but enough was enough.

"What happens on the Interstice? What are we going to do? How's it going to help us kill the King?"

Gabriel approached him quickly. He took hold of Owen's collar and pulled, lifting him off of his balance. He looked at the young man with terror and fury burning in his eyes as sweat descended down his pale and wrinkled brow. "Silence yourself immediately! We must be diligent here, more so than ever before. There are ears and eyes everywhere on the Island. Everything we see is his construction, his will made manifest. Secrecy, vagueness, it is a strategy. A necessity. Wisen up or perish, boy! I cannot save you here."

He slapped Owen backhand across the cheek. The blow stung.

"Sorry." Gabriel turned and walked back to the window, trying to swallow the condescended rage that flared up in his gut like fire. "I'm just sick of this waiting. I want to do something real and meaningful for the others."

Gabriel, deflating from the peak of his anger, laid the same hand he struck with on Owen's shoulder.

"You're the first of the devoured to reach the Island in a hundred years, you know. Janice has come close, many times in fact, but never once has she hit the shore. This is not to disparage her efforts. She is a supremely gifted dreamer. But you? You have little training, less understanding, and yet here you stand. A liminal engine in your own right, threading the line between living and dead, bound in some unknown form with the Beast itself. You are a freak of circumstance from beginning to end. It may come to pass that you are called to something great, some act that even now might seem incomprehensible to us. Such is the manner of fate. It is not for us to comprehend, only to fight or to follow."

Owen found no comfort in this. He knew he was nothing special and always had been. And nothing that had happened to him that had made him special in this way had been a good thing. Whatever it was that made him special, it was nothing he chose. Nothing he wished to be. He was the acorn that could fall and stop the gears from turning? Huzzah.

"I'll do whatever it takes," he whispered.

"We'll be leaving soon, you and I. We have something to witness. But first, have some ambrosia." He stepped back to the dining table, pouring the strange liquid he had been enjoying for some time from a glass pitcher into the second oak goblet resting on his desk. "It will steel your nerves."

Owen lifted the goblet to his lips. The liquid was bright and blue, silvery and mirrored like mercury or antifreeze. He had watched Gabriel drink enough to know that it was safe to consume and likely delicious given his frequent refills, but that didn't mean he couldn't struggle to find it appetizing.

Reluctantly, he drank it. At first, it had the bright acerbic bite of mint, but it quickly mellowed out, creating a cool glowing sensation that seeped down deep as bones. It was electric. All at once, Owen felt younger, flush with hormones and energy, wit and wisdom alike.

"That was incredible," he noted. Gabriel beamed proudly, patting Owen again upon the shoulder.

"My vice," he laughed away. "Every time I live away from the city, I crave it badly."

So Levi is 'away' to you, Owen thought to himself. "What is it?" he asked, taking another sip. "Not more spinal fluid, right?"

Gabriel shook his head like a cat as he poured himself another glass. "No, my boy. This is distilled astral seawater, mixed with the juice of the ambrosia fruit. To drink it is to taste the firmament of heaven. No bitter taste, no hangover. I call it proof there is a loving God. Even here."

Owen laughed heartily and drank his goblet clean. He felt his fear beginning to slip away, his weakness. Even, somewhat, his own distrust of Gabriel. His memory of the Pitters and their righteous anger, the war brewing inside Leviathan as they sat on fine carpets and drank their miraculous wine. All of it fading away, or weighing less heavy on his heart.

Gabriel filled his cup again. "You're the first new drinking mate I've had in a very long time."

"That's a shame."

"Aye. It is at that, lad."

The sun felt true and brilliant on his skin. The ambrosia flowing within him made all of the elements of this new existence feel luminous and solid, imbued with the original color and flow of the world. It was as if all at once Owen's real life, his half-life of mornings and evenings, work and vacation, love and loss had all been a shallow imitation, a decaying local theater with a dim backlight behind the frame. It made him feel sick to the root of his soul but the smile on his face refused to falter.

The streets were open and bustling with pedestrians, all dressed in gowns with wide sleeves of some thick yet breathable fabric. Some robes were silver, others teal or crimson, all worn loosely with no care for the weather. Many wore masks of brass and silver suspended over their faces as they moved about their business, talking, laughing. At some distance the sound of music wafted from some stringed instrument Owen had never heard before. Around them the alleys curved and bent, paved and polished cobblestone, matching the material of the walls all bleached and radiant white.

Bone, he understood at once. This was a city, an entire island of perfect, virginal bone. It curled upwards from the sea, rising upwards into a central tower, one grand central ziggurat like the curved colossal spine of God.

"The Spinal Mount," mumbled Gabriel, noticing his gaze. "Come now, cover yourself."

His hood was raised above his head, his face obscured with a corvid mask of blue stone. Behind it, his gleaming white eyes bore out. He took a swig at his wineskin for a fortifying splash of ambrosia.

"Speak little, or rather, not at all. Your voice is too modern to the ear. The newest citizens are the ones who are watched the closest. You follow?"

Owen nodded and put on his own mask, his recent death vivid in his mind. His fingers ran over where the bullet pierced his neck, where now no mark or scar remained. The memory of the tendrils coming up and through, grazing his vocal cords, made his stomach swirl in anguish. He hoped he should never feel anything so invasive or frightening again.

It became clear his stomach demanded attention. He pivoted quickly from the street and threw up quietly behind a bush. Gabriel patted his back as he relieved himself, both thankful the street was currently empty of passersby. When Owen rose, he grabbed Gabriel's flask and took another fortifying sip.

"All better."

And they were off. After a moment or two of quiet, they followed the central road as it curved down around the spine, the view of the island widening as they walked. The northern end of the Spine sloped down much wider than the south, allowing the city to spread and roll unfettered over verdant hills of green and yellow. On the southern outskirts where the soil was at its most vibrant, what looked like rows of orchards stretched on and on. It was a hauntingly beautiful sight, to see such rigorous, curated growth after so long in the bleak and wild interior dark.

Owen tapped Gabriel's shoulder and pointed to the rows of orchards, soundlessly asking for information.

"The Fruit," Gabriel explained. "The only food that grows here. Large, like cantaloupe but a tawney orange-red. Delicious, truly. As I said, it's half the mix of ambrosia."

Owen wanted to ask what point there was, to have food and drink when they were no longer needed, only to remember the Heartlanders' habit of discussing favorite foods from their lives before. Eternity with nothing but one fruit, Owen imagined. Could it ever be sweet enough?

"That's where we're headed," Gabriel continued, pointing slightly to the side. "Where the Festival is soon to be held."

Owen looked out at the wide coastline surrounding

the island. From here, the water looked dark and colorless, an undetailed horizon line obscured by a soft, ethereal mist. He remembered his dream. The stand, the turtle. The tree. *What tree was that?* he wondered. He'd seen none so massive or writhing since he arrived, but were it here it would be impossible to miss. He couldn't see the distant shore he had been to, even from this higher vantage point. There was the Island and the sea and nothing else in all directions as far as the eye could see.

Much of the city's populace seemed to be in motion, especially the farther down the hill they trekked. Between lit torches and homes of bone wreathed in fruitless vines and sheets of dyed fabrics of the finest caliber, the commotion of life seemed only to intensify as they descended. It must be that the population density declines further up the tree, Owen reasoned. *Even here, there's an uptown.*

Two women in azure robes walked arm in arm in front of Owen and Gabriel.

"Another Festival. The second in three years," one observed.

"Yes. They are coming frequently now."

"I find myself wondering, given the lay of our fair city, where the House of the Eldest expects to fit all these new acolytes. There is so little room remaining."

"Dear Sister, I must admit to bearing similar misgivings, though of course we trust the Heralds."

The first to complain now bowed her head in trained reverence. "Of course, of course."

Owen and Gabriel shared a glance, each softening their stride to listen in.

The second sister continued. "It would seem as though there are forty acolytes communing today."

"Forty?"

"This is what I have heard."

"That would make this the largest Harvest in decades, by a sizable margin. Does this not invite risk into The Labor?"

"You are right to question this, dear sister. It defies the slow procession of which we have all grown accustomed. It invites suspicion and concern, unless..."

The other sister turned to look her way in quick and sudden shock. "You do not mean-"

A hush fell over them both. They bundled their arms tightly together and skittered over to the left. As they moved, Owen understood what had interrupted them.

Ambling directly towards them, against the parting flow of foot traffic, was a lumbering beast some ten or twelve feet tall, with flesh that looked as dark and solid as stone. Its head was thick and square like a lion's, its body like an upright bear's, but it was hairless and damp, breathing hot steam as it ambled uphill. Its wide eyes looked like burning coals and they seemed fixated on Owen.

Owen felt a sharp pull rightward. Gabriel, soundlessly dragged Owen to the side of the road, averting the path of the grim behemoth. Despite this, the creature kept its slow, steady gaze on them both even as its path remained steady. For a brief moment, Owen worried he had been read like an open book. The sharp, hook-back claws of the creature seemed made for rending flesh from bone. From the force of his grip, Owen could feel Gabriel's worry and stern readiness, tightly chafing Owen's robe against his arm until the creature at last turned its head back the direction it was walking and disengaged entirely.

They both breathed a sigh of relief.

"Homunculi," Gabriel explained in a whisper. "Constructed demons, created by the Heralds. They serve the King with no real thoughts for themselves, building the city streets as well as destroying whatever must cease to be, object or person alike. We must keep moving. Stay silent."

No one in the crowded street, quickly resuming its original flow of traffic, turned to look at them. In that brief transition between fear and acceptance, Owen understood that even for the ones who were chosen, for the elected citizens of this eternal city, there was fear and uncertainty when a sigil of domination appeared before them.

Even uptown. Even in a deathless paradise.

"We're leaving the Lower Temple now and entering the Deepwoods," Gabriel noted.

The cobblestone streets had given way to roads of reddish, well-worn clay. Growing up along the edges were small bundles of bioluminescent wolf's bane and asphodel between tall bronze lanterns cradling calm but vibrant fires. The ethereal sea mist hung heavy and low, making everything feel slow and sunken, the shadows deep and murky as lakewater. There was some great dormant pressure in these woods that made him shiver. Everyone was silent here. All preceding in perfect order, in lockstep, a congregation of robed figures heading away from the core city, towards the hills.

They came to a craggy ridge demarcating the edge of the woodlands and passed beyond it. All at once, Owen could see it, bore into the sediment and soil: an in-ground colosseum, a circular theater gargantuan enough to house ten thousand or more. It was as if he were looking down a canyon's edge, the snaking pathways leading into the upper seats and the tunnels that led even further below. At the bottom of the colosseum, elevated in the center of the stage on three circular platforms was what appeared to be a well of equally colossal size, the darkness at its center full and absolute.

The pressure in this low place deepened. It made Owen feel weak, as if he were less a body and more a vase of flowers preserved in still water. He felt the light bending in and through him like he was a sheet of cotton dancing in the breeze.

Gabriel put his wineskin in Owen's hands. He winked.

Owen drank to keep from laughing.

"Look closely around the well. At the statues," Gabriel whispered.

In the pooling mist around the craterous well, there were silhouettes, forty unrobed figures all in all in stone repose. They were bland and featureless, carved as if a template of a body rather than a living, breathing thing. All their arms were low but raised as if in supplication in circular waves emanating from the center.

From the middle level of the colosseum, below most already seated (save the rows of an inner sanctum clad in blue and white) an altar came alight. All those present began to stomp in their seats, a rhythmic, orderly beat like war drums. Gabriel and Owen followed suit, doing their best to look the same as everyone. No way to tell if anyone was watching.

"Hark!" cried out a central voice, a priest in ritual finery emerging towards the altar. The stomping intensified, and the call matched with a "Hark!" from the masses. "Hark! Hark!"

Owen looked out at the crowd. The voices were all so deep and passionate, clear-lunged and meaningful. The precision and sameness of the shout gave him pause. Everyone here was fully committed, still. There was no way to tell from how things stood how old they were. Like in Leviathan, the people seemed ageless, but more like angels than embalmed corpses. These were the luminous portraits of the dead, not the decrepit flesh.

He noticed there were no babies or toddlers on the Island at all.

"One and all, bear witness!" cried the priest. His cloak was also a deep and royal blue, but it was embroidered with golden circles of thread and tassels and in their orbit well-set jewels that shimmered in the fire light. "The Interstice is upon us once again!"

Again, the crowd responded. "Hark! Hark!"

"When the Harmonies align, the many worlds draw near together, exchanging energy, giving and receiving, seeding the valleys of Atlantis!"

He continued, lifting a golden grail up into the light of the colosseum. "So it is that we welcome new strangers to our door! To our vaulted and sanctified halls!"

The crowd responded, chanting "Have they given penance?"

"It is so and it is so!"

A cheer broke out.

"Forty souls, forty new citizens of New Atlantis step foot on our grounds. Show them their fair welcome to the halls of Elysium, to our blessed shared *eternity*!"

Alan had doubted his footing since the moment he

stepped onboard the Order's great unmarked ship. Once it had departed and sailed off into open waters under the full moon, the feeling only intensified. Emily, standing just beside him, shared none of his concerns.

"We do this little nativity scene and then go home," she assured him during a quiet moment, the lights of the shore condensing into a thin horizon line to the west. "Should we get brunch tomorrow?"

The deck of the ship was lit with stout stone torches placed in measured intervals around the edges of the deck. Forty acolytes in robes of white, their arms low but raised in supplication, stood in circular waves emanating from the center. On the wood of the deck, sigil markings were barely visible beneath their feet, worn from decades of erosion from the sea air. Under the stage set by the moonlight, the stars were glinting closer than ever before as if also in attendance for the coming ritual.

The Herald in charge of the festivities stood before an altar that glowed with unnatural light, hands raised up as if pleading for the moon to fall.

"The Interstice has begun! Initiates, have you given tithe to the Spirit of the Depths?"

They all replied in practiced unison: "It is so and it is so!"

"Are you aligned with The Labor? Do you wish to live forever?!"

As trained, they drew from its sheath upon their waist belts the ceremonial dagger and held it aloft. They raised their nondominant arms, caressing the blade before bringing it downwards. Some cried out in pain. One man, unaccustomed to blood loss, fainted where he stood.

The ritual moved onward.

The initiates stepped toward a wide silver vase, about four feet in height, at the center of the deck. On the surface of the vase were carved a thousand faces, some in anguish, some in joy. Each and every face was different from the last, laid together in packed rows, their features blurred together in a shapeless mass. It was only under flickering torch and star light that the small eyes carved into the relief came alive.

One by one, the initiates let their blood run freely into the many-faced vase. Alan stepped forward, next in the spiral procession. He could feel the slash as he'd made it, clean and precise, stinging the carved flesh of his palm in the cold sea air. From the numbness and the lack of dexterity he deduced that he had severed the vein and tendons of his middle finger. It was his left hand, so no matter what he was unlikely to suffer any great loss of function, but still, his hands had always been precious to him. The sensation of pain was almost inconsequential compared to what the pain suggested.

He had been a surgeon before any of this. Before he met with his mother and her new husband and they talked about his future. Before his mother told him he had "spent enough time on other people." He hadn't really agreed with that. Most of his life had been about determination. *Go. Do the thing. Study. Practice. Achieve. Make. Take.*

It had been simple, no matter how complicated it got. Everything would fall to the wayside to get where he was going. He had never been a doctor to heal, but to do. Care is as much a challenge as a service.

They told him he should go into politics.

ȸ

In the underground Colosseum, the high priest in royal blue raised his gilded goblet to the hosannahs of the faithful masses. With a twist of his arm, he slowly poured out the dark concoction, allowing it to flow down into the large central well of the ground floor. He looked up at the crowd with practiced eyes of cold coalfire, taking stock of each and every resident of the city, challenging whatever doubt or lack of commitment resided in them.

Bellowing proudly, he spoke again: "From the depths of the Sea of All, we call forth the holy waters to rise and bless these frames with the possible, the eternal, the true! As above and so below!"

The people called back and recognized the act. A great howling wind rushed up from the well, as if at its bottom lived the eye of a hurricane that had only just awoken. In the stands, Owen did what he could to hold his mask and robe steady.

Despite the sudden tempest, the priest continued speaking. "By the Grace of the King of White Flowers and the Heralds, by the Blessings and Stewardship of The Fish of Dreams, we pierce the realms between heaven and hell! We extend our loving hands to our sisters and brothers shackled to the base soil! We assure them, we bear witness to their pain and say *NO MORE*! We call them to us across the tainted veil of Mundi, arms extended in good example!"

"By the tributaries of blood that coalesce into this bowl, great Fish of Dreams and King of White Flowers, we pierce the realms between heaven and hell, bind these souls to you, in the name of the Labor and the Dream!"

Alan looked at the moon and its sickly light as the attending Herald lifted the vase of blood high into the salty air of the night. He thought of the boy on the beach, of the dagger. His last expression, that of terror and recognition. Alan knew how much he looked just like his brother. His dead brother. Another of his works. The core price of his ticket upwards to the stars.

The ocean shook, a sonic wave like an abyssal foghorn shaking the ship, his skin, his very bones. Alan looked over to where he was sure his mother stood, but he could not tell in the darkness which of the robed figures she was as they all flailed around and steadied themselves on the deck. Only the practiced hands, the elder Acolytes, seemed unmoved by the disturbance.

The Herald walked to the edge of the ship and poured the blood out into the sea.

Another booming call, the black sea churning in deep ripples as if emanating from the ship itself. In the silver moonlight split open a tear of void from the reflective water. A great absence of light, like a wave, a wall, a mountain.

Amid the darkness, two great yellowed eyes came open.

The well began to sing, and from its depths came a silvery water, flowing up and over the wide lip of its edifice like a fountain. It rushed out with tremendous pressure, swashing against the heavy walls of the bottom chamber, breaking against the stone figures posed around the center. The figures, drenched and half-submerged, began to shimmer with an amber glow. The water rose already to their shoulders, but their light cut through it as if it were made of empty glass. Like it was a liquid mirror, a mercury lake.

Owen felt something inside. Something familiar, something painful.

The warm glow was transformative. As the translucent water flowed like a whirlpool, the figures warped and rippled below. The smooth stone was being eroded, or claiming new life through definition. They were becoming human, approximating flesh. They quivered with life, with breath but they were still beneath it all the texture of living stone, submerged in transpicuous well-water.

One's hands began to move, to flex themselves as if they had fallen asleep. Owen's stomach turned, or so it felt. What was this feeling? This sudden dread?

The figure's face was whittled down into a stable form.

It looked like *him*.

Owen rose in his seat. Gabriel grabbed his arm and whispered something, but the singing of the well was deafening. This feeling of déjà vu was overwhelming, driving him to delirium. Owen exited to the stairwell leading downwards. He needed to see clearly. He needed to know.

There was a sound of earth shifting deep below and all at once the water began to drain from where it had erupted, the abyssal well recalling its luminescent nectar. As the water subsided, the glowing stone was stripped of light. What lay beneath it was flesh, hair, but perfect to the point of distress. The many figures stood about, nude and silent, marveling at themselves and each other.

"Alan?" Owen called out from the edge of the lowest level.

Alan, Owen's brother, looked up at him, stone eyes wide.

"Owen?" A woman's voice.

Owen turned and saw his mother, changed somehow. A younger, painted echo of his mother.

"Mom?"

Owen became aware again of his surroundings. The colosseum was in uproar, the skies above them filled with dark winged creatures circling, clutching golden spears aloft that screamed in the light. The Herald who had led the ritual was pointing squarely at him, intoning in some strange and guttural language. Everything was in motion and horrid danger.

Owen felt unmoored. Foolish like never before. He had ruined everything. A hand grabbed him from behind and pulled him away from the railing.

"We must leave, now!"

It was Gabriel, eyes filled with panic and fury aplenty, sizing up the fast-approaching horde.

Owen remembered himself, his mission. As he was trained, he submerged his heart. He became air and light. As his body became the ash of dreams, he looked again with horrible pain at his older brother, the newest son of Atlantis, peering up at him like an abandoned child at the bottom of the ritual well.

XIX. Summum Malum

The skies above the lower hills of Atlantis were filled with winged homunculi, though their quarry, the two foreign invaders, had long since vanished from the city. Yet still they prowled about the skies in a murmuration, craving the completion of their task. It was not in the creatures' nature to understand travel between dimensions. There was little they understood at all. They were tools. Weapons. Constructs. Consistently useful in a way that man was rarely fit to be.

Herald Thomas despised them. As he ascended the central column to the Inner Temple, the peak of New Atlantis, he could not help but scowl as they fluttered overhead. It had been centuries now since he first saw them dissected, shaped and animated from the island's chalky soil. Many in Atlantis had grown fond of their hulkish forms and dull sedentary gaze, but he had never found a way to accept them in his heart. Now, they screamed like carrion birds across the horizon of utopia, a stain upon the divinity of eternal and unbroken sky.

Before Thomas had come to this land, he had made a point of rejecting what could not be empirically understood. He had been a man of learning, a rational dignified son of his mother country, and was known far and wide for his wisdom. He had taken great pride to stand against the idolatry of his time, to speak out against the hollow worship of spirits, though the fear of God's wrath was never heavy on his mind. This was, of course, before he crossed over the veil. Before he spilt his blood into the chalice and rejected death alongside his fellows at the King's Inn by the silver light of the moon.

Had I understood, then, what it was I truly had per-

mitted to enter in my soul?

He dared not think on this further.

Before him, at the height of the great staircase that wound around the perimeter of the central tower, across the chasmic distance crossable by a thin and solitary bridge lay the Thorn Doors that marked the House of the Eldest. Tall doors of coalish stone, carved with the likenesses of intricate roots and thickets that emanated from the central jewel. To enter required a sincere act of spiritual prostration before the gleaming crimson cabochon. It was uncommon, even for a Herald, to open these doors alone, without the fullness of the Brotherhood beside him to join in communion, but this was a rare occasion indeed.

And Thomas wished, for once, to stand before the King of White Flowers alone.

He bent down to his knees, letting his palms touch the polished ivory floor. There was no dust in Bensalem. Something in him craved the feeling of dust.

He muttered the words of unsealing as he had heard them many times before:

"The interior, revealed. Bask, ye who stands before the stone. In supplication, in surrender, ye who walks now in the garden."

With the shifting of a clunking interior lock the great doors cracked open, swiveling backwards unassisted, the central red stone splintering in twain. What once appeared as hard as crystal flowed like burgundy wine in a colorless glass, free now of its task of bonding door to door.

Thomas entered the House of the Eldest and climbed the interior stairs towards the throne room.

Before him, in the heptagonal chamber, cool light pooled in from above. The walls were covered in dark and colorless vines upon which bloomed white flowers of magnificent size. The flowers breathed slowly, eating the light and wind that collected in the chamber and digesting it into the coloring-matter that gave the petals their ghostly luminescence. The room, in many ways, felt more like a grotto than a throne room. And yet, at its center, bathed in soft slants of light sat the writhing tree of bone, its trunk a strand of cartilage, its branches fraying nerves, rods of ivory and veins all at once. Bored deep into its center was the Lord of Lords, the King of White Flowers, seated in his chair as he always was, his features withered and sunken, barely moving, breathing less, his eyelids hung heavy and low.

Thomas fell to his knees.

"King of Kings, I come bearing news. Our island has been breached. We do not yet understand how, but two men appeared as if from elsewhere during the Interstice. It is believed one of them was an Offering."

Thomas had not heard the King of Flowers speak in centuries, but in the slow, measured gaze of the immortal king there hid a wisdom beyond knowing, the accumulation of a life unending, entwined as one with the Fish of Dreams, the Leviathan.

He wished to hear his monarch speak so desperately that he could cry, but day in, day out, he heard nothing but the weight of dust. Only one member of the Inner Temple, the upper echelon could claim to know his thoughts. But why?

"Why do you only speak to him, Your Eminence?" Thomas pleaded. He crawled on hands and knees towards his king, towards his ageless dignity.

The king's eyelids hung low. From his marble lips, a soft, shuddering sigh flowed out.

From the entrance of the chamber, a voice, high and sweet as honey, called out. "Herald Thomas, he will not speak to you, no matter how you sprawl about. You know this well."

Thomas felt rage boil in his blood at the sound of this voice, but he kept himself contained. He lifted himself up from the ground, his eyes boring straight onto his silent monarch. He had no wish to look at the Lord Verulam. At... him.

"You heard me speak, then? Of the intruders?"

Verulam laughed, his angelic voice brightly echoing between the walls, softening against the petals of the abyssal rose.

"Yes, good sir. The fingers of the powers above do tune the harmony of this peace. Nothing shall harm the White City. Not one or all."

Verulam stepped forward, past Thomas, until he came to the right of the immortal king and took up his unmoving hand. Verulam closed his eyes and smiled lightly, ever fae and spry, features set as soft as water. The king shuddered again, and from his lips that holy breath condensed and formed like frankincense, curling and flowing like water of a thousand hues before it passed into nothingness.

Verulam's bright eyes sparked open.

"So it is time."

Thomas did all he could to bottle his indignation.

"Time?" he asked, as if that word meant anything at all.

"Time, Herald Thomas. The King has said it clearly. We have reaped what we will sow of the dark and bitter soil. It is time for the Final Harvest."

Thomas, deathless man of learning that he was, felt

himself shrink with fear. He had known this day was coming since the beginning, and yet it seemed as if to be an eternity away. But now, on this last Insterstice, the sun was truly setting on the world he remembered.

Verulam laughed again, stepping towards Thomas and offering his hand.

"Call the other Heralds. It begins at dawn."

XX. The War Within

Raffaele's head awoke with a gasp, startling everyone.

Sean began to cry in his mother's arms. Janice groaned, bouncing the baby in her arms, patting his back as soothingly as she was capable. When nothing worked, she stepped outside the cabin, slamming the door behind her. Serge, whittling a wooden rod down into a spear in front of the roaring hearthfire, laughed under his breath. Nina roused from sleep in the cot in the corner of the room, having enjoyed the first comfortable sleep she had found in a long time.

"What is it, Ledger Man?" she asked, reminding herself that it was alright that Raffaele was a severed head, that any of this was normal. She had come to expect some inherent level of strangeness inside Levi since she arrived, but recently the scales had tipped massively in one direction and not let up since.

"News from Gabriel," Raffaele offered, bouncing himself with his chin to face the others still inside. "Ill tidings, I'm afraid to report."

Serge looked up from his whittling, dark eyes burning. "What have they learned?"

"They witnessed the Insterstice ritual, but something went awry. It seems as if Owen's mother and brother were Acolytes, and in a deep panic, he revealed himself to the Islanders. We have lost the element of surprise."

Serge scoffed. "Idiot."

Nina thought of Owen, and the powerful sadness of what he must be feeling. She could still barely comprehend that he was alive. She had seen the sinews crawl like a spider's legs through the bloody hole in his throat, but yet she had heard his voice. He had worked to free her from the Heartlanders. And now, he was elsewhere, in what Janice had described as an astral sea, a dimensional ocean that all life flows into. It was there, she had said, where the Island of Atlantis stood. Where everything began.

"Is Owen to be trusted?" Serge asked. "Is he working with them?"

"Serge!" Nina exclaimed, throwing a nearby empty wooden goblet at him which bounced off his arm and fell to the floor with a hollow *clank*. "He's one of us, you ass!"

"Don't be a fool! Think with your brain, not with your heart. His family is connected to the masters of our suffering and now he has damned us even further with his folly. Is blind trust something to be proud of here? I say no."

"Owen has *not* betrayed us," Raffaele chimed in with a harrumph. "It is a hard thing to accept, that your family would ascend as you fall. It was a failure of our imagination that they could be in attendance on this particular day. Most initiations are not this populated for the Order. It suggests a sloppiness, or rather, a lack of concern for being discovered that is unusual to say the least."

"Do you mean, they *sacrificed* him?" Nina asked. "To join the Order?"

Raffaele sighed and did his best to nod. "Most everyone inside the Leviathan was, by someone important to them. It is a test of loyalty for initiates and a battery for the beast to grow as it has."

The three of them sat in silence for a moment. Nina wondered who it was who had sacrificed her, if anyone. She had not been swallowed alone. *At least*, she thought to herself bitterly, *it was not Mannfred. He had gained nothing from this.*

“So what does this mean for the revolution?” Serge inquired.

“Unsure. This is deeply concerning, to be sure. I expect that the Heralds, those at the height of the Order, will not accept this development without response. It is only a matter of time until they realize we act from within. This cabin will not be safe for much longer.”

Nina rose. “Where can we go? What can we do?”

“The original plan to infiltrate the island has grown much more difficult. Initiating you both to the Sea, to the Mysteries, was already a tall order. I am unsure if there is enough time now. It took Janice many years of practice to reach the level that she has.”

Serge scoffed. “What about Owen, then?”

“A rare case. It was his death, and more importantly, the flesh of the beast that claimed him as he died, that has made him what he is. This cannot be replicated by our own methods. Simply killing you will not inspire the Leviathan to act on your behalf,” he said, laughing slightly. “Or someone would have discovered this path already.”

Nina tried not to let his casual laughter bother her. There were more important things happening in the moment than to confront this severed head for his emotional disconnect, but she wouldn’t forget it. “Do we know why it did that to Owen?”

“If only we did. It does not seem to have been a choice of the Order. After all, they did not create the beast. It acts of its own accord as much as it does of their bidding.”

The door opened, stopping the conversation. It was Janice, with a calmer baby Sean sleeping in her arms. “As you were, soldiers,” she said with a sing-song flourish.

“Any sign of Pitters? Heartlanders?” Serge asked,

walking over to the door and peeking out the portcullis. Janice passed him by, sitting back down in the same chair Serge had tied her to not long ago.

"The only thing I saw or heard out there was little Sean. I'm sure if anyone is watching the cabin, they've become very disinterested. Has a plan been made?"

Nina shook her head. "We're working that out still."

Janice chuckled, noticing a smudge on Sean's cheek and wiping it off with her thumb. "If I try to enter the Island alone, they're going to kill me, you know. I don't want to die after all this waiting around. It'd be such a tremendous waste of my value."

Nina got up and started pacing, trying to work through her building panic. "The Heartlanders are going to kill me on sight for escaping. They're convinced I'm one of the Pitters, and in their eyes I've all but confirmed that fear. Now you're saying the cultists who are feeding us as sacrifices are coming for us. Isn't there some way we can escape from here together? Even if we don't go to the Island, there's an entire sea we could escape to."

"Hear, hear!" Janice cried. "I quite like that idea. Let's leave it all behind."

"So you would look away? You would bear witness to all this misery, this violence, and you would do nothing?" Serge asked, the flickering hearthlight gleaming in his eyes. "After all these years, I now know how to fight back against the greatest evil. After all these years of darkness, all these years of misery, there is a chance to end things, to set things *right*! We've been dead to the world for so long we have nothing to go back to. I say good. We were chosen to fight. To kill a false god and its hellish adherents. To better the world and avenge ourselves as well as everyone else who has been devoured since all this horror began. That's worth any risk."

"Alright, calm down," Janice said. "We need to solve the pressing issue. We need to leave Levi, no matter the risk, no matter the destination. Now, our darling Nina escaped her insulting cage thanks to the Holy Corpse you mentioned. Owen was able to channel energy through him, correct?" she asked Raffaele.

"Indeed. The Holy Corpse is a liminal engine, much like Owen has become, like Sean even. It is a result of the great whale's dreaming. Inside, we are subject to different laws than material reality. Once we are understood by the beast, we are preserved in a sort of stasis, a living memory of sorts. That is our blessing and our curse."

"Could we use Sean as an engine, then? To get us to the Island?"

Raffaele nodded. "That had been my original hope, but there will be too much danger. They will notice when we arrive. We will have no element of surprise. Against the Order, we lack numbers and power on our side, and there will only be one chance to kill the king."

Nina looked deeply into the fire. In it, she saw what possible futures lay ahead of them. No matter what would come to pass, there was little hope for victory and less for survival. All these years, she had only wanted to escape, to survive this torturous confinement, but Serge had been right. Mannfred had been right. She should have aged by now. She wasn't alive, not anymore. This half-existence was a dream. The world had changed outside, likely far beyond her ability to understand, and what none of them had dared to say aloud was that there was no guarantee at all that they could ever stand on solid ground again.

If the dream ended, it was only natural they would end along with it.

"What we need," she said quietly, "is a sacrifice."

The room turned to face her, but she could not look them in the eye.

"We have two engines. Sean and the Holy Corpse. We need to use them both." She fought her fear, her unease, to meet the eyes of the group, to communicate the seriousness of her ideas. "We could bring the Corpse to the Island, draw their fire."

Janice looked at her uneasily. "It would be a death sentence."

"I know."

Raffaele's brow furrowed. "Perhaps, if I were to form another body, you and I could go together. The Heartlanders may be less inclined to violence if I made a rare appearance at your side. But I am unsure if I can accomplish this quickly."

"I could also go. To protect you," Serge offered, blushing slightly.

"So then what, Owen and I siege the palace?" Janice asked. "With the baby on board?"

"With Gabriel, yes," Raffaele nodded. "He is more powerful than you imagine."

"I suppose you're right. Still, it feels somewhat pointless to try."

Serge shook his head. "Until today, they didn't think they could ever be reached. I doubt there is any standing army on the Island. The quicker we act, the more ironclad our purpose, the more chance we have of success."

Raffaele looked concerned, distraught even, but said nothing.

Serge continued, understanding what must be done. "We can't leave getting to the Corpse up to chance."

"Then what do we do?"

Serge handed her the wooden spear he had been whittling for hours. “We need to end the war. The Pitters are more likely to fight, more hungry for revenge. We tell them what’s at stake, we seize the stomach and the Corpse, we have an army.”

Raffaele mumbled something to himself before addressing the others. “Yes. I shall need to depart, then. I must consult Gabriel and begin my efforts to reconstitute my body. It will not be easy but I will move as hastily as I am able. Before I go, I will say this to you all.”

Janice, Nina and Serge turned to look at Raffaele.

“I have watched over the wretched souls devoured by this abyssal beast for centuries. In this time, I have seen saints and sinners alike take root inside and try their best to survive. I have always considered myself an observer. A witness. But as I look upon you now, as I hear in your voices the resolve and selflessness you demonstrate, I find myself doubting the path my own life has taken. But more than that doubt, I am left with a greater sureness that this moment, that your efforts, will lead to incredible things. Your example is the stuff of songs and legends, whether the world shall ever know it or not. Take pride, stay strong, and await my return.”

With a smile, Raffaele closed his eyes. His severed head transformed, decomposing into a pile of ash that lost its structure and faded into the dark shadows of the cabins’ ancient paneling.

The souls remaining in the Ledger Man’s cabin said nothing for a while. The gravity of the mission weighed on them, but as they looked into each other’s eyes they understood that the time for waiting, for suffering senselessly in hope of absolution, had passed them by for good.

All that was left to them was the bloody road towards freedom.

XXI. Immunity

It was dark in the tunnels of flesh. Dark, hot and pulsing pink and red. Nothing had changed and yet it was worse than ever before.

Since the war began in earnest, the tunnel lights burned dim or were snuffed out altogether. It was better that way, better for fighting, sneaking, but it also drove home a sickening truth: the tunnels, the ropeways, every bit of flotsam architecture men had created inside the Leviathan was not separate or safe from the ever-closing dark.

In the light, your eyes could lie for you.

A small contingency of Pitters snaked slowly through an interior tunnel. Six brave souls chosen for the task by virtue of their dexterity, wit, and comfort for violence. It was not yet time for the main attack on the Heartlanders' seat of power, for the great bloody night where all outstanding balances were paid in earnest. But the hour grew ever nearer.

Bill was ready, mostly. Sick of waiting around most of all. He'd been swallowed in the mid-90's off a pleasure cruise en route to Bermuda. It had been a corporate vacation, the first he'd ever taken in his life, and this was how it ended. But Bill had always been an unlucky guy, and he'd made peace with that. All he wanted anymore was to be warm. To have a little task to keep his hands busy.

He'd always had fidgety hands. His middle school gym teacher Mr. Callowy had said it was the sign of a disquieted mind with a tone of voice that implied weakness. Why did he remember that so clearly? He hated that guy, then and now.

But that's Bill for you, thought Bill. Shaky hands, weak

will, memory like an elephant. Gabriel knew he was dead meat and dead weight inside Levi, but why the Pit with the mad screamers and the criminal element? He knew he was being harsh in his assessment. He'd made a friend or two in the Pit, good people down on their luck, same as him, but he just never understood why he was picked to go below. Nobody ever explained any of it to him. Wasn't worth telling it to him, maybe.

All that's in the past now. Now it's war.

Bill could barely make out the front of the vanguard. The other five Pitters were all much braver and much angrier than him, so he didn't try to make too much conversation. This was a mission, a chance to even the scales against historic oppressors from a higher circle of hell.

"Watch where you're going," whispered Farrah before him. He'd bumped into her without realizing. Bill went beet red at the embarrassment of it all, but also as much the sudden feeling of another warm body against his own. That little moment of touch, accidental it might be, made him realize all at once how long it had been since he'd been touched, really held, at all.

"Sorry," he whispered back.

A harsh click of the tongue from the front of the vanguard. In the dark, the glimmer of cold steel flashed on what slant light reflected off the moisture of the tunnel walls. A chill ran down Bill's spine. It was the new guy, the Russian. His gun was raised up as if to silence all sound, Bill figured, and if he was wrong it wasn't worth risking.

He shut right up, quiet as a church mouse.

After a moment of total quietude the group shuffled onwards. The corners of the tunnel, pocketed between the intestinal lining and abdominal wall, were hard to watch too closely or too far ahead. They were rarely, before the war, used for much at all. A long abandoned throughway that suggested a level of trade and connection between the upper and lower societies that had long since frayed beyond repair.

Bill felt something in his gut turn. It was as if the darkness behind him had been cut, and he could feel it on the hairs of his neck. A sound rang out from far behind them, a shrill and powerful shriek. It didn't sound anything like a human being. Closer to a bird, a crow, but massive and thick-throated.

The vanguard stopped at once. "What the fuck was that?"

"Did you see anything?"

"Heartlanders?"

They all kept their voices low, still in the mindset of war, but this new fear had ended their ability to stay silent. Bill said nothing, did nothing, save watch the darkness for signs of danger.

A ripple shook through the flesh. The angle of the tunnel steepened as the Leviathan contorted itself. One of the vanguard, midway in the pack, slipped. He rolled past Bill, into the pervasive shadows with a full-throated yelp. The others tried reaching out to catch him but he fell too quickly to get hold of.

"We're making too much noise!" Another hissed. Bill could barely see anyone or make out who was speaking. The ripple continued. A dull pulsating tone filled his ears, shook the bones beneath his skin.

"Quick, light a torch!"

"The enemy will find us!"

"Do it. We're too loud anyway," Ivan snapped. He

tapped the shoulder of the man nearest him, who lit a torch and held it aloft, facing further down the incline.

Nothing stood out at first glance. They could see now, in the distance some twenty feet away, the slipped man climbing to his feet. He seemed a little dazed but otherwise unharmed, and gave the vanguard a quick wave to that effect.

Then, they heard it.

Behind the fallen man the sound of slick and heaving like steam and oil bubbling together in a pit. A mass appeared from the dark. A boulder of sinewy flesh and tendon, writhing limbs and hot white blood rolled up the tunnel, quickly dwarfing the fallen man whole, crushing him like a swollen grape against the floor.

Bill turned and saw it. He screamed.

The sinews flew to life, stretching out and piercing his body. He was lifted up from his feet by the thousand small hand-like appendages flowing freely from the visceral mound, ripping and tearing with abandon. The man struggled wildly, caught in unimaginable pain and fleeting terror, but the mass acted with methodical certainty, pulling vital strips and chunks of the man into itself bit by bit until there was nothing left to struggle in its grasp.

"*Run*!" Someone shouted.

No one needed convincing. Least of all Bill.

The mass did not seem to follow at first. They hauled ass further down the tunnel, all sense of subterfuge abandoned. As the torchlight vanished around the bend, only the polished bones of the risen man were visible when Bill stole one last glimpse behind him.

Another ripple and groan. Around them, the intestinal walls seemed to convulse with sudden life. From the living walls sprung things like bodies, or rather the opposite of bodies, skinless bone and marrow, muscle and blood. They screamed from places of dark hollow within and lunged at the running Pitters. One was caught. He hacked and hacked at the arm of the corpse-matter to break free, but around him many arms rose up to pin him where he stood.

The others kept running.

Bill wondered if he was going to die. It seemed quite likely now. He was already almost out of breath, fighting for each new step he took. *Why* had he been chosen for this mission? These others around him, these warriors, they were all just as terrified. All their ability and confidence meant nothing in the face of this threat.

A higher scream. Farrah saw the original mass rolling towards them from behind, its tendrils gripping the tunnel and pulling it forward as it rolled.

It was so fast.

A flash of light and sound. Ivan was firing his gun at the mass, one bullet after the other. It shuddered, deflating slightly into itself like a punctured balloon. He reached for his belt. Bill remembered him saying he had two magazines left, then that was it forever. What moments ago had felt like the perfect weapon of war now seemed like a toy against this encroaching evil.

"Enough," barked a deep voice from the darkness before them. A new figure stood on the walkway, also stitched together out of corpse-matter, but this one stood full and upright with a human dignity, the deep holes in its head glimmering with a silver light.

A thousand hands broke through the walkway boards, through the ceiling and the walls. They grabbed Bill, Farrah, the others who had not yet already been lost. The sinews felt so hot on Bill's skin coiling around him. He wanted to scream, but it was as if that part of his brain had gone dark in self-preservation.

Farrah screamed, shortly.

The central figure walked between the suspended Pitters being burned and ripped. It watched with cold clarity as they died, one by one, their bodies seizing with panic before falling limp, mute.

Farrah was gone.

Bill could not fully register the feeling, could not look down to see it with his eyes, but he knew his stomach had been opened.

The figure approached Ivan, kept low to the ground, quiet. Eyes that gleamed with ancient rage. Ivan looked to his pistol and where it lay on the splintered walkway, just out of reach.

"You are the one I was searching for," the figure said. "Liminal and bound to the corpse."

Ivan said nothing. Did not even blink.

"We cannot enter the field your brother creates, but you can. Finish what you started, and there shall be a place for you in the White City, far beyond this place. You shall look each day upon the glorious work and legacy of man made eternal. You shall eat of the fruit, drink, and be merry. You will be warm and loved for all days to come. Or, you will refuse, and die like these parasites before you."

The sinews tightened their grip on Bill's numbing extremities. He screamed, fading in and out of consciousness.

"What will it be?" the grim figure asked.

Ivan, with eyes of black fire, nodded his assent.

The figure laughed. "Good. Let us celebrate the compact."

He turned to Bill, the last of the Pitters, dangling above him, pulled upon from every side by vicious sinews of flesh.

"Let it rain."

XXII. Breakfast

Continental breakfast began at 5:30 AM at the beachfront Hadrian Hotel in Atlantic City, New Jersey, nestled just a mere hundred and twenty feet from the shoreline. For a seaside hotel in the subtle, dreamy lull of the off-season, there's not much to expect. Some shipped in blueberries, a stale cornbread muffin or two, your choice of seven name brand cereals dispensed at a plastic trough and coffee that tastes as if it had been cooled and reheated four or five times already this morning.

This was no secret. The reviews all said as much, on Yelp, Google, TripAdvisor, and elsewhere. The staff, for whatever reason, seemed disinclined to improve things. After all, they *could* perfect the craft of buffet-style breakfast spread, ready and able to address the dietary needs of an impossible to predict clientele who have no obligation or incentive to appear outside of their own convenience, but why?

It was the off-season. The beach was cold and the wind gales blew strong, brandishing the dagger-sharp taste of sea salt on its wings. All this weather suggested to the outside world was the wide oblivion yawning just beyond the shoreline. People only came to town then to gamble, to hide away where it was quiet and slow. At least, that was what tradition suggested, but on this particular day the hotel lobby was packed to the brim with tourists.

"I'm counting just under 40," one of the hospitality desk workers told her general manager over the phone, covering her mouth as she spoke. Despite the sheer quantity of patrons shuffling around and fetching their breakfasts, the atmosphere was eerily, pervasively quiet. "Think it's a conference of some sort."

"You're out of orange juice," one older man said, clutching a styrofoam bowl of dry pancakes cradling a few scoops of cinnamon oatmeal. "I can't drink coffee. Not even decaf."

The worker nodded, tilting the phone so her boss could make out every word. "We'll get that replaced right away, sir."

Alan cut at his pancakes softly, so as to not scratch the bulk order ceramic plate. Every motion, every bite he took felt loud enough to be blaring through a megaphone. It was hard enough to function and eat at all after what had happened the night before, but every little sound he made drew eyes, ears and a heavy pressure that choked the air from his lungs.

His mother seemed completely unbothered by the animus. She was on her third cup of coffee, going through the motions of cream, sugar, cream and stir with a slow, methodical hand. She hadn't looked him in the eye since the face of her dead son stared down at her from the colosseum railing in a world once described to them as idyllic, eternal. She'd barely said a word since the ritual ended and they returned to their mortal coils on a ship in the middle of bitter ocean darkness.

The Herald had said this disruption was a serious offense to the ritual and a portent of coming evil, but it could not yet be decided that it was a crime on their part. He had said, *the decision will come some time after dawn*. He sent them back, with the other Acolytes, each of them bewildered and terrified, to their pre-booked rooms at the hotel to await the news.

It was understood they were unable to leave. No one had needed to say anything.

"I wonder what the weather's going to be like," Emily

pondered, holding the cup of coffee up to her lips as she gazed out the seaward-facing full glass windows. The skies were gray and dull, a heavy but quiet front of clouds having rolled in since just before dawn.

Alan thought of the stars and the moon as he had seen them only hours before. He had tried sleeping, briefly, since they returned, but the moment his hold over consciousness slipped, he felt it: the dull, hard gap between his body and his soul. They had been bonded together, lightly, before, but now, having gone… elsewhere, he could feel it. The gap. The hollow.

His hand ached distantly as he scooped his cold eggs with a fork.

"I'm not sure, Mother," was all he could say.

She looked up from her coffee at him, her big eyes set in stone in their sockets.

"We've done nothing wrong, Alan. We followed their rules to the letter. There's nothing to worry about."

Alan could not hide his indignation. "I'm sure they'll see it that way. Rational bunch."

Emily looked around the room at the other Acolytes eating breakfast. As she did, they all turned on cue to make eye contact with her. Their rage and sharp focus was all-apparent. She couldn't help but smile and meet their glares head-on. She picked up a piece of buttered toast from her plate and chewed it vigorously, as if to taunt them.

"Cowards, one and all," she said, her mouth full of toast. "They're afraid. Little cockroaches exposed to the sun. They want to put it all on us. Every little thing they're feeling. This stress of being trapped together, seeing each other's faces after the fact. As if that changes anything at all!"

She laughed loudly, eating the entire piece of toast in

three bites. This caused her to choke, and she raced to wash it down with water and coffee.

Alan thought of his brother.

"What do you think he was doing there?"

Emily shook her head. "Haunting us."

"And you're okay with that?"

"Alan."

"You saw him. He was… alive. Or looked like it."

She shook her head tightly as if to deflect the thought entirely. "Atlantis is a city of the dead. They said so in the presentation. No one was alive there."

"But he wasn't one of *us*. He was an offering. How did he get there?"

"I don't know, Alan."

"Will he be there when we cross over? If we cross over, now? And they don't…. do whatever they do to people who ruin the ritual?"

"I don't *know*! " She was holding her butter knife up and pointing it for emphasis. Her hands were shaking. "I don't have an answer for any of this. But it doesn't matter, any of it, and you know that. All we can do is sit here and figure out what is in our best interests, together."

One of the hotel employees swung by their table, drawn by the conversation in an otherwise eerily quiet dining room. It's always best for a server to nip these sorts of outbursts in the bud.

"Is everything to your liking today? Anything we can grab you?"

Emily flashed a long-practiced smile. "Oh, dear, you're too kind. I could use a refill on my coffee. Oh! And also, I meant to ask, do you by any chance have a raspberry jam somewhere in the back? I hadn't seen any when I was up at the table."

"I'll check for you, right away, ma'am."

"Of course, thank you very much!" She waved her hand with a light flourish, like a fairy godmother or a conductor of a tiny orchestra.

The server hurried away. The smile melted from Emily's face in seconds.

"*Ma'am*," she scoffed, waiting for a reaction from her son that never came. She paused to drink her coffee, watching her disaffected son. "Tell me, Alan."

"Tell you what, Mother?"

She looked at him straight on. "Do you hate me?"

"What?"

"Do you blame me for all this?" she asked. "For your brother?"

She had startled him. "I-"

"Do you think it's all unfair? Heartless? Am I the root of all this pain in your eyes?"

Alan ran his thumb over the bandage of the fresh wound on his hand. "I don't know."

"You don't know."

He felt his face go red. "Oh, is that not fair to you?"

"I want an answer, Alan. A real answer, from your heart."

Alan wanted to say *Yes, of course. Your status, your ambition, they drove me here. Your favoritism, your self-centeredness, all of it led us here as a family. You said it was right to curse my brother, to kill him. Maybe you didn't believe it would work, not so soon or so strangely. Maybe you thought this was all a big act from rich bastards, some Halloween country club, but you signed along and convinced me to do the same.*

But he didn't. All he said was, "Sort of."

"Sort of?"

Alan sighed. All last night, he had laid in bed, thinking of the beast and his brother somewhere within. He knew the truth.

"I did it, too. All of it. I never said no."

Emily looked away at the window, trying to hide a tear forming in the well of her furthest eye.

"It goes back so much further than you or I, you know. I've spent my entire life feeling like a failure in my own father's eyes."

"Grandfather, you mean?"

She nodded. "He wanted us to be a family of means, Alan. He wanted me to be the model bride for some great, handsome mover and shaker. Instead I married your fool of a father. He never forgave me. And where did he get it from? This suffocating pressure for more. I just don't know. He never told me."

"We killed Owen, Mom."

"I know."

"He was an idiot, sure. But he was one of us."

The wrinkles around Emily's thin lips were deep as canyons, carving her face into a frown like a wooden doll's.

"I know my son."

They sat in silence for a while.

The hotel staff came and brought the coffee and the

jam. Emily nodded, her hand resting gratefully on their forearm. The person, a younger employee, recoiled slightly, nodded, and left.

Emily filled her cup with black coffee, then Alan's. They drank.

Outside, the sky above the water had darkened. Thick clouds, voluminous and shadowed, had condensed into a seastorm. What few people had been seen combing the beach, getting in an early morning jog, had vanished. Seagulls, hundreds of them, were flying in from the sea, squawking loudly. Behind the thick glass windowpane it barely registered at all.

One of the cultists, an elderly woman, short with well-slouched shoulders, was returning back from the bathroom when she stopped to watch the storm coming in. She stood there beside the glass, saying nothing.

She noticed that the water surface far out to sea was moving strangely. It was, for half the horizon-line, raising up as if buoyed by a sunken moon.

She turned to face the other Acolytes when it came: The old siren, an Atlantic City institution. The birds and the tide, receding deep.

From below the surface of the sea, below the world itself came a whalesong. Deeper than marrow, deeper than the soul, it trembled through the physical world, shaking the firmament. The tidal water began to refract, almost crystallizing as it ballooned in the distance, eating the visible sea, twisting it into a solid shell of liquid glass.

Everyone inside the hotel was aware now of what was happening. The Acolytes rose to their feet and crowded by the window in rapt awe. The hotel workers watched them do so with dread, unsure of what in the world could be happening, shaken to their cores.

"Is this an earthquake? A tsunami in fucking Jersey?" All they knew was this was the beginning of danger. Some began to leave the dining space, bolting for their cars or hotel rooms. Others got on phones, paging the hotel staff, anyone who might not yet have noticed what was happening outside.

The whalesong rose in tenor. The water broke, the whole great dome shattered into rain and white spray. Within it, in the eye of this great cathedral emerged the figure of the impossible titan they had seen a glimpse of the night before.

"It is *him*! The Leviathan wakes!"

From miles away, it stood at the height of a mountain. Its gray-white flesh, shining with the smooth texture of a sea mammal dripping with tonnes of brackish water, bore thousands of human faces like etchings of the damned, writhing thoughtlessly, some the size of buildings, others miniscule, half-formed masks in corpuscular piles on the surface of its colossal limbs.

"The Harvest has begun!" one cultist cried.

"Praise the Order! Praise the Great Labor!"

Alan and Emily exchanged a glance of understanding terror.

The first woman to stand at the window, crowded out by the others, walked over to her table in silence. She picked up her handbag and drew her phone, tapping with both thumbs at her phone until she had sent a text to her husband.

Afterwards, she set it down and picked up the butter knife resting on top of her half-finished pancakes. She performatively cleared her throat, but no one turned. She cleared it again, with all the emphasis that she could muster. This time, people turned.

"We are needed, Acolytes!" she said. "Return to The Island. This world has ended. As it should. We were promised the only true tomorrow! Seize what is ours! Long live the King of White Flowers!"

The elderly woman stabbed the knife diagonally into her jugular. Her blood sprayed against the window, across the nearby cultists by the window, but she had followed through.

Her lifeless body fell like trash to the carpet. A hotel worker screamed.

The Leviathan's song boomed forth from its lungs. It was beyond any sound Alan had heard before. A shout of a million voices, the song of some ancient and unknowable god. The soundwave hit the shore like a bomb, shattering the hotel windows.

Alan rose, his ears ringing and wet with blood. He looked around the room. Some of the cultists had died from the impact, from the heavy shards of glass blown back at sickening speed. He himself had been cut along his forearms. No arteries.

His mother was unconscious on the ground. From the pressure, not extraneous wounds. He checked her pulse. It was light, but beating. He had to get her away from here.

He picked her unconscious body up off the carpet. The other cultists, stirring, seemed to barely notice. The line had been crossed, after all. What lives they had dreamed of before, what benefits may come from a marriage to the Order were cashed out. Only the one and final gift remained.

Alan, exhausted, carried his mother out of the lobby just as the gunshots started. He didn't look back. Didn't hesitate.

He ran to his mother's car. His old car was in a shop

somewhere, out of state, being cleaned on Order dollars. All evidence of what he had done to the lifeguard was being erased, expunged, but that couldn't be counted on any longer.

He could see it from here, from the parking lot. The Leviathan.

It had begun to approach the shore.

Alan put his mother down in the back seat, checking her head for signs of a concussion. Nothing visible, but he couldn't take chances. He took her spare sweater she kept in the back and put it under her head to keep it elevated.

The whalesong pulsed again. From the body of the beast, the writhing faces clearer now in view began to slip loose from its skin, becoming eel-like spirits of the air that curled around its body like a storm front. The very clouds themselves seemed to follow suit, unfurling as a grand white rose of coming death.

The force was like a hurricane. A tsunami. It tore at the world like a knife through fragile thread.

Alan cleared out the shattered windshield glass from the front seat and started the car.

He was driving inland.

XXIII. The Far Shore

Far from Atlantis, there was a long and shallow shore that connected to greater land and yet never seemed to end. Large rocks formed a natural wall that blocked off the visible horizon, though the mind understood that something *must* be there. There is always something beyond. It was simply never seen. It could never be seen.

Owen was here again.

He was alone on the shoreline, looking out at the sea. He sat beside what once was the small wooden booth he had found in his first marrow dream. It had become damaged, waterlogged, covered in patches of dull moss and refuse. The water must have risen and receded here a thousand times. *Had it been so long already?*

This was to be the starting point. It had been decided back inside the Leviathan by The Ledger Man and the others. Gabriel, furious and sullen, had gone to reconstitute the fullness of his power. In the many years he had been inside Levi, he had sequestered parts of his spirit away in distant corners of the astral sea. Or so he said, as if it had meant anything at all.

The lessons had stopped abruptly since the Interstice. Gabriel couldn't accept what had happened, couldn't move on to better nurse the mission than his grudge. He had believed Owen to be a more stoic, strategic agent than he had proven himself to be in the pivotal moment. But all of Owen's training in astral travel hadn't readied him to find his family there in the Well looking up at him. To see his mother, his brother at the heart of an ancient ritual and understand exactly what that had implied.

"We have waited for so very long to act," Gabriel had

muttered before he left. "Now we must commit to the scene, to the risk of open war, or it has all been sunken, pointless time."

"Why?" Owen asked. "Why is there such a rush? Why can't we just... keep waiting? Why do we have to act?"

Gabriel had not answered.

Owen waited. He could not see the tree of bone from the far shore. He could not see the island. He knew well enough now that the sea was endless. It went on forever. As it bounded in all directions, it became the sea of everything. Below its waters, shape and light became fluid in ways the eye struggled to follow. Gabriel and Raffaele seemed afraid, almost, of what lingered within. It haunted them to ponder what the sea truly was, what it became and what it contained. And yet, here upon the cosmic waters lie the grand human project of New Atlantis, the beautiful and horrifying fortress of deathless majesty, sustained upon the spine of the abyssal beast that fed off wayward souls, some found and others fed, like Owen, by their own family and friends.

He wished that the coastal air of this far shore felt cold, or warm, or like anything at all. The sea moved like a breeze was blowing but he felt nothing but numbness, inside and out.

Behind him were footsteps, lingering without erosion in the sand. He lifted himself up off the ground and turned to find the woman from his first marrow dream, the strange booth worker, standing just beside him on the shore. Though he could recognize her at once, she seemed entirely transformed. In his memory, her every feature was blurred like cloudy water, but no longer.

"We meet again," she greeted, her voice high and soft, her pale green hair wet with seawater, the light gleaming in the pearls that were her eyes.

"We do, yeah." He felt awkward, slow in her presence, as did time and wind and sound.

"You are whole this time. Last you passed this way, you were a wisp, dashed upon the rocks."

"That makes sense. I was new to all this."

"New?"

"Yeah. I'd never been here before."

She laughed. "You've always been here."

He laughed too, but was unsure why. "I have?"

She nodded. "Like me."

Owen had no idea what to say.

"You never paid me for passage."

"I didn't?"

"No."

"Oh. Well, I didn't have anything to pay you with. Sorry."

"You had no clothes, either."

He turned away, towards the water. "Right."

"It's fine." She walked beside him, also facing the sea. She sat down on the sand, her white gown flowing soundlessly. "Pay me now."

"How?"

"Tell me a story."

Owen sat down, too. He rubbed his face, trying to wipe away the sudden blankness in his heart. "I'm not really in the mood for stories."

"Come now. It is owed, and so must be given. What care should I have for your feelings?"

The sharp bluntness of her question made him chuckle.

"Fair enough. You're a harsh one."

"I suppose."

He wanted to ask her what she was, where she came from. What this moment was, what anything was. But he knew, more than anything, he had a story to tell.

"Alright. So there was this family. Mom and Dad and two little boys. They weren't born yet. The Mom and Dad met and hit it off instantly. Dad was a wild card. It never really made much sense why he did the things he did. He just did them, and you either went along for the ride and got off the first exit. Mom wasn't normally that kind of person, but for a little while she was pretty happy about it. Going along for the ride. Two becomes three and three becomes four. The brothers, there's the older one and the younger. The older one knows what he wants. He goes for it, and normally, he gets it. But it's like when he gets it, he never wanted it. Luckily there's always something more for him to get.

"The little one doesn't quite work that way. He's quiet, mostly. Maybe not all there, maybe a little tucked back inside his head. He's not really like either of his parents, because he's really along for the ride. He doesn't need that much, want that much. He just wants to see things. To know things. To meet people. He wants to live, you know. As much and as little as that means.

"Everything's rough for a while, but there's love there. Four people, all cutting at the world in their own ways, bouncing off each other soft and violent, like atoms."

He paused for a moment, stuck inside himself. She tapped him on the head.

"Go on."

"Yeah. Okay. Anyway, it goes on like this for a while. Then four becomes three. Dad… goes. He's gone. And even though it wasn't all perfect, even though it wasn't alright, something's broken now. Some tether binding them all together. Mom goes off and looks for new love, new life. Brother goes off and looks for goals, acquisitions. And the little one, well, he just… hangs out."

"That's it?"

"Well, no. He meets some people. He sees some things. Does some stuff. But everything he does, everything he goes after, it's all temporary. It's a handful of sand."

"And then, somehow, he ends up here."

Owen sits for a minute, slightly embarrassed. "That boring, huh?"

"It was fine. Just not over yet."

The woman with green hair rose with a dancer's leap, like a deer on slanted green hills below an old trail. She began to sway and dance, looking at the water. It beckoned her.

"Do you remember the moon?" she asked.

"Yeah."

"Good." She twirled, lightly, her dress like steam clinging to her skin. Her limbs were muscular yet soft, unharmed by gravity or age, like polished marble sprung to life in a world without the cutting wind. "It would be a great sadness to forget."

They each were silent for a moment, and the far shore was silent, here at the edge of infinity.

"We're going back to the Island," he said aloud, feeling the pressure return. "All of us."

"You won't all fit on the turtle," she noted.

"We know. But will she help?"

The woman laughed. "Yes, she will be here for you."

"And you?"

She shook her head. "This is the last we will meet, I believe."

Owen wasn't sure why, but this sentiment terrified him. "Why?"

"Because this is the last." Her head tilted wryly to the side.

"Alright. But, before you go, may I ask you a question?"

She stepped closer to him, her translucent skin alight. "Can you pay?"

"I don't know."

"One question."

Owen thought to himself a moment. He had many things he wished to ask. So much of his existence, of the sea, of Gabriel and Raffaele. Of Atlantis. How did it begin? Would she know any of this at all? Would she answer with 'I don't know' no matter what he asked, and leave him alone on the beach?

He had one question.

"What is the Leviathan?"

She smiled. She stepped forward and offered her hands to him. He took them. They were cool. She led him to the water, past the crashing foam of the tide to where the water reached above the ankle. She lifted her leg and stepped up to the surface of the water and stayed there, hunched over, hands still in Owen's. He followed suit, and together they walked away from the shore until they were a good way out into the sea.

She let go. He panicked about his footing but the sturdy waves sustained him and fixed his balance from below. She laughed and began to dance, her footfall piercing the water. Where she stepped, light pooled and flowed like galaxies. In contrast to the light, the sea itself seemed to darken.

Soon, it was abyssal black.

She sang in a language Owen did not know, and as she sang the sea inverted so that the darkness was above and not below, so that the dull gray light was the water and the universe unfurled above them from the blueprints of her dance, from the harmony of her song.

It was the darkness of space, the deepest sea. The many million suns exploded to life and swirled in form and flow, ever outwards, ever rapid, too much for anyone to see.

Owen recognized the swirling detritus around it taking shape, becoming the heavenly bodies, the planets. They began to roll together, to shimmer and sing all their own.

It came from beyond. The dreaming thing. It landed first at the periphery. It was dormant, forever sleeping on its celestial journey. The dream carried it through. With bridges of light, it pierced the gap from one heavenly body to another. It brought with it an ocean, a flush of the astral sea and mundane shadow.

Owen could see it plain: The bridge. The song. The dreaming. The seeding of the earth. The continuation of the dream undying.

This was the Leviathan. He knew now what was coming. The dreamer would do what it had always done.

The woman had passed like a shadow into the sea, leaving Owen alone on the surface of the water, facing the unending shore.

XXIV. Nectar On The Vine

The spinal mount loomed large above the verdant sea-side orchards, the shadows deep and thrumming as if a storm could roll in at any moment, as if anything could mar that perfect astral sky. The homunculi still flew in concentric rings above the island of Atlantis. The Insterstice was marred by intruders for the first time in memory. The demons would not rest easy knowing this. There was a tenseness to the air, in the stillness of eternity. It was the universe, the dream, pondering the question of itself.

From an alcove high above the masses, above the winding paths that curled around the ivory tower and pierced the horizon line in solitude, the Lord Verulam stood and took in the deathless city. It had grown so very large since its humble beginnings, since the first dreaming. Since the day Verulam, in his mortal days, then living a different life with a different name, first met the King of White Flowers and his Leviathan.

He was but a boy. Precocious and fae, playing by the dark and churning sea. He darted from craggy rock to rock on the cliffside, laughing bright and free, following his new-found friend. The man before him, leading him to the sea, shined as brightly as sunfire. Verulam had known nothing and everything, then. What was death but some thin shadow on the wall in the heart of a curious, brilliant boy?

He could not remember entering the water. Only the smile and its silver light.

In the cold darkness, he had sunk like a stone, terrified and gasping, until he first heard the Voice. It sang so low, so sweet and all-consuming. It was, even now, at the height of his brilliance and his powers, beyond understanding. The memory alone caused him to shiver.

"Lord, the children are ready to begin." Herald Thomas prostrated himself as he delivered his news.

Verulam nodded. "Then let us attend to their work."

The two men walked up the grand spiral staircase of the upper central Spine. Ghostlight lanterns flickered as they passed, as if their bodies carved through wind, but this was just an illusion, or rather, human will made manifest, reflected by the flame. The light was unbidden, untethered to chemical reaction. It simply was.

"Any word?" Verulam asked.

"The Final Harvest has begun. Acolytes from the last ritual have understood and begun awakening in the garden."

"And what of the Leviathan?"

"The Heralds have entered the flesh. They will unroot the parasites in short order."

"Good, good." Verulam stroked his goatee. "All moves as it should."

Herald Thomas stopped in his tracks. "If I may…"

Verulam paused, taking in the hesitance of his elder accomplice with mild bemusement. "Speak plain, Thomas. I am always glad to partake of your counsel."

"Very well. If I must speak the truth, then I will admit I am… afraid."

Verulam laughed. "Afraid? Of the intruders? They are novel, but nothing more than a carrion fly nipping at the neck of a workhorse."

Thomas shook his head. "Not them in the slightest, Lord. No. I mean, of leaving."

Verulam laughed again, but this time hollow. "It is

what must come to pass, Thomas. You know this as well as anyone. It is the will of the King."

Thomas' thick eyebrows furrowed. "I know. And yet."

"And yet!" Verulam exclaimed, his soft voice raising in frustration. "Let no one else hear your praddling 'yets'! What has happened to the man who once spoke bravely of the need for calmer judgements, of trust in authority? Do you doubt our King?"

"Francis–"

Verulam slapped him hard across the face, sending the aged man tumbling down the steps. Were Thomas still tethered to flesh, the rough fall could have done great harm to his frame, but the soft marble of his body bounced off the ivory stone. He lifted himself up slowly, injured most deeply in his pride.

"Speak no further, Herald Thomas. Gird yourself for what is to come. I shall not speak of this with you again." Without a second word, Verulam turned and continued his ascent of the grand stairs. Herald Thomas, after a moment, followed mutely behind.

They reached the Lyceum in short order. The children were already gathered on the central stage, where class was held each day and the children performed and demonstrated their knowledge. They wore their ceremonial togas and laurels. Around the stage, Verulam saw the families of the children as well as the upper Acolytes. He had not made attendance mandatory, yet all knew this performance was to be of great importance.

No one spoke of the intruders, but all knew now. The implications were understood.

Verulam took his place at the headmaster's podium and steadied his nascent rage. He must not show his own weakness. His own small, budding fear before anyone. In this grand theater, he knew as well as anyone that every line, every movement, was worth its weight in gold.

"I thank you all for your attendance. It is a testament to our Labor that the Prodigals can, no matter what new challenges face us, rally themselves in noble form and demonstrate new brilliance, new light, to guide us through any darkness. Since the day this city was founded, we have held true to the Labor, no matter the sacrifice, as much for this opportunity as any other."

The Acolytes and Prodigals clapped in perfect unison.

"Children of the Light, you perfect cherubim, I thank you and praise you as the fruit of our empire, as the promise of our eternal majesty. I do not wish to pressure your performance, but speak for but a moment to your innate greatness. You are, all of you, preserved fire. You are the light of the world, just as you are. I trust your show today shall inspire us all to rise above our weary limitations and become something greater than before."

He sat himself down at the head of the room, as was tradition. He felt inside himself a painful wave of cold.

The Choirmaster rose and took his place before the children. They looked dashing in their clean white robes. Their bright eyes, forever young, rose to the ceiling, to the grand candelabra that gleamed like heavenly gates at the center of the hall.

Their voices rose like sweetwater and all were moved by the sound.

XXV. Cronus

Nina could not speak. Since she and Serge had left the Ledger Man's cabin behind, she felt delirious, thinly laid inside her body. *Was any of this real*? she asked herself again and again. What was real? she asked the depths of her soul, as if something would reply. She had lived inside Levi long enough to know she was alone. The hole where God should be was always fraying at the edge.

Serge was also quiet. He led the way with a small torch lit from the Ledger Man's now dormant hearth, his expression locked into a focused scowl. So much had changed since she had seen him flee from his cot, arms flayed and ribboned in some manic ritual. Since he had threatened Owen with his knife in a desperate burst of grief. He had been alone ever since. Stewing, brooding, emerging only to decapitate the Ledger Man, though in doing so had thankfully failed to kill him. And now, here he was, her rescuer, leading the way into darkness.

She felt no safety by his side, but there was nowhere in Levi safe for her. Not anymore. What little you could call life inside the beast a "world" was ending. She was returning to the gastropool, to her former oppressors turned peers turned captors. The war raging between the Pitters and the Heartlanders must end so that the true war could begin in earnest.

Nina had no will to fight. No matter the injustice, no matter the pain, it was not in her nature. She was a leaver, a survivor. She had left Europe, left home, and taken to the sea. She had left the Pit and her former lover behind. She left until there was nowhere else to go and kept on moving.

"Have you noticed?" Serge asked, his voice low and

dry.

"Noticed what?"

"The lights have all gone out."

He was right. The ropeway lanterns that guided traveling souls through the Heartland were no longer burning.

"Heartlanders? Pitters?" she wondered aloud.

"There is something else out there. I can feel it," Serge coldly observed. His body was tense, his eyes dark and wild. "Can you hear it?"

Nina tried her best to focus, to hear and identify any and every sound. She heard the normal ambient groans of bones and muscles creaking in frigid water, water dripping in cavernous pockets of flesh, the rhythmic pulsing of the Leviathan's heart emanating through every surface and the deep pressure of the sea collected in her eardrums in sharp relief. Her mind had long ago suppressed them to maintain some sense of sanity, but in her ragged fear and confusion, the psychic weight bore her down.

"Chanting," he whispered. "From every direction, chanting."

Nina gripped the ropeway railing tight as her blood froze. She tried again to listen.

There. She could hear it now. Like a man's voice. Or several, like a building whisper near and far alike, barely audible above the normal din. Despite the terror, Nina pressed herself to focus, to try and understand the chant.

Was it some language she could recognize? *No*, she realized.

Was it coming from the Heartlanders? Some echo?

No. It came from Levi. It *was* Levi itself, the yawning teetering mass of it, the structure of undying life. The walls, the flesh. It was the dark life, the devoured souls, thousands and thousands. Centuries of the dead. They were *awake*.

"We should not linger long," Serge muttered.

Nina grabbed his forearm and they ran as fast as they were able through the snaking, whispering tunnels towards the pale glow of the gastropool, not looking back or at each other for even a moment. They arrived at the upper thoroughfare, the same spot where not long before they had escaped in the cover of holy light. The luminance of the Corpse had receded since that initial supernova, but it still shone brighter than before, casting long shadows from the driftwood walls erected in a hurry to keep out the Pitters and anyone else not already inside.

Nina struggled to catch her breath. The air inside Levi had gotten hotter, drier, and all this exertion was taxing. Serge tugged at her arm, though he, too, was struggling.

"We need to get inside. Now."

Nina nodded. She walked up to the central gate, now doubly fortified, and banged on it.

"Let us in! Let us in!" she cried, hoarse and weary, but there was no sound from beyond the gate. "I have a message from the Ledger Man!"

Wooden slits slid open in the barricade. Spear tips emerged, jaunting out like falcon's claws. Serge instinctively pulled Nina backwards but one spear ripped at her shoulder as she fell backwards. She screamed. Blood flowed quickly down her arm, staining her tattered tunic. She felt lightheaded.

"You bastards!" Serge shouted, setting Nina down before drawing his knife. "I'll kill every last one of you!"

The spears recoiled slightly into the slits, their tips pivoting in waiting towards him. Serge seemed unworried, or rather, undistracted. Nina grasped at him with her bloody arm, putting pressure on her wound with the other, and pulled at his leg.

"Serge, no." She struggled to lift herself up without her arms, fighting back the overwhelming pain. "We surrender!"

"Are you a fool?"

Nina looked deep into his eyes. She could see the darkness of war swimming in their center. He was losing himself to the dark instinct. "Remember the mission."

Serge sighed. Even worked up, these words carried through. The knife in his hand dropped onto the tissue below. "Stay together," he whispered. "Stay human."

He stepped closer to the barricades where the spear tips curled in waiting and raised his arms, the torchlight illuminating his ritual scars. "You bastards happy now?"

Nina looked out at the gastropool from her vantage point on the central stage. Though her hands were bound tightly together, the Heartlanders had been kind enough to bandage her arm wound. It was quite the courteous gesture before her execution.

She glanced across the central podium to Serge, who seemed to also find humor in the rope harness coiled around his torso. He was mumbling something to himself, but amid the commotion of the Heartlanders, she couldn't make out a single word.

Everyone was watching the stage. In the perpetual gleam of the Holy Corpse, the Heartlanders seemed hollow and ragged, their eyes deep-set in their skulls. The constant pressure of the corpse light and the paranoia of the war had changed them, degraded the sense of community and conviviality they once maintained together. Nina felt a pang of guilt. Her escape had pushed these people even further into despair. She gazed painfully at them, fragile, mad things, and saw Mannfred in her heart.

"Good people of the Heartland, look upwards!" boomed the fiery voice of Hans, ascending the rickety steps onto the second stage. Behind him loomed the silent, stone form of Edmund. Both seemed as sleepless and manic as the rank and file, but where the others skittered and shook like ship mice, they had grown more pillarous and solid. Whatever doubt they once knew had vanished with the Heartland's last flickering shadow. "Today, two lost souls, traitors to our noble cause, return to us to face their final debt! Death to the enemy!"

"That's all you have to say?" Serge laughed, prompting a swift, punitive kick from Edmund that buckled his knees. The ravenous crowd cheered.

Hans climbed to the podium and waved his hands, calling all eyes again to him. "It's all gone on long enough. All this noise and nonsense. Your double-dealing ways are all played out, you hear me? You both left when the going got rough, when the dark turned against us! How are we to trust a word you'd say, any argument made in your defense? You're self-serving worms, through and through. The only use for you is feeding the beast. Edmund!"

Edmund yanked at the pulley from the back of the stage, hoisting Nina and Serge up off the ground. With forceful grunts, he spun the large wheel on, pulling them farther from the stage until they hung suspended in the air directly above the deepest point of the acid. With the force of the drop and the distance from any climbable surface, there'd be no chance of survival.

Hans continued his pontificating, but the sound of his voice melted away to the pounding of blood in Nina's ears. She had known this was a risk, coming back. She'd known what the Heartlanders were feeling, what everyone inside Levi was feeling. She knew what men did when pushed to the impossible brink, time and again. They chose to savor the taste of death. They chose to surrender to the bloody shortcut, the spectacle. And still, knowing all too well what she would encounter, she'd returned.

A distant scream pierced through the cacophony, silencing the rabble at once. It came from beyond the lower barriers, from the darkness where the corpselight did not shine.

Another scream, piercing and brief. The Heartlanders broke into a panic.

"It's the Pitters! They're coming!"

Another cry rang out: "A trap! It's a Pitter trap!" They pointed at Nina, dangling above the acid, as if she had planned this, like somehow, bound and held at razor's edge of horrible death, she held the cards for victory. Despite the terror rising in her breast, she felt a cheap sense of pride at that. Even now they feared her.

"Calm yourselves!" Hans shouted, already scaling down the steps, rushing to the barricade. Edmund watched his stalwart leader from his place at the pulley wheel, eyes darting back and forth between him and the dangling traitors, unsure of what to do.

The screams continued. Despite her own danger, Nina wondered what was prompting those hellish cries. They sounded more like blank, animal fear than any performance or war cry. It chilled her to the bone as she remembered the chanting murmurs of the Leviathan's flesh building in the tunnels. How the souls of the dead had awakened. If that was what the Pitters were facing now, some rank manifestation of the Leviathan's hatred, then those screams were likely very real.

"Battle stations! Readymen, arms! To your posts, your posts!" Hans stood on a box, hoisting his harpoon aloft into the air. "Together we weather the storm! We bleed the Pitters to their last. We alone are the chosen!"

The great bell rang through the hollow of Leviathan, and the war chants rose like storm tides crashing against the docks. The Heartlanders were feral, whipped up like galewind to rip and howl, to kill a fellow man desperate for better days ahead and call it victory.

The screams came closer. The agitated Heartlanders grew quiet. Even the most mad could tell these were not the sounds of warriors. These were death cries.

A crash of bodies suddenly pushed against the barricade, causing the guardsmen to twitch and ready their spears, but as they did the sounds of the Pitters rose:

"Let us in! Please! Oh, God! They're coming! Hurry! Please!"

The spearmen held fast to the wall. The Pitters pounded on the barricades with fists and open palms, begging and dismantling with everything they had. They were desperate to escape what lay behind them, preferring the spears that jut out towards their faces. The Heartlanders looked to Hans, who seemed to falter at this display of desperation.

The chorus of Pitter voices grew. So too, did the screaming.

"Do not lose resolve! Do not falter!" Hans cried, but it helped little.

From the darkness, a high, proud voice rang out.

"Hans! Parley!"

Nina smiled reflexively. She knew that voice well. *Carmela.*

"It's you, she-witch! You think I'd trust a parley from you anymore?"

Carmela laughed as if she had nothing to fear. "You fucking *buffoon*, wake up! The war is over!"

"Says who?" Hans called out. "Not I!"

"The flesh is killing my people, Hans! Our soldiers are all but finished saving the weak! The dead have risen, you fool! The end has come for us all! Let us in! Our people do not deserve to die like this!"

"Oh, the dead have risen, have they?" Hans laughed dismissively. The panicked Heartlanders around him chuckled in halting mimicry. It made the thought more bearable.

"It's true, Hans!" Nina called out from high above the acidpool. "The flesh is speaking! We heard it on our way back, and we came to warn you. Please, let the survivors inside!"

"She's right!" Serge added. "The Ledger Man sent us. The Leviathan is purging itself. You're all next unless we join together!"

"Join together? With the enemy?" a Heartlander cried out. "Against what, Levi itself?"

"If it wants to kill us, we've done something wrong!"

"There's no point in fighting! If Levi dies, we die anyway! There's no hope! No tomorrow!"

The crowds began to panic. The outer guard, their resolve shattered, fluctuated between breaking rank and doubling down, thrusting their spears through the slit of the guard walls at the terrified Pitters, killing some. This did nothing to quell the pressure on the walls.

Hans tried to rally the crowd but his voice was drowned in the chaos. Carmela, from the other side of the wall, also tried to direct momentum, but from Nina's spot above the gastropool she could not make out a word. It was pandemonium on every level, madness and fear like never before. The Heartlanders' sense or rather illusion of safety was gone in its entirety and all at once they remembered they were living on driftwood in the stomach of hell's great sunken king. They had always been nothing but fodder. Worms for the fish. Bonemeal.

Nina looked at Serge, desperate for some clue in his eyes, some way forward to make a difference. The others had counted on them to do this. They were preparing to siege Atlantis, to break the shackles once and for all.

Serge's face was furious but resolved. He was facing the acid, wriggling beneath the coarse ropework that held him suspended above.

Nina could see it clear. He was planning how to swim.

Nina looked up at the Holy Corpse and thought of Owen, somewhere in the Astral Sea. She wanted to join him there outside this perpetual darkness. She wanted to see what lie beneath the water.

Owen, can you hear me? She called out from within, sending her heart to the world. Could she connect to the infinite, to the liminal world? *Owen, let's escape this hell together. Let's see the wide world. I want to survive, somehow. I want to live!*

The holy corpse began to glow. Tendrils of light like the arms of a giant squid poured forth, coiling outwards into the acid. This was a far different light than before, more tangible and organic than the pulse of brilliance the others had pushed through the body before.

The light emanated a sound, high and clear yet thin as a whisper, like the memory of horns removed entirely from physical instruments. It was the sound of life, accelerated far beyond the scope a human mind is capable of understanding.

From the acid, the tendrils of light pulled forth a skeleton, decayed and frail, stripped of all remnants of flesh. The tendrils coiled round the bones, filling in their form, branching out like roots of a tree or nerve endings. The skeleton, suspended like Nina and Serge, began to convulse as it was threaded by the strands of sentient light.

The onlooking Heartlanders were transfixed, barely noticing the Pitters continuing to press hard against the battlements, still avoiding attacking at all. They were merely attempting to break through. To risk everything for some small chance at safety. Hans, lost in the valleys of his furrowed brows tilted up at the puppeteer corpse, was speechless.

LET THEM IN, came a booming voice, traveling through the light.

Nina recognized that voice, distorted and inhuman as it was. She looked over at Serge, whose eyes were wet and glimmering with tears.

IT IS I, GABRIEL, COME TO YOU AGAIN AT THIS LATE HOUR. YOUR WAR HAS ENDED. THE TRUE WAR HAS BEGUN.

The Heartlanders fell down upon their knees in bewildered awe. Hans wheeled back to the battlement guards.

"O-open the gates! Open them! Let them through!" Silhouetted by holy light, he had become a shadow with stars for eyes.

As the barricades opened and the Pitters poured

through, one by one, they looked to the source of the light and shielded their eyes. In the darkness of the Pit, there was no light that pierced the senses quite like this. They fell to the ground, one after the other, grateful to bathe in the light.

But only so many came through. Nina, from her place closest to the holy corpse (averting her eyes so as to not be blinded entirely) felt disturbed by the numbers of Pitters passing. This was a fraction, a third maybe, of the original population.

Carmela entered, helping a crippled Pitter cross beyond the battlement. Her eyes turned to the light for just a moment, but she did not blink. Instead, she smiled. Though she knew it was impossible to see her, Nina smiled back.

The moment of greatest brilliance passed. The skeleton of Gabriel was now ensconced in tendrils, dangling from the corpse like a shimmering cocoon. Each tendril dulled as it drew closer to the coil's center and the body within, becoming something more than light. Becoming flesh. Life.

Hans, in the chaos , had ascended back up to the center stage where Edmund stood clutching the rope lever that kept Nina and Serge suspended above the acid. He pushed the silent Edmund aside and took over, grinding the old wheel back and reeling them slowly towards safety.

Nina felt a shudder ripple through her as she realized that Gabriel had saved their lives. But, she could not help but wonder, *what had happened to change the plan? Was the Ledger Man with Owen? Would they be alright in Atlantis alone?*

Nina's feet touched the wooden stage. Hans walked over and drew a knife from his waist and began to cut at her bindings. His hands were shaking. He could not look her in the eye.

"It's him," Serge was saying, again and again, barely audible to anyone but Edmund, also indignantly cutting him loose. "It's him."

"Yes," Edmund agreed. "It is."

The cocoon of light unfurled into particles of dust. At its center, the reconstituted body of Gabriel floated, slowly lowering to the level of the battlements, towards the Pitters. Naked, the bizarre newfound youth of his frame was clear to see.

The Pitters studied him with disgust and terror in their eyes, save Carmela, who stood strong and equal against his gaze. This was the man who had populated the Pits, had instituted an "order" of above and below. She would not easily forget his sins.

Gabriel met their gaze head on, saying nothing. He made his way like this through the teeming crowd of Pitters and Heartlanders alike. Some Heartlanders reached out to him, to see if he was flesh and blood again like their eyes suggested. Their hands grazed him, skin meeting skin, but he did not linger there. He passed among the throngs of the devoured, coiling around the perimeter of the gut until at last he had reached the center stage.

He climbed up and came face to face with the judges and convicts alike. Edmund was resolute, stone. Hans, once a ball of fire made manifest, was nothing now but ashes. His rough outer shell, his inner darkness, had been stripped from him. He was a child again, lost at sea before the man he saw as father and god.

Serge patted Gabriel on the shoulder. "Good to see you."

Gabriel nodded, his eyes weary with the knowledge of collapse. "I am glad none of you were fully lost."

Nina did not wait to see if he would look at her. For some reason, his resurrection enraged her. It had saved her life, it had stopped the madness all at once, but to see him reconstituted in the beast, as if death and suffering had done nothing to him but give him a vacation, struck her as a horrible crime.

But now was not the time for that. "Speak to them, Gabriel." It was all she could say.

Gabriel understood.

He stepped up the podium and the din of the gastropool fell to a murmur.

"It is good to see you all again, Heartlanders and Pitters alike. It has been some time since I last walked among you. It pains my heart to recognize that many others have perished since my own death some time ago. Our ranks have fallen thin, and there is no one to blame for this great loss more than myself."

"Bullshit!" cried a Pitter.

"You be quiet!" cried out a Heartlander. The two sides, agitated, seemed to bristle against each other.

"Enough! There is no time for petty squabbles. Heartlanders, the Pitters have undergone a hell you cannot currently imagine. Ask them what awaits us in the darkness. The lights have all gone out. The beast has awoken."

To Nina's right, Serge's guard went up. His eyes began to scan the crowds frantically, slinking slightly back towards the duller corners of the gastropool so he might move with less attention.

"What is it?" she whispered.

"Something's not right," he mumbled.

"Do you see something?"

He held a finger to his lips. "Watch Gabriel. Don't follow me." And with that he disengaged entirely.

Gabriel continued. "The time has come for the truth to be revealed to you all. None of this will be easy to hear, but I must ask that you listen. It was a difficult thing, returning. But it will have been worth it and more if we can come together now. It is the great task of our age. It is why we have fought so hard to survive, day in and day out. Everything you have done to save yourselves, to save each other, have led us to this day."

Gabriel paused.

"It is easy to forget, living day to day inside the Leviathan, that none of this is natural. That all of us struggle to understand just what this beast is, where it comes from, what it means that we have been able to survive in this… unnatural mode. It is easy to forget, to look away from that core question. Granted, there is so much we will never understand about its origins and how it came to share the seas with us. But the true question, the question of 'Why does it exist?' is answerable. What we call Levi is the product of man. Our fates, the ends of our first lives and our awakenings in the dark, all of them have been the design of other men. Our hell is a living engine, a dream created by a man once swallowed, the same as us, hundreds of years ago."

The crowd broke into an uproar, but Gabriel continued, his voice booming through the gastropool propelled by newborn lungs.

"Each of us eaten, each of us digested, consumed, feeds the Leviathan. In doing so, we fuel the *other* dream, we give it power and life. That dream is not the sunken entrails of a god, but a land of plenty and peace. It is a city like no other, a heaven of the mind. They call it New Atlantis. The ones who live there come when they are ready, when they have enjoyed all they wish for in life. When they have paid their dues and fed the Beast with the souls of the innocent."

Nina tried not to watch Serge, or at least, to not be obvious about it. He crawled slowly along the periphery flesh, blending in well to the crowd, his eyes slowly scanning the crowd. Nina wondered if he had actually seen something dangerous, or if he just felt as though something bad would happen. He had become quite paranoid since Gabriel died. Could he not accept that things might just yet improve?

Did it all sit too heavy on his heart?

"We are the sacrificed!" Gabriel cried out. "We are the lambs upon the altar! And yet, despite our deaths, we live on. The Atlantaens and their Order did not know of our existence, our parasitic liferaft of a home, until just *days* ago. They assumed us all to be digested whole, forgotten, abandoned by time. Now they know that we have not yet surrendered to their will! They now know that we hang on by the blessing of the Leviathan, by its power! We are, in our suffering, as much the chosen children of this great creation as they are! And they are *terrified*!"

Cheers rang out from both camps. Heavy, painful, furious cheers.

"The Pitters were the first to be struck. The creatures in the darkness move at the bidding of the Order. They seek to cleanse the body before their 'Harvest' has ended! To be rid of the danger, the sin we represent once and for all! But the great fools and devils have given us, in their final hours, the tool we need to strike back."

Gabriel extended his hands towards the lighthouse glow of the Holy Corpse.

"Through the Corpse, we can bridge the dreams of heaven and hell! We can leave this body behind and descend, together, upon the shores of Atlantis! We can seize the lands of Providence from those too corrupt to earn its fruits and usher in a golden age of mankind! Together, we can reshape this fallen world into a place of true harmony! Will you stand with me? Will you fight with me?!"

The crowd became one. The ones most aggrieved had been given an outlet. A revenge. The most fearful, dreadful confirmation: they *were* already dead. There was no life to keep here. Only the hunger awaiting to clean its plate.

This was their only chance at life, or something like it.

"*NO*!" cried a voice from the crowd.

It was Ivan, the Russian. In the confusion, he had slipped in with the refugees, obscured his features, but his pale blond hair stood out against the crowd, and the cool steel in his hands glimmered like a prized jewel.

He held his pistol up, pointing at the Holy Corpse, the liminal shell of his own deceased brother. Ivan's eyes were bloody red, his veins varicose and dark against pale skin.

Nina saw Serge spring to life. He was still some distance away, ripping his way ferociously through the crowd. Those closest to Ivan screamed in fear. Others were still cheering, oblivious to the threat of all hope spilling away at the very precipice of its renewal.

Nina ran to the podium and cried out "Stop him!"

She pointed at Ivan.

The world seemed to stop on its axis. Ivan turned and pointed the gun at her. Even at this distance, it felt like how it had before, when Owen died. When Ivan watched her go with an abyssal stare. When it came time to kill, the void of his heart could step right into control and see him through the storm.

Nina felt her body recoil. She fell back and hit the stage floor, numb to the weight of her own body. She could see the corpselight above her, glimmering bright and unbroken.

Blood splattered across her face. She lifted herself slightly to see Hans standing where she had been seconds before. He turned back to check on her as he fell to the ground beside her, his face mangled fiercely, his one remaining eye wet with tears, locked onto her face.

Shock compelled her to stand and look away.

In the crowd, more shots rang out. The bravest of the crowd rushed Ivan. There were too many for him to ignore, to focus on the Corpse. One fell, and another. Someone grabbed him from behind with a chokehold.

Ivan, resisting the pressure, shot the man slack, clutching his ears from the pain of the visceral ring.

Nina watched Carmela leap from the crowd and stab a spear into his gun arm. Ivan called out, toward the shell of his brother as one spear after another pierced his frame and pinned him to the floor of the gastropool. He writhed about in anguish, musculature twitching and reaching for his gun, but it was over. Life had been drained from him. He fell silent, his broken body suspended on broken shafts of driftwood.

Gabriel cried out from the podium. "There will be others! The time for hesitation has ended! Look to the Corpse! Ready your souls for war!"

With that, he raised his arms towards the Corpse and began chanting in some distant tongue. The body, for so long stiff and Vetruvian, coiled into a fetal position. Around them all, ensconcing the gastropool, a great barrier of porous light, like the surface of water under a brilliant sun, grew thicker and more brilliant.

It enveloped everything.

Nina, knowing what was to come, began to cry.

XXVI. New Jersey

Alan was driving west on the Atlantic City Expressway towards Philadelphia but the traffic was unreal. At this point, most of the population of the city had made it to their cars with one goal and destination in mind: Get the fuck away from the shore and the marching Leviathan.

Alan's hand throbbed as he gripped the steering wheel until his knuckles went white. Cars were passing by on the left and right shoulders of the highway, peeling out rather than risk waiting for the traffic to disperse. The sounds of collisions and car horns rang out for miles, but there was no normal flow around them. Just deadlock, panic, and fear, covering the sound of the radio.

News reports indicate that Atlantic City is quickly becoming submerged. Authorities assure all those in the area to evacuate in a calm and orderly fashion. We repeat, the Southern coast of New Jersey is in a mandatory state of evacuation-

Alan looked back through the rearview mirror at the image of the lumbering Leviathan, its pale, damp flesh swarming with eel-like wraiths that flowed like great winds around the eye of the storm. The spirits broke off asynchronously, swimming through the cold, foggy air. A few miles back, Alan had seen one swoop low into someone running down the street.

It seemed to pass right through the man, causing him to lose his panicked momentum. He stopped, shook like a popcorn kernel and burst with a sickening *pop*. Bits of him splashed against the rear window, obscuring Alan's view.

They seemed to be flowing now in greater numbers. Harvesting. Flowing and feasting over the wide flat land.

"Was it always going to end like this?" He whispered to himself, looking back at the unconscious form of his mother, resting like a shattered statue in the backseat.

He switched stations, trying to find something to calm him, distract him from the unfolding nightmare. Screams rose and fell in the distance.

The end has come! God has sent his divine angels to the earth to purge all sinners from the earth! Get on your knees NOW and pray with all your heart that God understands and forgives you for your sin!

Switch. *For a limited time, get a footlong sub for $7.99-*

Switch. *Has you or someone in your family been exposed to dangerous levels of asbestos in your home? If so, you may be entitled to-*

Alan slammed his fist into the radio, accidentally switching the player to CD. Franz Liszt began to play. All at once, memories of the past flowed through him. He had taken this woman on a date not long ago to see a philharmonic orchestra perform renditions of Franz Liszt. He had purchased this CD sometime before, to get a sense of the composer, only to find he hated his music. Dull. Dark. Mild.

The date had gone by without incident. What was her name?

Oh god, he thought. He'd forgotten her name completely. They'd had dinner and a show. Sex had almost come to pass if the signs were to be believed. But now, listening to the music, transported back to that moment in his life just weeks before, it felt impossible to remember.

There had been nothing wrong with this woman. She was sweet, if quiet, with bright eyes. She said she worked at some medical software agency somewhere, something administrative. She had been a calming date, pressed him on nothing he said all evening, even entertained his poor excuse for small talk like it was real entertainment.

Maybe something could have happened there. Maybe he could have found something with this woman, some other kind of life, even for just a few weeks. Would the Leviathan have woken now, if not for him? Did the end begin when he saw his dead brother looking down at him from inside New Atlantis?

Could he ever have lived a regular human life?

The sky roared, split open. Fighter jets flew over the expressway, clouds of jetsmoke splitting into smaller trails as missiles volleyed forth, passing overhead. Alan turned back to watch them fly towards the lumbering titan, well inland now and swarming with the dead.

The missiles barreled closer until they suddenly exploded in the sky. The spots of air they struck rippled outwards, revealing some shimmering sphere of translucent energy swirling impenetrably around the beast. No hole was torn or pierced within the barrier and yet the Leviathan screamed, lumbering jaw distending with a shake. The visceral wail shook the metal frame of Alan's car and filled his eardrums like a tidal pressure.

As the mutilating howl rang out, drivers on the expressway peeled out of any orderly flow with hysterical momentum. Alan's car was struck, sideswiped by a minivan. Emily ricocheted against the side door legs first, waking up in anguish.

Alan came to face first against the dashboard, head swimming with pain and shock. He stepped out of the car on lame legs to check on both cars and the other driver. Around him, people were abandoning their vehicles en masse and running for the woods further down the highway. A sprinting woman slammed into him and kept running, climbing over the cars ahead of them.

Alan saw the other driver in the wreck, or what was left of them, coating the interior of their car, the voracious hellfish wraith curling in the open air overhead. His head was pounding, the peripherals of his vision faded and graying. He could barely muster the instinct of fear at this unearthly threat. He began to wonder if he had a concussion.

"Alan!" It was Emily, from the back seat.

Alan opened her passenger door to find her left calf deeply bruised and distended, seemingly broken. Adrenaline and terror gave her tremors he felt when she gripped his arm and pulled him close to her.

"What the hell is happening, Alan?"

He looked back at the Leviathan, unsure of what to say. It was so colossal now the visible details of its face were faded from the atmospheric distance.

"It's all over, Mom."

Emily tried her best to sit up, wincing and cursing under her breath. Once she had risen fully, she was able to see it, and understood what he meant. The crowds around them passed like blurs of flesh, crying, bleeding, screaming, reduced to animal fear in sight of this colossus.

One of the cars behind Alan's rental was a police car. Alan could see someone in the front seat slumped over. He broke free of his mother's grip and stumbled over to it in a lull. The officer in the car was still, laid silently against the wheel.

Alan understood what he was seeing. He checked the door. It was unlocked. He reached inside and confirmed his theory of what had happened.

The officer had checked out.

It made sense, Alan thought. It wouldn't be long now until the Leviathan reached them, even if it kept ambling slowly, gorging on Jersey like an apocalypse buffet. It was heading this way, and for anyone hoping to escape, forward was no longer an option. The expressway was packed with abandoned cars, littered with the corpses of the dead.

Alan remembered that statistic about gun ownership and suicide as he reached over the officer's waist and grabbed her handgun.

He shut the door and walked back to his mother. He got back into their car and sat down in the driver's seat, turning so he could face her in the crumpled backseat.

"I've been thinking, Mom. About everything. I don't want to look at everything around us and think it's all our fault, because it isn't, not really. But we're not guiltless in this."

"Now is not the time, Alan. We need to get out of here!"

"I need you to listen, Mom!" Alan screamed, surprising even himself. The throbbing in his head was making him sick. "The other Acolytes seem to think, if they die now after the ritual, that's where they'll go. Atlantis. I don't really think Atlantis is the paradise we were promised, especially for you or I. But I don't think there's paradise for us anywhere anymore. And maybe we don't deserve it, for the part we played in everything."

Emily watched him speak with furious, static eyes, the way she used to look when Alan's father was alive. He recognized that painful glare. How everything you threw at it slid off its bright stillness.

"My brother is still… alive, or conscious, where we were meant to go. I don't know if he needs help. If he'd even want it from me. But I've been trying to think of something to do with myself for hours since that fucking *thing* stepped out of the sea, and this," he emphasized, lifting up the handgun, "is all I've come up with."

Emily, silent, shook her head, tears forming in her eye ducts. "Don't you dare abandon me, Alan. Not now. How *dare* you."

Alan sighed. "I'm sorry, Ma. I love you. I wish… I wish it could've all gone differently for us. For Owen. For Dad, too. From the beginning. I wish we could have been a normal family. I wish you could've been a happy grandmother, watching our kids learn how to go swimming in a pool. Maybe teach them how to ride a bike or something. I don't know, I don't really get kids." Alan laughed. "I didn't get how to be a kid even as a kid. Maybe the problem was always me."

Emily reached out and grabbed his arm. "Alan-"

Alan shook her hand off. "Do what you need to do, when I'm gone. Follow me or keep yourself safe. If you stay behind, stay safe. I don't know how those fish things are picking targets, but as long as they miss you, it'll be okay."

"Alan!"

He rose and shut the door. The jets came round again just like before, peeling off missile after missile, striking the invisible barrier. Conventional weaponry seemed pointless against the Leviathan. Alan wondered if nukes were being considered. Would the government hit Jersey to save Philadelphia?

He realized half the government was probably gone now. Gone to Atlantis, same as him.

Invite only.

He cocked the handgun, his left palm throbbing badly. He never would have been able to do surgery again.

He'd cut too deep. If he really cared about saving lives (he knew he didn't, not as much as he should,) it was all down to this one last stupid gambit.

Would they know to keep him out of Atlantis? Would it matter? Would *he* matter?

He laughed. It didn't really matter if it mattered.

He was excited to try.

XXVII. The Light on the Shore

On the forested shores of New Atlantis, not far from the Well of Souls, a great light erupted from a centerpoint high above the shoreline. The light rose up into the sky and came down in a central column. Around it, seeds of light came open, growing and unraveling into human forms, extending in either direction like the extended wings of an albatross, blossoming into sunflowers.

ȯ

From a hill nestled into the Lower Woodlands, Hermit Kelpius of the Order of White Flowers sat on the periphery of his solitary cave. This cave had been here for centuries now, and few on the Island knew of its existence. Even fewer knew it was where Kelpius, once a shining star of the Order's highest caste, lived in a state of exile.

He spent his time here, day in and day out (as though there were days and nights in Atlantis and not periods of waxing and waning dull light, never fully extinguished or set aflame) in silent meditation, away from the bustle of the Order and the utopian society of his former fellows.

Herald Kelpius had done as was instructed in his mortal life and grew the ranks of the Order in the developing colonies. In secret, he found luminaries and influential persons in search of higher purpose and introduced them to the Great Labor. In doing so, he had guaranteed himself a place in the White City as an honored emissary. Though, when he had shed his mortal flesh and ascended to the island in the astral sea, he swiftly discovered it was not the place his heart had dreamed of, his faith believed in. It was a pale and hollow light upon the hill. A lie.

By asking nothing in return but isolation, he was granted it. This freedom had given him much. Time to travel outside the boundaries of flesh, to understand a thousand sacred truths that had no name. As a sparrow, his soul flew above the wide reaches of the astral sea. In time, he mastered the art of parting the veil and trafficked his awareness high and low, ever in search of possibilities and legends come to life, and then, at the end of it all, he had come back to his dark cave, to his place of silence in the shadow of the dreamer's spine. No matter how far he flew, he must always return to roost in New Atlantis.

It was this bitter regret that led him to the interior of Leviathan and the people clinging to life, to their nascent efforts at survival. There he found his people. The very people sprouting now in the sky, seeded on the divine wind of the Holy Corpse brought to port.

It was the revolution he had borne witness to and helped to kindle in the darkness.

Kelpius rose from the cold stone floor of the cave. Though the cave went deep into the soil, he knew better than to venture further than he had. This was no cave of Earth. This deepness was the fathoms of infinity. What darkness became, unbounded by all rules, no longer interested him as it first had so long ago.

He stepped slowly into the light. Though he had spent years dreaming up a life inside Leviathan, sparing only moments to check in on his 'true' body & the comings and goings of the Order, his eyes did not need to adjust. They were, like all flesh in Atlantis, animate stone. A gift of the Dream Fish. Bone and soil in equal measure. Soft yet firm, pliable yet study. The body as a tool, stripped of its own will and powers to forever serve the pilot light of the tainted soul bound to it by blood and magic.

It was time for him to head south, away from the pillar of light and its tragic, desperate army. He was needed on the opposite shore, where the ambrosia fruit grew in tender groves. Where the eyes of the Upper Spine would not be looking.

Kelpius laughed at himself as he tried to remember how to walk like a regular man. He had been Raffaele, wretched corpse, severed head, for far too long. It would be slow going, but the turtle was ferrying Owen and Janice to shore and he must be there to guide them. They would have the baby in tow, the liminal child. The key to new life.

It was imperative they made it to the throne.

Dong, dong. Kelpius stopped in his tracks at the sound. It was the tenor of the Great Bell, housed in the center of the Tower, ringing out. Once, twice. *Dong, dong. Dong, dong*. Three patterns of two.

He understood at once. They were sounding the keening bells.

Atlanteans all knew the harmony well. It was imprinted on their spirit, waiting in the depths of the heart for confirmation. It meant to signify the world of the Island as it was once written was over. *O, Mourn the Labor of Atlantis, dear subjects. It is dead, drowned in the coming blood of war. Our noble project is besieged by Death and all her mortal contracts. Heaven is forbidden. Hell is rising.*

Lower bells, stationed across the width of the woodlands, rang out in response, resonating through the dense treelines, imitating wind. Patches of soil began to quake and splinter open as if something were unhatching at the beckoning of the bellsong.

Kelpius knew time was of the essence now. The Order were waking the Delights.

XXVIII. The Delights

On the shore of Atlantis, below the light of the Holy Corpse, the devoured citizens of Levi were summoned down, each a thread through the eye of the needle unspooling from a central source and tying up in knots until light became flesh and flesh again began to breathe. They fell like pollen onto the chalky sand, drifting into being.

Nina felt sand between her fingers. She was on her hands and knees, naked as everyone around her, on a long strip of sand overlooking the treeline and the sea. Through all her senses she felt numb and gasping, but the air was thin and still. But there, behind her, was a horizon. A vast ocean, churning slowly, a universe of motion.

It was the first sky she had seen in decades. She had craved this moment for so long. The unburdened soul can never understand how painful it is to lack the horizon. To those deprived of it for long, it carries the weight of a miracle.

Pitters and Heartlanders alike began to cheer around her as they found their voices in their reconstituted flesh. The light of the astral realm was dim yet full in a way the corpse-light and acid glow had never been. There were colors all around them, warm and cool hues of refracted light. The trees swayed slowly, thick leaves rippling and sliding like fabric against each other's limbs.

The remade souls, freed of the abyss, forgot their purpose here. All they could focus on were the signs of the earth before them. It ached beyond measure as it healed with every breath.

In the distance, the sound of bells tolled low and mirrored, emanating from several points further ashore. Though they could not understand their meaning, the melodies of bells upon the open air were more like music than danger.

A gleaming rose of light descended from the Holy Corpse, forming Gabriel anew. He reconstituted on both feet, unphased by the transubstantiation. He did not look at the squirming horde, the reveling exiles around him. His eyes were to the woods, to the treeline. Towards the keening bells.

"Stand!" he shouted. "Stand now!"

They did as he commanded, their joy cut brief. Nina scanned the crowd quickly, spotting Edmund and Serge. Carmen was already patrolling along the forest's edge for movement. Like a cat, she seemed to never be caught off-footed no matter the balancing act.

Hans had not crossed over. She remembered him then, trapped forever in the dim gastropool. All his efforts and his folly, only to have his killer alone to keep him company in an abandoned hell. Despite everything that he had put her through, had put them all through to claim control of their fates and assert the strict boundaries of loyalty, she felt pity for him. A man made small by the weight of the dark, left behind to rot.

The bells rang out again. Strange noises, like the roaring clatter of exotic animals, rose up from the forest primeval.

Gabriel wheeled about to address the former citizens of Levi.

"There is no time for me to prepare you for what is coming. You must steel your screaming hearts! We have but one chance at this. Our objective is clear: Cut through the forest, past the Well of Souls to the lower rings of the city. As you go, start fires, make noise! Become the hell that was done to you! Do not hesitate but for a single moment. Remember:

we are already dead! We are the ghosts of the living! This dream is *our* dream to rule!"

A frantic cheer went out before the ground began to tremor. A throaty yawp, shrill as a bird call, broke close enough to feel on the back of the neck. In the distance, from the direction of the looming spinal mountain broken at its vertex by a solitary tower of cartilage and bone, the sight of heavy wings and bodies loomed into view.

The forest trees began to groan and crack as the figure of a man's face, pale and placid, loomed above them, grafted to the body of an elephant's, seemingly constructed of eggshell and cartilage. On its head a bulbous flower of green and purple foliage grew, resting on a silver platter populated with chattering death birds, bare-skulled, pinioned and starving.

Gabriel raised his hands toward the Holy Corpse and spoke in a whisper. From the corpse-pillar sprang forth a hundred bolts of light that rained down on the beach, kicking up sand as they pierced the soil. Each bolt bloomed and faded, leaving firm spears of wood and bone. Pieces of Leviathan. Their prison.

Gabriel lifted one aloft and let out a warrior's cry. In his spare hand, a horn of light sprang forth and from it he blew a terrible cry that shook all the roots of the island.

"Fast, move the sons and daughters of men! Let fate's call spill out in the horn of your vengeance! To war!"

The sound of a host grew nearer. Nina, unsure of herself, drew up a spear. She had escaped the Leviathan. She had *survived.*

Nothing would change that now. The sea was at her back.

Figures like men and birds, living gargoyles with

great claws like femur bones, grotesque shapes in ill-fitting armor were met on the forest's edge with screams of fear and fury, spears held high and all else lost to abandon.

XXIX. Reunion

The great pillar of light on the northern shore was all but obscured by plumes of smoke from the island woodlands. The people of Atlantis were fleeing upwards, where the great concentric gates permitted, or else outwards, away from the city, to hide from the coming carnage rolling through like a tsunami of blood.

No Atlantean, no member of the Order, was eagle-eyed or stable-hearted enough to notice three strange figures passing between the city's buildings. Not one observed that, besides the elderly man leading them between shadowed alleys and gleaming streets, that these people were not made of stone as they were, but rather constituted flesh, as if alive in the original sense, their chests heaving with labored breath, their skin soft and sun-starved. They even seemed to miss that one carried in her arms an infant boy, the sprouting seed of life frozen in the amber of the Dreaming.

"Quickly now!" Raffaele whispered harshly as homunculi shuffled down the window cobblestone, gaining force and momentum enough to leap like gorillas, until their heavy wings could unfurl and slam themselves against the wind, propelling them in uneven bursts and glides through the air. "Into this residence!"

Raffaele shut the door behind them. In silence, they surveyed the residence, passing into each room and scanning for signs of activity. The house was a mess, quickly evacuated in the chaos, papers and fabrics strewn about across every surface and floor.

Whoever lived here was gone.

"Good," Raffaele mumbled to himself, peeping through the curtains out towards the rising smoke. "This will make a fine staging ground. Our goal is the House of the Eldest and the Thorn Doors. Making it there under a siege will be challenging. Our movement must be steady and precise."

Janice nodded, stroking Baby Sean's smooth scalp to comfort him. She had noticed, since their arrival on this astral plane together, that he had fallen into some tremendous sleep and no amount of chaos and sound had disturbed him. She was worried, somewhat, but carried the faith that she would recognize if he was in some true, internal danger. She was a mother armed with a mother's intuition, after all. Not willingly or very well, but the role had bestowed some gifts upon her all the same.

"You'll be leaving then?" she asked.

Raffaele nodded. "Stay in this residence for now. Avoid the windows, as much as you can. Should a homunculi notice you are a foreign body and attempt entry, there will be nothing I can do for you. Though here in the astral realm, you two may yet hold power you would have never imagined before."

Janice looked at Owen, who nodded wearily at this strange turn of phrase. "You mean, we have some kind of power here?" she asked. "Like in the marrow dreams?"

"This is a marrow dream," Owen replied. "All of it."

"The deepest of the dreams," Raffaele concurred. "The Dream of the King and the Whale, bound for centuries to the fate of the God Flesh."

Outside, the screams of their compatriots from Levi rose up the urbanized hillside. Some number had made it through the woods.

Raffaele stood close to the door, feeling the sounds and footsteps rattle the ivory door on its hinges. His eyes were alight, as if terrified and yet deeply entertained.

"There is little time remaining, but now that we are shed of the others it is time I tell you the true aim of our desperate mission. Listen closely!"

Owen and Janice both sat down at a table in the center of the dining room. Raffaele came and stood at its edge, his eyes darting between them and the pointed arch of the window frame, scanning for movements and shadows.

"The Heralds, under the auspicious power of the King of White Flowers, have spent years cultivating this city. Their goal was originally noble: Create a sanctum for civilization. Separate from the world of men, from the horrors of war and the tyranny of foolish, selfish kings. Inside this waking dream, the aim was to construct a storehouse of all great human thought, a catalog of history and science, reason and art. In this way, we could outlive our empires, outlast the earthly erosion of our artifacts and fragile bodies. But the plan was led astray as the years went on. The hunger for growth grew stronger than the love of fellowmen. After so many years of isolation, of deathless death severed wholly from the common bonds of life's hardships, what could mortal men become in our eyes but another crop, another beast to raise and lead to slaughter?"

Raffaele sighed bitterly, the weight of it heavy on him, before continuing. "The blood of many thousands are on my hands. All my life, I sought the way of peace and harmony. I was delighted at the chance, the offer made to me to stand beside the greatest minds, to find new horizons and to commune with the spirits of the deep. What curious mind could turn away such a promise as eternal light, a translation of the self into a new existence at the time of my mortal undoing? I took that price and spread the word to the New World, awaiting my reward. And here it is. Here it all is."

Janice and Owen exchanged a glance. *Raffaele is one of the Order.*

"So you live here?" Janice asked. "You… sacrificed someone, too?"

Raffaele nodded. "When I sailed upon the Sarah Maria Hopewell. I… kept no record. I could not face it in ink."

"Like my father," Janice noted, acid on her tongue.

"Or… My family, I guess," Owen whispered, mostly to himself.

"Yes," he confessed, rubbing his scalp with his palms. "Like them both."

Owen covered his eyes from the light, struggling to speak for some time. When he finally could, his voice was weak, dry. "But you chose to live with us, inside Leviathan."

"It was a penance, of sorts. I took to projecting my soul away from this realm. I could not bare it, this white city, gleaming forever as if unstained by sin. In my wanderings, I found my way to the Leviathan in the depths of the Earth's oceans. I found the Inner Dream, the hell that pays for this heaven. That was the true beginning."

Raffaele laid his shaking hands down upon the table. "We have precious time. I must press on. As I said, the goal was noble but the fruit was bitter. It has fallen so far now that the Heralds, in their hubris, believe the Earth to be beyond saving. They are gorging the Leviathan. Preparing it to leave."

"Leave… Earth?" Janice asked, incredulous. "Towards the stars, you mean?"

"Where it came from," Owen offered, surprising both of them. "Where it was always going to return."

"How did you know this?" Raffaele asked, brows furrowing. "This is…"

Owen laughed awkwardly. "Good guess? I don't

know. Continue, Raffaele."

Raffaele also laughed, that fear and entertainment dancing in his eyes meshing like stormfronts with the frustration of intellectual surprise. "You two may just yet be who we need. Good, good!" He clapped his hands together. "It is time, long very past, for a new King and Queen. For a rebirth."

"Excuse me?" Janice asked.

"We cannot abandon all these works of human genius, all this *potential* to be more than simple apes bound to the soil, but the King of White Flowers and his Lord Verulam must be overthrown. Someone must take the throne, someone still human who yet can truly dream! Both of you, through fate's design, have developed the Gift and are suitable to do so. And best of all, young Sean, in his strange liminality, holds the greatest promise of all. He is a weapon and a seed, all at once."

A loud scream piercing from above, falling close and coming to a brutal stop. A homunculi had lifted someone, a fellow of theirs from Levi, up from the cobbled city streets, only to let them fall screaming from that terrible height.

"They are growing close, too close," Raffaele mumbled. "I must go. Stay safe and wait for my return!"

"Raffaele–" Janice began, grabbing his cool marble arm, only to be haunted and silenced by its touch. Though he was more vital and animated here, he was less human than he had been inside Leviathan.

He laughed, his stone eyes gleaming with light like a torchlit river bore in white stone. "Call me Kelpius. That was my name."

And with that, he was gone. Janice quickly shut the door, holding gingerly to the handle, her mind racing with questions. Across the room, Owen rose, walking over to a table. He lifted up a pitcher, smelling its contents and chuckling to himself. "Hey Janice, come here."

"What is it?"

As she approached, Owen turned and handed her a goblet. "Ambrosia. You'll love it, trust me."

Janice looked down at her cup and the strange concoction inside. Her eyes returned to Owen's, desperate for some sign of crisis inside him, but all she saw was the same defeatist smile he had worn the entire conversation. She took a sip of the ambrosia and found herself in love with the taste until the silver shimmering feeling overflowed within.

She sat down and swirled the mixture. "This is *astounding*."

"Isn't it? Just insane."

The two laughed quietly and drank with distracted joy.

"You know, you've changed," Janice noted, that spry tone in her voice again.

"Have I?" Owen asked. "I don't really feel that different."

"Right, of course. You feel exactly the same. Nothing's any different. How could it be?"

Owen rubbed his neck, averting his eyes to scan the room around them and all the abandoned finery of this Atlantean's home. "Fair enough."

Janice followed suit, rising from her seat and pacing the room, studying the tables and chairs, the oriental carpet laid on the pale ivory flooring. "How did they get these things here? Is there some sort of astral maritime economy? Do they trade sundries with the physical world? Pop into the world of the living for some silk and magazines?"

"Good question. It's… a bit much, isn't it?"

"A bit? Gaudy, cheap imitations, all of it. The shadow of elegance. It's sad, really."

They sat in prolonged silence, the chaos of the street a distant lull, raising and falling like the tide. For all the fear, uncertainty and violence around them, the moment became an oasis, a chance to sit in the silence of good company and think. Janice's mind drifted to her father. She knew that somewhere, in this vast city of the dead, her father was living in the lap of luxury. All he had needed to do was sacrifice his daughter and her newborn son. Her mind returned to the cold ship, the long dark of her last night on Earth. Now, a century later, she was approaching a coronation.

"Can I ask you something?" Owen asked.

"Yes, my king?"

Owen laughed awkwardly. "Right. Royalty status. Immortality. The keys to the kingdom."

Janice refilled her glass of ambrosia. "Wasn't that long ago we were huddled in the dark, dressed in rags, floating in acid. The journey a life takes, eh?"

"Is this really what you want?" Owen asked, his brow bent by doubt. "All this power, this… weight."

"Me?" Janice laughed. "Funny."

"Why?"

"I've never really thought much about what I wanted for myself. Most of my life, I was told what I should want. If I deviated from that, well, thinking wasn't very involved in that process."

"Do you want to be queen of a place like this? Is that the right thing for us to do? I just don't know."

"What about you, Owen? What do you think? Do you think you're of sound mind and body to become the king of hell?"

Owen said nothing, listening to the screams of death float upwards into the open canvas of the astral sky.

"You don't know either, do you?" she asked. "So what point is there in wondering now?"

XXX. Blood and Thunder

Nina was sure her death was close at hand. To escape it, she had hidden in the dark alcove of an ivory chapel, fires raging by the splintered doors. The entire right wall of the cathedral had been broken in by the corpse of a gigantic bird, its pallid body littered with driftwood spears. The bodies of Pitter and Heartlander alike lay strewn about it. These were people she had known, people she feared and strived with day by day, crushed and broken to take down one demon among a thousand.

Nina held in her hands the top of her shattered spear. In the mad dash through the forest, chaos had reigned supreme in the shadowed darkness. Strange shapes and figures prowled in search of the invaders, brandishing weapons, biting and clawing for blood. To her left and right she watched others fall screaming, but still the masses pressed on. Nina had rushed through and beyond the carnage to this point in time, this cold chapel corner, watching inhuman silhouettes cast themselves against the leftmost wall.

The figures were that of fish-men, guppies with silverpool eyes, clutching daggers in their webbed appendages. They moved slowly, their mouths flapping soundlessly agape as if to taste the air, all to assist in tracking their prey to swarm them like bloodflies.

Nina knew now, more than ever before in her long, strange life that she was no secret warrior. No matter what she told herself, how she framed this moment in her mind, she could not bring herself to face death head-on, to take a life (even one so soulless and cruel) before her own was taken from her. She knew that it was necessary, that the lives of many hung in the balance, that this was as justified a fall towards animal instinct as any human being could face, but still.

She held the spear, tip facing down, and tried to steady her breath. The fish-men were fanning out, one towards the door, another towards the center altar, a third towards the furthest alcove. Towards Nina.

A voice in her head slammed like a gong hammer against her skull. Survive. Survive. Survive.

The nearest fish's head jerked in place, its left eye dimly scanning the room.

Fight. Fight. Fight.

Nina tried to imagine it: Running forward, stabbing the fish-man. Aiming for the soft flesh beneath his gills, like gutting and cleaning the catch of the day. The others would surely notice. She would grab the dagger, abandon the spear and run for the craterous exit. She was quicker than them, or rather, she had to be.

Live! Live! Live!

Nina tried to keep herself from shuddering. She needed all her lungs, all her body's might. She had seen what these things could do to a human being.

Not her. Not today.

Kill! Kill! Kill!

The roar of a crowd came from outside, and thunder rang out from above. The fish-men twitched and clattered, jittering in place. One turned and ran outside the church, following the sound. Another hesitated, clicking audibly with some bone or cartilage inside its body, before following suit.

There was only one remaining. The closest of the fish-men. It was distracted by the screams and the others of its kind leaving in a rush, but it hesitated to follow. It tasted living blood in this chapel air and it wanted to feed.

Nina rose without meaning to. Her body was sluggish, resisting its own demands for power, but the engine burned on. She screamed from the pit in her gut, from the painful fire of hard-earned inner light.

The fish-man twitched and turned to face her. It clenched its finger-like appendages, steadying its blade for battle. It stepped towards her on half-vestigial feet, swinging the dagger widely, left and right.

Nina was sure she was going to die, but she could not stop herself anymore. She stabbed forward, missing the gills but piercing the upper half of the fish-man's arm. The arm convulsed, flicking the dagger back instinctively and slashing Nina's chest below the breast. The slash was glancing but Nina *felt* it, falling backwards in shock.

The fish-man's wound widened from the swing, its arm falling limp. Its dagger fell against the stone flooring with a loud *klang*. It kept trying to swing its arm, to stab forward as if unharmed, like it could not feel the trauma done upon it.

Nina, horrified by her own blood, *could* feel her flesh split open, scream white pain into her brain, but all her limbs still answered her call. She lifted the spear again and stabbed with an upwards tilt, breaking through scales. She lifted her leg and kicked its torso with fury as she pulled the spear tip free, knocking the fish-man from its feet.

As it fell, she stabbed at it again, but the spear tip bounced off its body. She lifted her makeshift weapon again, gasping for air and with a scream brought it down into the fish-man's eye, spilling out the vitreous fluid. It made a noise like heaving and rolled to the right, causing Nina to trip. When she fell, her body hit the stone at a bad angle, striking her chest wound against it and ripping the flesh around it open.

She screamed.

The fish-man kept rolling away, horizontal like a log free-floating down a river. Nina could not find her spear, could barely see through her pain.

The fish-man rose and rushed at her with sickening, sudden movements, its working arm clawing the air in front of it.

Nina saw the glint of metal to her side. As the shadow cast upon her, blocking the light, she fumbled for it. Her hands clasped around a blade. It stung to hold, but there was no time to secure a better grip. She clutched the blade close and lifted it, stabbing the fish-man in its gut. It shuddered still again, and she grabbed the hilt, long and silver, until her raw and bloody fingers felt the jutting handle. She pulled and pushed with it, rending, ripping anything she could.

The fish-man squealed atop her and wriggled, shuddering in anguish. It fell backwards again, still swinging as it did, but this time it did not rise. It could not any longer.

It was dead.

Nina laid there, on the cold stone, clutching her bloody chest, feeling the stump of her missing finger try to close the envelope of her flesh.

She was alive.

Some distant voice inside reminded her the danger was not over. The other fish-men could return at any moment, or something worse. She could not afford to lie here, dying or otherwise. The mission awaited them all, under the booming thunder of Gabriel: siege Atlantis.

Voices grew nearer. "Through here! Hurry!"

Shouts, rising and falling like seafoam on the shore.

Footsteps shaking the earth. Even these few small men and women, these lost souls could birth new tremors in the soil.

Nina wondered if she might meet the one who chose to feed her to the Leviathan. Had she been a precious sacrifice, or just a bit of fodder? Collateral damage? Who, in her own life, would have singled her out as their dearest lamb to take to slaughter?

The idea of vengeance was appealing, but she struggled to get much lasting fire from it. She'd had a feeling that she knew the truth: It was Mannfred who was sacrificed. He'd been the prize. He'd come from fallen money, some dwindling aristocratic house gutted by the European wars. He abandoned his dwindling estate, his family name, to study the sea, sealing his fate and her own.

But here she was, alive, where he was long gone now. She'd have no idea how to avenge Mannfred or who to avenge him upon. All of this blood and thunder to end the endless empire. The life-water spilled out in pools to flow into the earth and drain out into the astral sea.

Was there really freedom at the end of this craggy path towards tomorrow? Was there something, anything more than pain?

"In here! Someone's moving!" Shadows danced on the wall, one and another.

"It's Nina! She's alive!"

A cheer went out.

Nina tried to lift herself from the ground.

"Parker?"

The Irishman nodded, laughing as helped her up with a soft palm on the back. "Look at you! Last in line for confession, with enough fish to share with everyone."

Nina burst out laughing, only to feel the deep gash in her chest yawn, sending white hot pain coursing through her veins. "Fuck you."

"Oh, that looks nasty. Let's get that covered for you."

Nina, wincing, watched as Parker rushed over to the alcove, ripping some fabric curtains into strips. She tried to keep upright but contorting her torso made the pain feel that much more fresh. Apologizing, she laid back down on the ground as Parker gathered dressing for the wound.

It wasn't long ago that Parker and the others had feared her, and wished her dead. Now he was trying to keep her alive.

Parker came back with the velvet strips and set about wrapping Nina's chest with them tightly. Nina looked at his face, covered in sweat and dried blood, concentrating as he worked.

"Parker?" she asked.

"Yeah, Nina?"

"Where's… Fernando?"

Parker's left eye twitched. He avoided eye contact. "Still in the woods, yeah. Like a lot of them."

Nina's mind flashed with memories of the mad dash through the forest.

"Oh," was all she could say.

"We'll go back for them," he whispered, as much to himself as for Nina. "When we kill that bloody King, we'll go back for them all."

Nina wiped a tear from his cheek. "Once it's all over."

"Ready to get back out there?"

She grit her teeth as Parker put her arm around his

shoulder. "No time like the present."

The war raged on, ascending the spiral hill around the Spinal Mount towards the Inner Temple. In the skies, a host of flying Delights and homunculi swarmed the Holy Corpse, now a lesser sun above New Atlantis. Tethered to it by hundreds of strings of sinuous light, Gabriel, like some great angel of wrath, threw forth bolts of lightning that fragmented the sky. Beast after beast splintered and came raining down to the earth, splintering into fragments of stone.

Below, the frantic hordes spilled out in all directions. The residents of Atlantis, marble-fleshed, fled for their immortal lives or held their ground against the furious hordes of Pitters and Heartlanders alike.

"They've broken through the lower gate," Parker noted, squinting at the far-off figures of Levi dwellers almost entirely around the bend.

"Are we… winning?" Nina asked, unable to believe it herself.

The two moved slowly, avoiding any obvious confrontation. Both were weak and tired but unable to surrender to their fates. Neither said as much, but the quiet resolution to choose a meaningful death gave them common cause, if any such death were possible to them.

The curving road up to the lower gate was desolate. The bodies of other survivors lay strewn about, bloody and ragged. Around them lie the fragments of the statuesque undead, half-mask heads and porcelain arms devoid of the spark that turned them fluid in the imitation of flesh. This hill had been a chokepoint only moments before, but already the deep silence of death had permeated the air.

Nothing is real around recent death. It siphons sense

and reason away, leaving a stain in the shape of life.

Nina felt a sudden sense of horrible danger like a finger slowly traced the interior of her skull, lingering upon the nape of her neck. She craned her head back on instinct to see its source, a shadow, descending from some higher rooftop.

Three times the height of a man, it walked on piercing rib-legs like some abyssal spider. At its center was a hooded figure, draped in tattered rags of thick and ancient smoke.

Two lost lambs, it intoned, beyond the senses yet clearly understood. *Simplicity itself.*

"Parker," Nina whispered, but Parker did not answer.

You taint the bones with lesser blood, sinners.

It crawled closer, one blade at a time in a weightless scurry, graceful with the pride of the hunter. Nina could see the blooming seed of a fleshy body at its core. This was no Delight, but one of the Order. This was some manner of man.

Back to rest, it shuddered.

"HERALD!"

The roar of bullets cracked through the air of death, piercing the creature's form, causing it to lose its looming foothold. It was Serge, descending quickly down the city hillside, holding the gun of Ivan aloft with the clarity of a soldier, a dagger in his steadying arm.

Parker sprung to life, leading Nina to the side of the street, away from the Herald spider and Serge. Behind Serge came Pitters to his left and right with wide white eyes like dying stars.

The Herald screeched, bone against bone, and charged them. Nina could hear the sound of piercing flesh and the cries of death behind her.

"In here!" Parker whispered, limping with Nina on his arm into a nearby building.

In the dark shadow of the unlit entrance hall, Parker sat Nina down against the wall. The sounds of battle grew fiercer outside, bullets and screams, some feral piercing screech from the spiderous Herald. Parker kept looking back at the door, his expression wracked with guilt and terror.

"Nina, I…"

"It's okay."

She understood.

He smiled at her, joyless. "I'll… find you, when it's all over."

"We'll find Fernando together, and the others. Don't forget."

"Not for a second. Stay low, lass."

She nodded.

He rose, standing by the door frame for just a moment, unable to re-enter the street, to face the awaiting hell. He looked back at Nina, eyes begging.

"Fuck it all, right?" He asked, laughing pale and haunted. "There's no other way it ends."

"I don't know, Parker."

"Right," he muttered. "Right."

And with that, he was off.

The sound of fighting outside seemed to fade away, further down the street and up the hill. Nina realized Serge and the others must be trying to lure the Herald away. She didn't want to think about wounded, terrified Parker joining the fray. What little he could do against a thing like that.

Even Serge, the former soldier, the one who seemed

most equipped for war of any Heartlander or Pitter alike, could do nothing. The only one fighting like survival was an option was Gabriel, high above the killing fields. Gabriel, who knew all about the city, who understood how things worked in this foreign world outside of space and time.

Up in the sky, bellowing thunder, he was a moth-flame swatting at pests while the rest of them died like pigs. Nina fought the urge to scream from rage and pain. Her whole system was aching, the adrenaline of near-death giving way to weakness and misery.

In the chaos, Nina had not noticed the trail of blood from the front door, leading further in. She wondered who it belonged to. Not an Atlantean, that was for sure.

With some effort, she lifted herself from the ground. Her legs were shaky, so she held a hand against the wall for balance. Her other arm around her chest for pressure, she pulled herself deeper into the building, following the blood until she came upon a wide, circular room filled with row after row of books and scrolls.

It was a library. One of the finest Nina had ever seen.

In the center of the room, the blood trail led to a figure slumped over against an overturned table, haloed in light from the oculus at the top of the domed roof of the library.

"You found me," Carmela said, laughing.

Nina rushed over, fragile on her feet. "Carmela?!"

"It's good to see you again, dear. I was afraid you died in the woods like the rest of us."

Carmela was covered in wounds, deep gashes across her arms and legs. Her hands and torso were soaked with blood, but still her eyes were lit with mischievous lightning, like everything was a game. Even death.

"You're..." Nina started.

"Not long now."

Nina fell to her knees, stroking Carmela's hair, pulling her wiry strands free of the caked blood on her cheek and pushing it behind Carmela's ear. Nina was crying. It had just started, with no resistance from her eyes.

"Now, now," Carmela purred, her eyes flickering to stay open. "Don't make me feel things."

Nina looked around the room. "There has to be something to bandage you. I'll-"

Carmela grabbed Nina's arm, her grip loose but willful. "Look around you, Nina. What do you see?"

Nina was reminded of Carmela's condescending steak. "What do you fucking mean? Books, okay? I see books."

Carmela laughed, stroking Nina's hand with her finger. "Ever since I... well, crawled in here, I've been thinking. About these books. About this city."

Nina fought back her tears.

"I loved books, Nina. I read every day. Even when I sailed to war, I was reading. It was... the joy of my life." Carmela shuddered. The emotional pain made her physical wounds cut that much closer. "It hurts to see them here. To think of them all reading in the light."

Carmela coughed, and blood splattered over her dress. Her lungs were filling quickly now. She was drowning. "Burn it. Burn them and me together. Let them lose this place, at least."

Nina nodded, sobbing mutely.

"I wish..." Her hand lifted to Nina's cheek, her thumb resting on the edge of Nina's lip. "I wish I could have laid in a meadow with you."

Nina held Carmela's hand against her cheek and felt her grip go loose. Nina's mind went blank. She cried, loud and deep, wailing in the light. She forgot to be afraid, to be herself. All she could be in that moment was pain.

From the shadows, a statue figure stepped forward. Nina looked up at it and tensed, expecting her imminent death, only to see a face that looked like Owen's carved in the living marble of Atlantean bodies. The figure held an open torch aloft.

"Let's do as she said, then."

XXXI. House of the Eldest

Far above Atlantis, on the highest rungs of the spinal mount, Herald Kelpius, once the Ledger Man, led Owen and Janice in a frantic race. Janice, clutching Baby Sean to her shoulder, struggled to run at pace and keep the baby from rattling, though his state of near-comatose sleep seemed unchallengeable.

All around them, pillars of smoke rose, wafting on the still air, obscuring the path ahead. When they reached a tall set of stairs, Kelpius stopped, the smoke and fire fully registering in his mind for the first time.

"What madness."

Owen, slightly behind, struggled to catch his breath. "We wanted a distraction, right?"

Janice chuckled grimly. "Nothing like a barn fire to rattle the chickens and foxes."

Kelpius shook his marble head. "That fire there," he pointed out towards the middle, where the largest fire burned bright and tall, "is the Great Library. There are tomes and parchments in that storehouse that no longer exist in the mortal world! Reams of ancient knowledge, history, science, philosophy. The legacy of all humanity. I cannot fathom our loss."

Owen said nothing, but watched Kelpius closely. Though the shadows sat the same on his statued face, contorting in the manner of skin, he felt a great distance from him. He missed Raffaele, the old man in the dark room, the man who bled to preserve the memory of the devoured. Owen realized, more than humanity, it was the history, the separated data of life and all its happenings that held true weight for the ancient man.

Kelpius sighed. “The fault lies squarely with the King and his advisors. Their failed rule salted the earth. If we are to save anything of this city, we must press on. It is time for a new dynasty, young and noble, to lead.” The thought seemed to comfort him, though Owen could recognize the flicker of doubt creasing the edges of his eyes.

“How much further is it?” Janice asked.

“This is the last exterior stair. At its zenith we shall find the great bridge and the Thorn Doors that bar the way. The House of the Eldest awaits.”

“How will we overthrow the king?” Owen asked. “He must be…”

“Powerful? Aye, he is at that. But you will see the truth of him when we reach the throne. It is not him I fear. It is Verulam and Thomas we must overcome if the day is to be truly ours.”

Something about the name Verulam made Owen’s head pulse. It was as if he was floating underwater and a great ship began to pass overhead, shaking him at his foundation with sound and pressure. Somehow, beyond his senses, he felt a strange light calling from above at the height of the tower. A dim light and a low song.

“Quickly now! We must make haste!”

And so they ascended, Kelpius at the head, Janice and Sean close behind and Owen pulling up the rear, looking back at the fire and up at the invisible light. The stair curved alongside the central column, wide, short steps of carved bone, jagged and coarse to the step for better traction. There was no guard-rail to protect the careless. Only patience and surety would lead one to the top.

The steps grew thinner as they curled around the

edge of the edifice, until at least they fed into an alcove, framed with ornate columns well-lit with blue fire. They had arrived.

"My god," Janice muttered.

From the alcove, the great bridge, long and thin, was visible. It was barely wide enough for two or three, and with no guard or handrails to speak of. It was a flat path suspended on great pillars of bone that descended far beyond the eye could follow, bridging a chasmic drop between the exterior column and the House of the Eldest. At its end, three times the size of any man, stood the grim and beckoning Thorn Doors, finely detailed with a relief of roots and veins entwined carved upon its edifice.

"It is time," Kelpius said. He raised his arms aloft, away from the bridge and the Thorn Doors, out towards the island. With a whisper, a green light rose from his breast and traveled up and out of him, ascending as rapidly as a bird. As it did, it unfurled and sparkled, bathing the city skyline in a brief flash of green. There would be no one, above or below, who missed its glow.

"What was that for?" Janice asked.

"Reinforcements."

White thunder cracked above them, and from some great vicious tear came Gabriel, transformed beyond recognition. On great wings of light and lightning, he landed on the alcove on one knee, head hung low. The great tendrils of light that had connected him to the Holy Corpse and fed him power had now bound their two frames together. Half corpse, half body, flesh and light in active fusion, Gabriel had become something greater and lesser than man. He had become a liminal angel of war.

Kelpius approached him. Resting a hand upon his

misshapen shoulder, he sighed.

"Rise, Gabriel."

Gabriel's living head rose to meet his accomplice. His eyes, once so piercing and dark, had become glossy and placid, though his face was still contorted in fury.

He rose.

Owen could not hide his fear or revulsion, and so he looked away.

Kelpius spoke to them all. "The enemy knows we stand at the gates. There is no time to rest."

The group departed from the alcove. Kelpius led the way across the bridge, with Gabriel slowly, glacially following the rest. Owen and Janice exchanged a glance of worry and fear, but both knew better than to speak.

"Watch your step," Kelpius instructed. "This chasm goes deep below the island surface, below the Sea."

Janice looked down at the darkness and fought her burgeoning sense of vertigo. "Fuck's sake."

Though no wind blew on the Astral Sea, the bridge seemed to writhe and sway beneath them, rocking slightly on its central tether. With each step forward, the world outside the spinal column disappeared behind the major vertebral wall, leaving only the smoke and distant cries from the city and the dull groan of the abyssal deep below.

A tremor rippled through the bridge, extending from the central tower and the House of the Eldest. Kelpius froze, his arms raised in warning. He turned back at Gabriel, his stone eyes wide with fear.

The Thorn Doors began to open.

A thick incense emanated from within like sea fog, flowing and curling around the platform at the end of the bridge. As it pooled outwards, the great cloud of smoke seemed to replenish itself as if it were an endless sea of fog its very own.

"*Kelpius*," a low voice, sourceless on the air bemusedly called out. "*Hawkins*."

Gabriel growled. "Separ."

"Hawkins?" Owen asked.

"A dead name," Gabriel responded, shame heavy on his tongue.

No name etched in bone may be lost, no bill left unaccounted.

A tall, rakishly thin figure emerged from the fog, arms extended in supplication. Wet, silver flesh glistened beneath a heavy robe, and two red eyes like sunken, black-red rubies peered out.

"It has been some time, Separ," Kelpius greeted, fury in his throat. "I see you have grown well into your role."

Separ laughed, removing his hood to reveal his strange, damp skin and rows of dagger teeth from which rot-lunged air lolled forth.

Someone must commit to The Labor, Herald Kelpius. Someone must honor their vow. Or should we all become spoiled children, dirty-kneed in Our Father's woods, pretending to be knights in your example? Have you finally found your honor and courage with this mummer's farce? I should hope so, given what it has cost.

Owen reached out and put his hand on Janice's back. He felt powerless and terrified facing down this demonic priest at the end of a narrow passage, but he did not want to die here. Janice, pale, nodded thankfully at him. In her arms, Baby Sean began to stir.

Gabriel stepped forward, his bulky, misshapen flesh and massive wings leaning fearlessly over the edge. "We have been led astray long enough, Separ. It is time for a new line. Stand aside or die."

Separ laughed again, haughty and proud. *Noble commander, seller of men, driftwood king. You are nothing to fear.*

"Levy your insults, worm. I have laid waste to beast after beast, Herald after Herald. You are nothing but the next."

Our Lord Verulam has spoken. Traitors to the Labor shall not enter the House of the Eldest. You signed your soul to our King. To his great Labor. There is no greater vow to make in all the world. There is no greater cost.

Tendrils of light sprang forth from Gabriel, forging another spear from light. "Enough of your tongue! Face me now!"

Silence. Open your ears, heretic.

Owen could hear it. It was coming from below, a breath of ancient law, a fact like fear or love.

Oath-breakers, You stand above the pits of hell. Above the roots of the world. What is signed is delivered. What is owed, is due.

Separ lifted his arms and began to sing.

Kelpius grabbed Janice and Owen, his cold stone hands trembling.

"One of you must make it inside." The bridge began to rattle. Owen fell to his knees, grabbing the edge of the bridge for safety. Kelpius held tightly to Janice and Sean, steadier than them both. "Should the door close, speak these words: *The interior, revealed. Bask, ye who stands before the stone. In supplication, in surrender, ye who walks now in the garden.*"

"What the hell is going on, Raffaele?" Janice asked, staring at the darkness below.

Separ stepped forward. *The root-biter comes. The adder comes, and with him comes the water.*

A tremendous superheated pressure rose from below like a subterranean vent letting off the heat of a planetary core. Wind, with all the fury of a storm, carried that heat skywards, shaking the bridge even further so it swung loose in the middle. Black roots rose along the outer column, growing upwards with impossible speed, each gasping strand an unending snake slithering out from a cave.

IT AWAKENS! IT COMES!

From below and in all directions came a serpent of muscle and wood and stone and steel, of darkness and mud, leering with a hundred eyes and forty mouths, a creature beyond understanding. The sinews of its flesh were like bark and blood, the raw base undercurrents of the world. It writhed about mindlessly, each fiber of its form a grasping, hungry will, eclipsing Separ in its sudden, fluid grasping.

Separ laughed and turned to face it, to greet it with joy, only to discover one such mouth extending from the central mass and swallowing him whole.

A pillar of the beast coiled around the bridge, rapidly closing the gap between its form and the rebels on the bridge. Gabriel's body glowed brilliantly, every inch of skin in a transformative sheen. With a bestial roar, he lost himself fully to the fight, ascending off the bridge and piercing the coiling flesh of the demon worm. As its main growth came up from the bridge, its lower body tightened its grip on the bridge, causing the bone to splinter and crack.

"Run!" Kelpius screamed, pulling Owen and Janice

up and forwards, towards the Thorn Doors. Above them, a host of mouths flared from the worm, launching at Gabriel's wings. His body burned with the sacred fire of the liminal, causing many of the mouths to turn at once to ash, but dark is as light does and the worm must feed and bite.

Gabriel screamed in pain as his shell of light was breached, but he carried on, pulling the worm up towards the ceiling of the world.

The bridge, squeezed to the marrow, splintered at the end and broke. It swayed even looser, and the closest pillar to the break shattered in turn. It was tilting off its frame and crumbling to bits.

Owen could not bear to look backwards. He held tight to Janice and Raffaele, his eyes locked firmly on the Thorn Doors. Nothing felt real. Nothing had weight.

In his heart, he was back at his old apartment with Ciara and Bobo. It was ten o'clock in the morning. The light was warm and solid coming in through the bedroom window. He was looking up at the ceiling and smiling, trying to remember some joke from the night before, the weight of loved ones pressing on his arms. He could smell Bobo's little belly like it was heaving there beside him.

Janice screamed as her footing gave out.

Kelpius's hands shimmered as he grabbed tightly to Janice and Owen. With a heave, he pulled them up above him, the transferring light causing them to linger in the air, like gravity was lessened on them.

The bridge fell and with it Kelpius, like a stone into the deep of a lake.

On instinct, Owen floated upwards, arcing towards the Thorn Doors, his hand clasped tightly to Janice's. Together, they softly hit the remaining walkway. Above them, above the darkness, the worm, lifted above the column walls, turned into itself towards the light of Gabriel, devouring itself to reach him.

The two figures, light and dark, man and snake, reached a peak before combusting like a frozen flame, twirling as it fell, leaving a streak of light behind it like a comet as it disappeared back into the deep.

Janice and Owen laid gasping for a while, watching the darkness below for any signs of danger or of life. Neither could speak, could fully process it yet, but reality began to assert itself.

Raffaele and Gabriel were gone.

Baby Sean began to speak, big dark eyes bouncing open. Janice was surprised, but she felt a tremendous sense of relief to hear him wake from his slumber. Sean's small hands reached out, grasping, towards the smoke of the Thorn Door. He cooed like the smoke was a toy, as if there was nothing at all to fear.

Janice rose to her feet, still numb to the loss of her tutor, friend, and surrogate father. Whatever awaited them both down in the darkness below, she hoped it would not pain him long.

"We should go," she worked out from a dry throat, fighting back her tears.

Owen laid there, stunned by the enormity of the moment. What had that demonic creature been? Root-biter? It had made quick work of Gabriel. In the Astral Realm, beyond physical reality, great wills and greater beasts seemed to bend the fabric of space and time to suit them.

He understood nothing. He could do almost nothing, other than swim. What awaited them there, at the peak of the ivory tower, resting above the total darkness carved out of the eternal sea, and how could they ever mean to match it?

For the first time since his throat was pierced by the bullet in the depths of the Pit and the Leviathan claimed his dying form as its own, he felt true and absolute fear. All his hard-earned confidence, what surety he had mustered had collapsed into itself.

"Owen!" a voice cried out.

He looked up. Across the broken expanse, at the ruinous alcove that marked the way down was Nina. She was alive, bloody but alive, with another hooded figure close behind her. She waved at him with tears in her eyes, her other arm clutching her chest.

He stood up and waved. "Nina!" He too began to cry. "You're okay!"

Nina looked at where the bridge had gone and her momentary joy dried up. "What happened? Where's Raffaele and Gabriel?"

He wasn't sure of how to respond or what to say. All he could do was look down at the darkness and back to her. Let his eyes tell the story.

She understood at once and sighed.

"Find a way across! Let's leave. The city is burning. There's nothing left to fight for."

Janice put her hand on Owen's back. "We have to press on, Owen."

Owen felt the pressure building in his gut. He did not want to let Raffaele and Gabriel's death be for nothing, but the city was ruined and many Heralds were dead. What else was there in the House of the Eldest for them but death itself, waiting in black wings?

"Owen." Janice looked at him with cool darkness at

the heart of her eyes. “There’s no going back.”

“Owen!”

Owen’s blood ran cold at the sound of another voice, familiar as rain, as sickness. The figure next to Nina stepped forwards, removing his head. It was the marbled face of Alan. All at once the gap between the Thorn Doors and the alcove felt as much an inch as a mile, and Owen felt sick.

He screamed some frantic, furious and deeply damaged howl, like no sound he’d ever made before, flooding his gullet with caustic, searing acid.

Alan did not flinch. He did not speak.

The two brothers stared across the chasm at each other, at the weight of the world between them. Owen’s heart felt a violent pain as he remembered the days of their youth. the death of their father, the solid, stoic break between them and the years of distance that led them to this moment, worlds away from their shallow, boyish lives and thrown headlong into the shadows of the inbetween.

“That’s enough,” Janice said. “Remember the dead. Our pain’s not special, Owen. Just our opportunity. Say your goodbyes.”

Janice nodded at Nina before turning away and stepping through the fog of the Thorn Doors, disappearing wholly from view. Owen did not watch her leave, but as her words sank in, he lifted himself slowly up back onto his feet.

He looked at his brother, or what was left of his brother, and imagined what choices he had made to be here now, standing besides Nina as a companion. Nina would not trust an Atlantean this quickly without reason. She was too smart for that.

There wasn’t time to learn what path Alan chose to take, or how he came to be here. The distance was too wide and time was running out.

"Nina," he shouted, his voice hoarse and faltering. "There's a turtle on the southern shore. It's a friend."

Nina laughed and cried and nodded. "It's good to see you again," she shouted back.

He laughed and nodded, too. He looked to Alan and tried to speak, but nothing came. Neither moved or looked away, twin anchors, mirror and water, the moon and the sun.

"Take care of yourself," Owen said, his voice faltering, becoming something closer to a whisper. "Live well."

There was nothing to look forward to, nothing to hope for in the tower. Only the chance at something different, something final, that might put the long game to rest, or start it all over. Owen wasn't sure of himself or his footing, but his body couldn't bear to hang back on the periphery of fate a moment longer.

He turned and followed Janice into the smoke. It covered his skin, filled his senses, blurring the synaptic gap between sight and feeling, sound and smell. He could feel the light again, hear the song of the world as if it rose from within him, from the marrow of his bones.

XXXII. The Genius Of The Dead

Janice could not see the beginning or the end of the fog, nor the interior walls of the House of the Eldest. She could not see the light of the island or the Thorn Doors behind her. All was lost to the impermeable miasma. All but Sean, cooing in her arms, and her own two feet to carry them forward. She had a sense it had been a grave mistake to not take Owen by the hand and walk into the seat of their enemies' power together, to stand as a united front for what unknowable dangers awaited them.

But she was tired of waiting. Tired of Owen's simple pain and fear. She had thought for just a moment, drinking the ambrosia together and discussing their uncertain tomorrow, that he had changed, become a surer version of himself than the chewed up boy still finding his sea legs inside Leviathan. After a hundred years of living hell, she had little room left in her heart for pity.

All she had left to call her own was calcified rage and a need to press onwards.

She wondered with some dedication exactly what sort of trap she had wandered into. The mental exercise was somehow entertaining. There must be some Herald, mind and body warped through the power of the Leviathan's dreaming, leading her astray with the patience of a flycatcher, biding its time in some dark crevice for the final opportunity to pounce. She was unsure what she might do in such a situation. For all her astral traveling through the marrow dreams, she had never learned to wield it in the manner of Gabriel, threading light into lightning, bringing storms of rage beneath his heel like some wine-drunk demigod.

"Listen, you," she whispered to Baby Sean, stroking

his soft crown, unchanged in its weakness and primitivity in the century of unlife they had shared.

"I know you're capable of tremendous things. I've seen it, you've seen it. You need to be ready to do them again."

Baby Sean looked up at her with his void black eyes and giggled.

"I've done a lot for you over the years, you know," she continued, "and it hasn't been easy. Not even Mary would've reared the baby Jesus if it meant he'd scream and cry and soil himself forever. I know I've said some cruel things in the heat of the moment. I didn't want you, after all. But I never let you die a second time. I never left you behind."

Sean's eyes watched her, blinking passively.

"I wouldn't have chosen this life for either of us. Not from the start. But I never thought I had much choice." She sighed, feeling a rare and buried pain rise within. There were more words, more pains, but she had not forgotten her danger and all of them felt pointless to say.

"So stay awake with me, little one. Eyes open."

She never knew how much he understood. The thought was haunting. She never entertained it long, but in this strange moment it felt as though he did. That was enough for now.

Step after step, the fog remained. If Janice had any sense of distance or proportion for this space, she would have sworn she had walked in an unbroken, level line far further than the House of the Eldest seemed capable of extending. If she was going deeper, or climbing upwards, there was no sense of it, no incline, no step.

Wherever she was, the simple laws no longer applied.

Ahead in the fog a large silhouette bore heavy into view. It was a figure in a stone chair, alone in the darkness.

"So the day has finally come, kitty kat. You have wandered far and wide in a cold, uncaring world, until at last you found your way back home. I feel so proud."

It was her father's voice coming from the chair. He rose. Around them, a concentric ring of torches flickered to life, dissipating the fog, leaving only light and darkness, father and daughter and son.

"Hello, Daddy." Janice fought to keep herself steady, to speak with strength. "Of course you'd be in the House of the Eldest. Why wouldn't you? You always found a way to worm your way into an interesting party."

Her father laughed, his voice thin and hollow in a way it had never been, like he wore himself as a mask.

"Glad to see you paid attention."

Owen passed through fog and shadow, guided by a solitary strand of light.

"Janice?"

She did not answer. Before him, the light grew evermore radiant and welcoming until at last Owen felt nothing but the warm glow of it against his skin. Despite his fear and confusion, he smiled, as if he were waking up on the river raft that last summer's day and none of this had come to pass.

It was hard to open his eyes and face the truth, but he did.

Owen had passed from nothingness into a heptagonal chamber, cool light pooled in from above. There was no door behind him. The walls were covered in dark and colorless vines upon which bloomed white flowers of magnificent size. Bathed in pale light at the center of the room sat the writhing, colossal tree of bone, its trunk a wheel of cartilage, its branches fraying nerves and rods of ivory veins. Carved into its center was the figure of a king, features withered and sunken, eyelids hung heavy and low. His garments were modest, a dull white, though atop his thin, silver hair rested a thorny crown of silver, inlaid with streaks of gold and laid with ruby inlets. It seemed to be a wreath of laurel and bone, vine and blade, interwoven as if in natural and harmonious order.

This was the Lord of Lords. The King of White Flowers. Though Owen had never seen him before, something in his visage, bound up in the great tree, felt alien yet deeply true. It was a god and a corpse, a tree and a grandfather, a statue and a man all in one. His breath shuddered as Owen stepped into the light, and his eyes pulled open with surprise.

In the space before him was a wide wooden table, with two plush velvet chairs on either end. At its center was a small fountain from which ambrosia flowed in a burbling perpetual motion and two glasses on either side, set as if for a dinner party.

A figure emerged from behind the bone tree. It was a young man, vibrantly dressed in a bold blue cloak that glimmered with the light reflecting from his curly blonde hair and shock of white collar.

"Ah, you have arrived," the young man said, voice high and bright. "Welcome, my dear Owen. I have eagerly awaited this day."

Owen paused where he stood, speechless. Tense.

"I'm sure you must be apprehensive about all this. I can read it plainly in your eye. You came here expecting some grand climactic showdown with a demonic vizier, some epic duel of fate against an ageless terror and not some old man in a chair and his foolish yet caring attendant. It's only natural to doubt me. And after all, you have suffered so very much to arrive here, in this sanctified city beyond the mortal world. Led a grand uprising across the astral sea, allies at your side. One can almost hear the music swell behind you as you enter our humble hall, you limber creature of tomorrow's legend! Perhaps we should have a tussle to start, so as to not disappoint the children who shall one day hear stories of this day."

"Who the hell are you?" Owen worked out, feeling dizzy.

The blonde man laughed again, his hands gently draping over each side of the nearest chair. "Quite right, quite right. Please, have a seat. There is so much for us to discuss."

The man's sparkling pupils watched Owen with great interest, trying to hide a clear impatience between a thin veneer of magnanimousness. It was apparent he was playing a game of sorts, a strategy to disarm Owen, to set the tenor for their encounter. Owen could either refuse outright and try to begin a fight or sit down and see what may come of a parley.

Part of Owen's soul blared with anxiety from this abject manipulation. Outside, the Pitters and Heartlanders were dying, one by one in some unknowable landscape of horror and rebellion. To sit with this man, who was almost certainly a Herald, was to insult their sacrifice. But in equal measure to this sure indignance, doubt crept in. Doubt that this man was a true foe or a distraction, an illusion or a threat. He had referred to himself as a foolish, caring attendant. Was that the sort of thing a Herald might say? Kelpius and Gabriel were Heralds once, and though they too had sacrificed the living to the beast and "earned" their titles, so too did they fall together in the dark, coiled in an undying embrace with the horror from below. Was he also a pawn of the King, or the true threat?

Owen finally found his voice. "I won't do anything until you reveal your identity. This isn't a social call."

The blonde man nodded, curled locks bobbing in the light.

"Very fair. I've come to this conversation pre-armed with knowledge of your past and nature. Your family crossed the threshold, and since then you have been quite involved in our affairs. I feel as though I know you very well, Owen, though I must admit I have some reservations about you I would love to address. But let us circle back to that. Introductions are in order."

The blonde man did a formal salute, pounding his hand against his chest and smiling broadly. "I am known by my former title of the Lord Verulam, though there are many names and titles in my past. You may call me by another name, if you would like. I was born Francis Bacon, son of Sir Nicholas, Lord Keeper of the Great Seal."

Owen felt as though the name felt familiar, aristocratic, but he knew very little about Old World lineages. Before the Leviathan, he had not cared much for history. He had always loved the present most of all.

"You're a Herald, aren't you?" Owen asked.

"In a manner, yes. But also, in a more important sense, I would say no. My current occupation is High Grandmaster of The Order. For many years now, I have led the construction and settlement of this great Island. By the grace of His Majesty," he motioned deferentially to the quivering figure on the throne, "I have gathered a society of thinkers, poets, merchants, criminals, jesters and children under one banner, under our one true king. Together we have built out, hand in hand, the closest expression of heaven that all of humankind may have ever known. Until your lot came around, of course."

"Heaven?" Owen blurted out, incensed at this careless, proud admittance of power. "You think this is heaven?"

"As much as God permits a mortal soul to know. He holds his truest secrets behind the veil you cross but once, the true and final death. But in Atlantis, there is no hunger, no sickness. The people rise and slumber as they wish, committing their time to science, art, philosophy or merry-making. There has never lived a city so brilliant for so long without the shadow claiming its due. Atlantis will rise from the ashes again, I am sure of it."

Owen could bear it no longer. His fists slammed into the table. "What about the Leviathan? All of us sacrificed, suffering for centuries on end, all at your command!"

Francis, Lord Verulam, smiled, eyes glimmering like a fox's at play, bounding in a snowy field, painfully bright.

"I will admit to some surprise when I learned there was an Inner Dream. In all my studies of the astral realm, never did I imagine that the Fish of Dreams might sustain what it consumed in yet another plane, physical yet astral all the same. I learned only what I could from His Majesty, so many years ago now, before he fell into the Deep Time. Back then, he was luminous and spry, a living star fallen to the earth, gleaming like the sun. He was the first, you see. The first of the devoured."

"What do you mean?"

Francis sighed, looking over at the living corpse of the king.

"I have seen it in his dreams, visiting them from time to time. The way he is now, it is… a necessity. It is how I understand his will. I can see it now like a painting rendered before my eyes: The forest primeval, green and dark, bent and ancient growth. Men in armor, shouting. Torches in the pit, cutting the night. Here is the boy prince of a dying line, orphaned in blood, scrambling for somewhere to hide in the dark. The common way, once, for the beginning and ending of things. Science, art and a true faith were seconds to the sword and the coin. Same as it ever was.

His Majesty fell then, during this hunt, into the deep of the sea. There it found him. The Fish of Dreams! So different then, nothing like a human being in shape or visage, but still very much alive, still carrying the gate to this world within, unopened."

Owen looked over at the corpse king and felt a dangerous pang of sympathy. His guard was slipping, but he must remain diligent. He could not let Verulam rattle his convictions.

Sensing Owen's doubt, Francis doubled down. "I met him on land, on a visit to the royal court of my own time. He had many names then, and many more to come. He could do this, create a dream of flesh that even the living believed. You could feel his warmth like a hearth-fire, his laugh like a storm. He told me, before I committed myself to my studies in law and science, of a world beyond this world where reason and fairness won out. He offered to take me there, one day, at the end of my life. He led me to a clearing one night beneath an open moon and asked me for my blood. He was so beautiful, so terrifying, Owen, like lightning on a cloudless night."

Francis paused for a moment, fiddling with the rings on his middle and pinky fingers.

"He said the dream awaited us. Any of us, who gave our blood to the Fish. He had found his way through blood and so he thus taught us the way. In time, he led us over, a few at a time, to see the island where his soul resides. Here, we found a paradise to call home, to plan for our great paradise.

The kings of our world and their petty power struggles were but a mummer's farce compared to our shared vision for Atlantis."

Owen felt himself sweating. The still air was cool inside the heptagonal chamber, stillness emanating like a soft chill from the bone tree and its tethered king, but he felt delirious, sick. "So you think this was the moral path? Building a city on the bones of the dead?"

"Is there any other way? I have not found it."

"What is wrong with you? How can you act as if there's no cost, no downside to this?"

"I do not deny the cost. Regardless of how you perceive me, Owen, I am aware of the weight of a human life. In my own life, long before I came to found Atlantis, I was not just a scholar, not just a statesman, but a judge. I weighed the lives of men and women on the scales of justice. I tried, as best as I was able, to be fair upon the bench, to give each soul its due, and to that I speak of the victim, the accused, and all those who lay ahead whose lives might be affected by precedent.

I will tell you what I learned then: It is the nature of the world for those living to fight to live. In the wilderness, does not a wolf feast upon the lamb? Would you curse the wolf for eating what it must? Would God, in his creation of Earth, of the Astral Sea, so design a world in which some souls are damned for seeking sustenance? It is not a pretty subject. It is heavy, and painful, but it is true. There is some manner of luck, or chance, really, that determines what shall kill to live and what shall die to sustain. The same for the animal, the same for man."

Francis reached forward and grabbed a glass, pouring ambrosia into a cup and swirling it before taking a sip. His expression softened from a stern, painful grimace to a contented sigh.

"Pardon me. Do you see how this subject upsets me? Now, to continue my point. If that is the nature of the world, to live and die, to kill and be killed, then so be it. But, if God has truly designed all, then so too did he create the Leviathan. The Fish, unlike all other beings I have observed, seems to break this cardinal rule. I do not know its age, but it is far beyond our ability to measure. It eats, but often needs nothing to sustain itself."

Owen could not keep silent. "You're telling me it doesn't need to eat?"

Francis laughed. "I thought that might pique your curiosity. Not as it once was. It feeds not on matter, but on potential. Liminality. In this way, it is a minor god, or heavenly creature. It is not of the Garden or its need for tending. So long as it sustains its dreaming, it may continue for eternity."

Owen thought of the Heartlanders, happily soaking themselves in stomach acid, believing it to be a necessary pain, a service to Levi. A tribute of the flesh.

"It is not the Fish that needs to be fed," Francis continued. "It is the King, the human half of the Leviathan. To live and rule and dream eternally, to grow in equal stature to the Fish of Dreams he has been bound with, to shape the body and grow it to his needs, all to preserve Atlantis, humanity and all its promise, he must feed. And so we have fed him countless mundane human bodies that fell into the blue Atlantic. African slaves and European freemen, sailors and soldiers living and dead, shaping human history with their potential to better fulfill his dream and build a world that could evade erosion, escape the petty cycles and final certainties of life on Earth. Human nature paid for human divinity. Same as it ever was. There was no other way for us to climb up from the mud and ascend to this place of true potential."

Owen stared at him, mute, feeling the weight of history like oceanic pressure, crushing his shoulders, crushing him to dust.

Francis rose from his chair. "I should hope you'll drink with me. Enemies or not, the ambrosia will keep you clear-minded and energized, the best version of yourself. I would like to settle our business together with dignity. After all, you and I, for all our differences, are equals here. Two champions of a civil war, ministers of fate elected by higher forces to address the final question. I stand for the King, and for some strange reason, the Fish has preserved you time and again and brought you to the throne. We should enjoy this moment together on the stage of the universe."

His luminous smile stung like a knife. "Let the revels begin."

In the vast inimitable darkness of the tower, encircled by a ring of armless fires, Janice stared at the visage of her father. Though he looked much the same as when she saw him last, on her final astral visit to the sinking of the *Empress of Ireland*, white-haired and fresh-faced, something was off. Something of his face, the way expression hung on the muscles of his cheeks and eyes, rang hollow.

Had he truly become so foreign to himself he forgot his own smile?

"Fair daughter, what brings you here to the House of the Eldest? What is it you seek to do?" His voice was low and thin. "Your presence here disrupts the Labor."

"Then I am accomplishing my goals, Father."

Her father laughed at that, rubbing his hands together. "Spiteful. Understandable, given your ordeals. I must try to be more respectful in my speaking to you. After all, even the Lord Verulam and the other Heralds were surprised at the chaos you and your friends have wrought, tearing a hole in the sky, burning and pillaging as you went."

"Was that too violent of an entrance? Have we embarrassed ourselves?"

"Yes, you have. You have damaged the creation of all mankind, the cradle of eternal civilization. Perhaps not beyond repair, but at such a critical moment, during the Final Harvest. It borders the unforgivable."

Janice spit on the ground. "Unforgivable? A father, selling his daughter like cattle to be slaughtered? Consigning her to the worst sort of death imaginable, stuck in the belly of a devil whale for a century, slick and pale with no release, no light or hope or love to be found? You speak of unforgivable?! I should kill you where you stand, you tiny man! I loved you, I admired you, I did everything you said because I thought you loved me too. I trusted you so much that I feared you. I was right to fear you, but not like some great ruler. Like a worm. A sniveling, earthsucking worm, burrowing holes and leaving rot in his wake."

Her father sighed. "This was the wrong approach. You are sharp as a blade, yet far more ruled by base emotion than I hoped for someone groomed to power. Perhaps it is the fault of this face. I apologize."

Seams in his face began to show like the unraveling of fabric. Bits of stoneskin, follicles of hair began to droop off the frame and fall into the dark. In the flickering lamplight, Janice could barely see her father's face shed and peel, becoming another man's, one she did not know.

"Forgive me," spoke a new voice, the high and quivering voice of an old man. "I was wrong to deceive you. I had hoped familiarity would soften you. Let us meet again. My name is Thomas."

"W-what?" Janice stuttered, clutching Sean to her chest tightly to balance against her fear. "You're not… you're not Father?"

"No. Well, sort of. When I realized you were approaching, I brought him here and absorbed him into myself. He was only a lesser citizen, no great loss for Atlantis, but I hoped to glean some insight from his past to prepare myself for dealing with you."

"So, he's gone? Completely?"

Thomas smirked, looking up at her with only segments of her father's face still clinging to his own. "Yes. Does this please you?"

Janice searched her heart, desperate to make sense of this. She knew why she was here, truly. It was not revenge, but as Raffaele had said, it was for justice. She had lost herself for a moment in the chance to hurt her father, to avenge the woman she could have been had he never interfered, but that was pointless now. All his scheming, all his tyranny and this was all it had amounted to.

"No," she said. "It doesn't."

"Just as well. Then I would prefer you and I speak frankly. I understand your pain, I do. But I must ask you to cease this pointless rebellion. Whatever injuries upon your person, whatever abuses you may have endured to arrive here, you cannot be allowed to continue. It is the will of the King of White Flowers that the Final Harvest take place. That we leave the Earth behind once more and return the Fish of Dreams to the stars where it belongs. If mankind is to survive, we must accept his will."

Janice stepped forward, trying to reclaim her inner fire, to do Raffaele proud. He had fallen to get her here, he had given everything for her to live and rise to the task at hand. She would not be swayed so easily. "Compelling argument, Thomas. I'm afraid I disagree."

"It is natural to focus on the negatives of power, especially as its subject. I understand. But ask yourself this: Should you accomplish your goals and overthrow His Majesty, what then? Will you rule Atlantis as a queen? Do you believe yourself fit to the task of administration? Would you lead the Acolytes through the rituals, would you master the homonculi and Delights? Would you rule harmoniously and fair over your subjects, tireless and selfless, from your throne? For in all our history, never has a regent lived with such ability and ambition. Never has a King accomplished such great Works for his people, for *all* people. Could you possibly match his level?"

"I don't know. But I don't believe that he is quite as brilliant and selfless as you see it. I see a despot to be overthrown. Let tomorrow be a new start."

Thomas's face twitched, as if something she had said deeply wounded him. His eyes gleamed from their upwards glare to be confident and serious, unshaken in will, but his body seemed to disagree, to doubt.

"You see in him the abuses of your father. This is natural. But it is in the nature of all men and women to be creatures of domination. I do not think you are immune to it, nor I. It is in all of us to suffer domination. It is only when one is elected to be supreme, elevated above others, that the rest of us are free. If we can never achieve the ultimate power then we are free of the burden of doubt that drives us against our fellow man. In the world of the living, Janice, unruled men turn feral and tear each down over the smallest of slights. It is the rule of the powerful that stops them and nothing else.

If we are to ever know peace, ever be free of constant pain, we must surrender ourselves. You must see this. Do you truly believe yourself, or that boy you brought along with you, to be capable of this? Your body still remembers its weakness. It still remembers servitude. Can you rule unburdened, absolute?"

Janice thought of Owen, likely in the House of the Eldest by now, and what trials he must also be facing. She wondered if he had what it would take. If she herself did, not because she accepted Thomas' framing of power and its necessities, but because the question remained. There had been no time to think about this before the war began.

As Janice spoke, she felt her heart return to the years of marrow dreaming, dry and comfortable in Raffaele's room, permitted to disappear wherever she would go. "There must be other ways of being. Of ruling. The sea is vast, and in it, many forms of life rise and fall. You act as though this is it. The only way. All your language, your feelings, are fixated. Stuck. It's quite sad."

Thomas growled, deeply offended. "I am not stuck! How dare you? I have spent living centuries deep in thought and study. I have watched this city rise from nothing, been a part of its grand creation. What we have built here is the product of man's most educated and talented citizens, from their unceasing desire to achieve the tallest heights of society and governance! You act as though possibilities are endless in human nature, but you are wrong. Even the wisest and most selfless are bound to innate tracks of behavior, to simple needs and failings! Man must be held at bay from his darkness!"

Thomas' eyes flickered between Janice and baby Sean. He began to circle her, restless, his body shifting beneath his robe. Whatever in him was no longer human was aching to take action.

Janice put her hand on Sean's chest and felt for his heartbeat. Sean's small hand coiled around her index finger, and he cooed as quiet as a whisper as his skin began to glow.

"Especially you, it seems," Janice said.

Thomas laughed, coarse and joyless, as if his throat were filled with spiders and they had begun to crawl towards the light.

"Especially me."

Owen drank ambrosia in his chair and watched as Francis kneeled and spoke with the King of White Flowers, whispering into his decrepit ear, who delivered shuddering smoke wafting from his lips in reply. Francis rose and approached the table once again.

"The King has spoken."

"And?"

"He appreciates your visit and considers you an honored guest. When I told him of what had happened to you in the Inner Dream, when the flesh preserved you as you are, he understood what that meant. You are special. Chosen by the Fish. By God, as the architect of fate. The way he was a thousand years ago. He himself was not chosen for strength or intellect, but by providence and the Fish itself."

Owen rose from his chair, glass empty. The ambrosia had calmed him, steeled his nerves. "I don't particularly care. I'm not here to curry favor with you. Either of you. I'm here to set things right. Step down now or…" he hesitated a moment, struggling until the words bubbled forth on adrenaline alone, "or die by my hands!"

Francis laughed, truly and deeply, as if he were a child again playing in a field of green. "Yes, you command such terror. Unarmed, untrained. A meek boy playing at revolution. We have no choice but to comply!"

Owen sighed. He knew he had never been imposing, but this wasn't a matter of respect or confidence. He had experienced too much sorrow, seen too much pain, to not try to end things. Violence was never his preference or ability, but he would have to find it in himself before the day was done.

He thought of Gabriel on the Far Shore, teaching him of liminality. *Will is water and light*, he had said. *What can be is what will fuel what will happen.*

His hand was warm and began to glow, threading through the air, pooling and condensing into the shape of a blade.

Francis raised his hand as if conducting a symphony, and the light beckoned to his will. He now stood armed and eager.

"You know the Arts."

"I guess I do."

"Do you have the fire to wield them? Do you believe your abilities to surpass mine? Experience makes masters of us all. In a dance of swords, one false step cuts short the symphony."

"I figured as much."

"I will bring my fullest abilities to bear. Are you ready to die?"

Owen sighed. "Yeah. Sure. If I have to."

Francis stared deeply at Owen, his eyes taking in his stance, the blade of light in his hands, the dull, unmoving light in his eyes. Francis's smile widened until his white teeth gleamed like animal fangs. He dropped his sword of light, letting it unravel into embers.

"Magnificent! Just what I might have hoped for. Your will is steady, your light strong and expanding. I would hate for this to end in blood between us, Owen. I have found too much respect for you."

Owen stepped forward. "Enough mind games. It ends now."

"Yes. It does." Francis dropped to his knees before Owen. "It is settled. You have passed the test of the King. He congratulates you, as I do, and offers you his throne."

Owen looked up with shock at the King. The bound corpse was looking at him, eyes open with a wide yet joyless smile.

"What?"

"The King will honor the wishes of the Fish. He said to me, "*In a thousand years, none save you,*" Francis points at himself, "*has been worthy to supplant me. But here now comes a true prince.*"

Owen felt his arm go slack. "Just like that?"

Francis rose in a theatrical half-bow. "Just so. The King wishes for mankind to survive and ascend. He says that he built Atlantis, became the Leviathan in order to protect the soul and memory of mankind, to keep the original line from breaking. If one made and chosen in the same manner should appear to say he has failed in his Labor, he would honor the wishes of the Fish of Dreams. He would hand over the crown, the throne, to you, to lead our people to a new tomorrow as if he were his own flesh and blood."

Owen was unsure what to say. What to do.

"...and if I say no?"

On his throne, the King's eyes lowered.

"You sadden His Majesty after such a tremendous, historical gift. If you must know," Francis said, his voice dripping with poison, "the Leviathan will die. It is currently walking towards the city of Philadelphia, and its corpse will fall there. It will be like nothing the world has seen before. The death of a god, liminality ceased. Like cutting a sun in twain."

"...What?"

"Of course, Atlantis will sink. All of our great work, all our sacrifices will be lost to the sea. Every soul remaining on the island, as well. You. I. All your little friends setting torch to literature and history in the valley below."

Owen thought of Nina, of his brother.

"The Earth will continue to boil. Without our doing, mankind will render this Earth inhospitable. In a century or two, the face of the planet will be unrecognizable. No vessel created by man, no rocket or ship, shall successfully plant a seed of life on another. Humanity will rise and fall like summer grass and a grand stillness shall take the place of a beautiful song."

Francis stepped forward, extending his hand to Owen.

"So what shall you choose? Shall you become the next King? Or shall you be the end?"

Janice's body ached tremendously. Her skin felt raw and the gash above her eye was deep, filling her left eye with blood. Sean was sleeping, still clutching her finger. The fight with Thomas had tired him out. All the same, Janice was thankful.

She would not have survived Thomas without his help. Not after what the Herald had become.

Around her, the tattered organs and monstrous bones of Thomas' true body lay scattered about across the room. The fog and the darkness had lifted, leaving ivory walls and simple pillars beneath.

She could find her way around now, through the halls. The space made sense, as if lit by the pale and pooling light of dawn.

There was a circular staircase going upwards and below. It seemed in some manner to go on forever below, though the light could only carry so far. Despite everything she had learned, everything she knew, something in her felt curious about the steps below. She wondered, if not about the very bottom, then about the rooms and worlds that awaited behind those thousand doors.

She had come to love the world of dreams. Falling into them, watching the shapes blur and bend. Things too sturdy or sure felt less real to her. Like they were pretenders.

But all that was for another time. She had to find the throne room. That would likely be above.

It was slow going, for the steps were steep and her body was barely keeping itself going. With each step, she felt thinner, shallower. She wondered if this was from leaving the astral sea level behind her and traveling upwards. Like how air was thinner on a mountaintop, the soul shallowed as it separated from its source.

At the top of several flights of stairs sat two doors embedded with white stone flowers and a crimson ruby, much like the Thorn Doors had been. She caressed Baby Sean and held her hand up to the doors, which began to glimmer and open before her.

There was silence in the heptagonal chamber. Janice looked at the bone tree at the center of the room, at the table knocked on its side leaking ambrosia on the floor. Sitting in the throne was Owen, his body covered in pale white roots, boring into his skin as if to suck him dry, a silver crown resting on his head.

He looked at her and tried to smile, but the pain was far too great.

"Janice. It's you."

She stepped forward, struggling to trust her good eye. "Owen?"

"Yes."

"What's going on? Where's the King?"

Owen struggled to speak, the bone roots traveling around his esophagus.

"Gone. Francis, too. Though I can still hear them, from inside the tree."

Our revels now are ended.

"Oh."

Owen tried to smile again. "They told me everyone would die if I didn't take it. They weren't lying. The Leviathan… Atlantis. All of it. You. Sean. Nina."

"They tricked you."

"No. I knew what they were doing. I just… couldn't do it. I couldn't let it all end. I had to try."

These our actors,

As I foretold you, were all spirits and

Are melted into air, into thin air.

"And now you're king."

"I'm leading the Leviathan back to water. They were

killing everyone, Janice. It was feasting on everyone. They were preparing to leave, to go to space. Everything was going to be fucked. Everything is fucked."

"I know, Owen. I heard."

"What should I do? Everyone will fear us. They'll all know about it now. Do we leave? Do we stay? I don't know. I'm trying to figure it out but I don't know."

Janice sighed. "You couldn't wait a moment. You couldn't let me sit there, could you? It had to be your sacrifice, your story."

"Janice, it hurts. It...I can't-"

"Of course it hurts. Look at you."

Owen began to cry.

And – like the baseless fabric of this vision –
The cloud-capped towers, the gorgeous palaces,
The solemn temples, the great globe itself,
Yea, all which it inherit, shall dissolve.

"I was scared, Janice. I didn't know what to do. What do I do?"

"You're no king, Owen. You're a fool."

"I know."

"We can't leave you like this. It's wrong."

"But what about-"

And like this insubstantial pageant faded,
Leave not a rack behind.

"Enough. The longer you sit there, the more you'll lose yourself. There's little time. Is it back in the sea? The Leviathan?"

Owen shook his head. "Not yet. Almost. Moving it… feels strange. Every step feels like a mountain splitting in two. I don't… I'm not here, I'm not me. I'm it, Janice. This is just a seed, a face."

Janiçe stepped up towards the throne, well enough to see the thorns sprouting through his flesh. With every moment, he was becoming a part of the tree.

"No. You're Owen. There is no it. It's a dream. It's all a dream."

We are such stuff

As dreams are made on, and our little life

Is rounded with a sleep.

Sean's eyes opened. He began to laugh and glow in Janice's arms.

"You and I can't be what's next. It's just the same thing. We remember too much."

She reached out and touched Owen on the cheek, her own light mingling with Sean's.

"You're too weak to sit on the throne. That's a good thing, Owen. Get up."

Owen looked at her with human eyes. Elsewhere, he was walking towards the shoreline. The glorious sun shone upon his back as the clouds twirled and played around his neck. It was intoxicating. Below him, the rest of the world looked small, a faded tapestry in royal blue. Even the missiles and bullets seemed like bugs in summer, a chattering, enveloping part of everything. It was so very peaceful and the sea looked cool and inviting.

Sir, I am vexed;

Bear with my weakness; my old brain is troubled.

Be not disturbed with my infirmity.

"Owen."

He saw her again, sharing her light with him.

"Let go. Get up."

He smiled and felt a warmth touch his heart.

"You're a good friend, Janice."

"Sure I am."

If you be pleased, retire into my cell

And there repose.

"The shoreline is just ahead."

"Reach it."

He felt the chill of the ocean touch his toes. It felt like home. He stood up from the throne, the roots ripping and pulling at his bones.

"It's time, Sean," he heard Janice say.

A turn or two I'll walk

To still my beating mind.

XXXIII. The Sea

Atlantis broke in two.

The wooded valley was splintered, upheaving in chunks, bits of dirt and stone falling down and shattering the dense tree branches as they fell.

The city bent until breaking. Pillars came unmoored and roofs collapsed into themselves. The cries of the homunculi Delights in all their ravenous number were caught unawares. Some, still picking their teeth with Heartlander bones, felt themselves crushed beneath tectonic plates before they realized what had happened.

They seemed numb or unaware of the threat of death, moving on basest possible instinct.

Around the island, the sea grew choppy and violent as deep movements rippled through the water. The still waters of the astral sea had come awake, hungry to claim the rebellious island once and for all.

Nina tried her best to move quickly. With Alan's help, they rushed their way down the Spinal Mount. Buildings untethered to foundations crashed and shook around them.

"Quickly!" Alan screamed, holding out his stone arm to help Nina cross a divide.

They had little direction and no sure plan outside of Owen's last words. *There's a turtle on the southern shore. It's a friend.* There was no time to think about it and less time to doubt it. Atlantis was sinking, churning back into base elements.

Nina heard a great crack behind them. They both turned to watch the Spinal Mount groan and break above them. At its peak, the tip of the House of Eldest dipped low, beneath the peripheral column walls.

In her gut, she knew at once what it meant. They stood in silence for a moment, thinking of Owen, Janice and Sean, thinking of everyone interred forever on the island.

"Come on," Alan whispered. "Let's go."

The bells were ringing, masterless, punctuating through the sound of rubble and tectonic plates crashing side to side and the feral screeches of demons and men alike consigned to horrid death.

Nina looked out and saw the wide horizon ahead of her. The sea, though not her own. Not the beautiful blue sea of Earth. Still, even amongst the chaos, after so long without a distance, without a wide world to look upon, it had a soothing effect. Everything was ending, collapsing, but the truth of the sea remained. It called to her as one of its own and she heard its voice like a memory.

They passed through the orchards, wide and green, the last of the island to remain unbroken. This fruit was not of the Earth, and it grew large and wild on the vine. Would this, too, be lost? Or were there other islands, other vines along the infinite horizon? Was there some warm hill, some bit of sun, unbroken by the stain of history? Could someone find it one day and bite into a hanging fruit and taste its sweet nectar without fear or sadness or regret? Nina could not shake these thoughts, even as her own past and present fell away.

It was ending. All of it was ending. But here she was.

"It's the shore!" Alan cried.

Before then, the white sands of the southern shore carved a sliver through tall grass and dark, churning sea. As if a blessing, Owen had spoken true, and with no need of combing the shore, they had arrived to find the turtle. It rested on the white sands, eyes open, watching the fall of Atlantis was a kind of innocent smile.

It craned its head slowly to the two, regarding them with calm interest.

They approached, Nina clutching tightly to her chest wound, bleeding again from the exertion of their frantic escape. Her head was swimming, struggling to follow through from thought and feeling to language.

"Hi," she said.

The turtle blinked.

"Oh. You can't speak, I guess. Owen said you were a friend."

The turtle's expression remained unchanged.

"He…I…" Nina had no idea what to say to her.

"Can you take her away from here?" Alan asked. "Someplace safe?"

Nina looked at him, confused. "*Her*?"

The turtle nodded, surprising them both.

Alan turned to face her, his stone face stoic, implacable. She wanted to press him on this, more out of fear of loneliness than anything else, but she could not bring herself to do so. She knew what his arrival had meant. His brother was still on the island, after all.

She nodded. "I hope you find him. I really do."

"Thanks," he replied. "Me too."

The shattering of the island drew closer, judging by the sounds of breaking trees and rending soil. The island was breaking into smaller pieces, built on a thin foundation above an endless sea.

"You should go," Alan said.

She climbed onto the turtle's back, wide enough for her with room to spare. The turtle barked gently and shuffled backwards on its flippers, beginning its journey towards the water. As soon as its fins touched seafoam, it seemed to find a remarkable new speed and with a shove shot out like a marlin into the open ocean. The waves were tall and surging. Nina pressed her tender chest against the turtle's shell, gripping the edge tightly.

She lost sight of the island for just a moment, dipping below a cresting wave. On the ascent, she realized that Alan was already gone.

She was alone at sea with the turtle. She was alone.

She was alive. Tears began to fall, heavy, hot tears.

She was free.

The turtle barked lightly back at her. The bark made as much sense as human language. *We're going below.*

Nina didn't understand why she understood. She didn't need to. She put her hand gently on the turtle's neck and it faced forward, ducking its head and tilting its body forward into a coming wave.

Nina held her breath and closed her eyes as the wave came up like a wall of water and crashed down upon her head.

They were swimming. Descending. She could feel it.

Underneath the water, her body felt lighter. The pain of her chest wound felt soft and warm, and in the low pressure of the water she could hear a strange song coming from every direction, as if it were the song of the sea itself and all things in it in polyphonic harmony.

She opened her eyes.

Below the surface of the water, everything was different. There was color, vibrant gorgeous color, and bending bits of light. Strange vegetation and trees, like a sunken petrified forest made of every hue and form, loomed all around them, pulling them in.

She looked down at her body and saw it shimmering with light. It was changing. Everything was changing.

She opened her mouth, letting the ocean fill her lungs, and found that she could breathe. For the first time in so very long she could breathe.

XXXIV. Sunset

Emily didn't remember falling asleep. She didn't remember anything after her son got out of the car. There had been some great large figure in the rear view mirror and swirling creatures in the air, and people dying to the right and left of her.

In the middle of it all, she'd fallen asleep. She couldn't feel her legs well at all. As she came to, she looked down at her feet and tried to move her toes. She was a proud jogger. This had never happened before, this lack of feeling.

She felt numb all over.

"She's awake," she heard someone say. She looked up to see who was speaking. *Was it Alan?*

She struggled to see in front of her, she was so very numb. The figure grew close, suddenly holding up something bright into her eyes. It was not Alan.

"She's conscious!" The figure called out to others nearby.

"I can't feel my legs very well," she explained. "Could you help me stand and stretch them?"

Someone cried out in pain in the distance and the voices of men and women ran off shouting in that direction.

"You can't feel your legs?" The nearby figure asked. It was a young tan woman with strong eyebrows and a steady smile. "Show me."

Emily showed her.

"It looks like there's some movement there. Thank god. We're going to need to find you a hospital. I'll be right back."

The young woman left.

Emily, dazed, tried to look around her. Where was the car she had rented? Where was Alan? Her head hurt terribly.

"Ma'am?" It was the young woman. "I found a volunteer willing to drive you. The nearest hospitals are all filled up. We're going to need to get you to one the next state over. This man is going to drive you, okay?"

"As I live and breathe!" said the man. Emily's eyes adjusted to make out a somewhat familiar face. "Didn't think I'd find you here! I was working at that conference you went to a few weeks back. I met you and your son, he showed up late, we ate donuts together! Do you remember?"

"Oh, god," Emily said. It was the security guard. "It's you."

"*It's you*, she said!" the security guard laughed. "Oh, she's a firecracker," he explained to the young medic. "We've got a fantastic rapport."

The young woman seemed unsure. "Do you feel safe driving with this man, ma'am? We need to get you to a hospital but, well…" Her eyes lingered on the stretch of highway around them, covered in automobile wreckage.

Emily was silent for a moment as she found her bearings. "Sure. Whatever."

The security guard laughed. "Killer sense of humor on this one."

After the young woman took down identifying information on Emily and the security guard (first name: Jerry) and threatened him if anything went astray, they were off. He helped carry Emily, legs still numb to the point of uselessness, to the passenger seat of his red and white striped 1990 Dodge Ram pickup truck, the truck bed filled with old junk like a faded loveseat, seven rusty sewage pipes and one and a half construction pallets.

"I work on her to keep her running every year. She'll die when I die!" he said.

The two drove off in silence, making their way slowly off-road to avoid the congestion of abandoned cars. Emily looked out the window, silent, taking in the sight of the horror, all the blood and metal and depressed soil where the Leviathan had stood. She realized her husband must have done what the others did in the diner. As they'd been taught to do.

"They say all of a sudden, it turned around and ran right back to the sea," he explained. "Like nothing nobody's ever seen. Apparently there was a struggle in the White House. Most of the military wanted to fire a nuke to take the thing down, but cooler heads prevailed. It fell back into the sea, right by where the boardwalk, well, used to be. It kinda lay there for a while until it slowly started slipping back into the water. That whole stretch of coastline? Kaput. Just like that. A grand tectonic clusterfuck. My damn apartment? The storage unit I used to hide my valuables from the litigious ex? Davy Jones got all that shit now. Bye bye. Well, whatever. At least they didn't drop the damn nuke, let's say a prayer for that."

Emily remembered Alan getting out of the car. She wanted to ask where he was, but she didn't. She just stayed silent.

"You lose anything?" he asked, not taking his eyes off the road ahead. "...Anybody?"

Emily looked at him, her eyes bloodshot, and said nothing.

He nodded. "You got a home to go back to?"

She too looked straight ahead.

He sniffed and cleared his throat. "Like everybody, right? Well that's okay. Sometimes before bed, I like to watch these Youtube videos. '*You'll Never Believe What Happened Next*,' '*7 Impossible Survivors*,' fun stuff like that. I don't always think they're true or whatever, I mean everything's made up these days. I bet even that giant motherfucker isn't what we thought it was. Watch it turn out to be some kind of government-funded Godzilla or something. Doesn't that beggar belief?"

He laughed, watching her out the side of his eyes for some sort of reaction. He received none. Relentless, he continued on.

"So, in these videos, these people are always interviewed after the craziness went down. You think they'd be traumatized, shook up. Nah. Most of the time, they're happy, like they finally got it all figured out, always saying some shit like '*I found out what's most important in my life*.' That's just wild to me. How can you have a whole life of good and bad stuff happen to you and not have your shit mostly figured out already? Were you not paying attention the whole time?"

"Anyway, that's how I used to think. But not anymore. Not after all this. Did I lose just about everything left to my name? Yeah. I did. But I got my head on straight, I got my truck, and most importantly, I got more tomorrows ahead of me, hopefully without anymore giant people crushing us all into pulp. That sounds pretty sweet to me, all things considered."

Emily listened in silence until she could bear it no longer. She broke out into a big, ugly sob.

"Aw, I'm sorry, miss. I'm just trying to cheer you up

some."

"I have nothing," she said. "They're all gone because of me."

"No, it's not your fault, it's not. Nothing like this has ever happened before."

She cried all the harder, her head falling into her hands.

"Listen. You don't have to be alone if you don't wanna be. I know it's hard, and people like you and I on the older side of it all. We don't have forever to start something new. But look, the way I see it, you only get one shot at this life. You only get to be awake so many days. Even if it's all gone to shit, there's still… you know, sunsets. There's sunsets to watch."

She couldn't stop crying.

"I know you don't know me well," he continued. "I'm just some security guard nobody named Jerry to you and I get that. But if you feel alone in this world and you wanna watch sunsets with somebody, I'll be there. We can have a beer or two and chat about our days. We don't even gotta talk to each other if you don't want to. We can just sit there and watch the light go down and all those brief and beautiful colors come up."

The truck neared a collapsed highway bridge, encircled with confused and listless people waiting for someone to help them.

"Man, what a mess," Jerry muttered. "Anybody know where they're going?"

www.ingramcontent.com/pod-product-compliance
Lightning Source LLC
Chambersburg PA
CBHW061651190726
48289CB00006B/1822
* 9 7 8 1 9 4 9 1 2 7 6 0 7 *